"This book is a speedball, with lines as beautifully sad and weary as John Berryman's lines, and a premise as wild and lit as one of Philip K. Dick's premises. Stevens is a writer who makes you want to slow down and read each sentence carefully, even as you want to race forward and see what happens." —BENJAMIN NUGENT

"One of my favorite writers has written another imaginative and attentive marvel. *The Visitors* is about business: the business of staying alive, the business of being with others, the business of staying sane, and the business of business." —RIVKA GALCHEN

"*The Visitors* is such a unique gem of a novel—an intimate and affecting character study that is somehow also a DeLillo-esque container for diamond-sharp insights into big data, eco-terrorism, and the subprime mortgage crisis—that, like the garden gnome who haunts its protagonist, I'm half-convinced it couldn't possibly exist. But it does, and it is dazzling, and Stevens's readers are incredibly lucky to have it." —ADAM WILSON

"An orgy of synaptic firing and flourish, *The Visitors* is a novel of longing, lostness, and late capitalism told with roving imagination and warmth." —TRACY O'NEILL

"Stevens's frighteningly brilliant new novel is both a bold reimagining of the recent past and an all-too-likely prophecy of what's to come. Caustic, intimate, and consistently surprising, this novel cements Stevens's place as one of the great chroniclers of our cruel and terrifying times." —ANDREW MARTIN

"Stevens's scalpel-fine prose—slicing with wit and pathos—belies the bewildering scope of *The Visitors*, which lays bare everything from the audacity of modern finance to the visceral costs of debt, love, and success. Yet while collapse looms nigh, every page beams with defiant jubilance and gut-punch insights. Equal parts revelatory and moving, *The Visitors* cuts to the core of the delusion and disillusionment of our era." —JAKOB GUANZON

"Amid credit scores and talking specters, revolutionary impulses and the indissoluble truths found in a lifelong friendship, Stevens paints a brilliant and richly captivating portrait of an artist teetering between her own past and an American collapse happening in real time. Stevens's intimacy with history borders on the telepathic. *The Visitors* is transcendent and astounding in every way."

—MICHAEL ZAPATA

PRAISE FOR

The Exhibition of Persephone Q

"Finally a book that exposes how dull Occam's Razor has become after all these years. Adroitly crafted, *The Exhibition of Persephone* Q is a fun, urbane look at the faulty heuristics of perception and authenticity. Proof positive that in the age of Photoshop and Trumpian Denialism, the simplest explanation no longer applies."

—PAUL BEATTY

"With a voice both lucid and searching, Jessi Jezewska Stevens depicts the great illogic of love, as well as all the small, strange quiddities of being a body in a material and virtual world. Lit up with melancholy, humor, and perfect oddness, this remarkable debut casts an afterglow long after its final pages."

—HERMIONE HOBY

"An intimate and obsessive exploration of the act of seeing and the act of being seen. It's also a metaphysical detective story, an investigation of absence and voids, and a darkly comedic treatise on the art world and living in a series of apartments and rooms in New York . . . *The Exhibition of Persephone* Q mostly reminded me of taking a walk at night alongside a brilliant companion who has a keen mind, and an eye for absurdity."

—PATRICK COTTRELL

THE VISITORS

The Visitors

JESSI JEZEWSKA STEVENS

SHEFFIELD – LONDON – NEW YORK

First published in 2022 by And Other Stories
Sheffield – London – New York
www.andotherstories.org

1 3 5 7 9 8 6 4 2

ISBN: 9781913505288
eBook ISBN: 9781913505295

Editor: Jeremy M. Davies; Copy-editor: Larissa Pienkowski; Proofreader: Sarah Terry; Typeset in Albertan Pro and Syntax by Tetragon, London; Cover Design: Luke Bird; Printed and bound on acid-free, age-resistant Munken Premium by CPI Limited, Croydon, UK.

And Other Stories gratefully acknowledge that our work is supported using public funding by Arts Council England.

Supported using public funding by
ARTS COUNCIL
ENGLAND

FSC
www.fsc.org
MIX
Paper from responsible sources
FSC® C171272

```
[~]$ install aptitude GNITE
vim visitors.txt
:g/rat/s//irr/g
```

"What exactly can the one-who-waits do, so that faith, while not magically attracted, is not excluded? . . . Exactly when this transformation will come to pass and whether or not it will happen at all is not at issue here, and at any rate should not worry those who are exerting themselves."

SIEGFRIED KRACAUER
The Mass Ornament: Weimar Essays

"After having artificial flowers that imitated real ones, he now wanted real flowers that imitated artificial ones."

JORIS-KARL HUYSMANS
Against Nature

```
exit
```

This is a work of fiction. Any similarity to actual events, probable or improbable, is purely intentional LOL.

```
CREATE OR REPLACE PROCEDURE impute_missing(
    in_table_name "visitors",
    in_attribute "prologue",
    in_impute_method DEFAULT "irrational"
) IS
```

off the grid, along the border, up north, operatives fit new batteries into gear, slip backups into pockets, and set off into the dark; there are no hikers, no tourists, no botanists from Vancouver trailing the lost cause of flora depleted by fauna adapting too well to a warming earth; *ha!*; with night-vision goggles, you see through the skein of things to their authentic core; shoot a deer from four hundred meters, hoist the shadowed body onto shoulders, make your way back to HQ, a trailer, an outline in the night; inside is everything you need to survive; the carcasses hang from a sturdy branch of a tree, the bloodletting tree, letting blood into a bucket; the skin peels away at the touch of the knife in a greenish night-vision scheme; stretched on a frame and placed in a clearing to catch the sun, it becomes a hide; a row of potatoes out back, a book for identifying mushrooms and poisonous plants; psychedelics sprout in the compost of the operatives' own manure; they shit pure; list: venison, scavenged plants; no chemicals, mood stabilizers, anxiety killers, erection enhancers, progesterone supplements, beta-blockers, amphetamines, vitamin B complexes, Tofurky, vegan ice cream, soy-based eggs, hormone-enhanced chicken breasts, undigested margarines, I Can't Believe It's Not . . . !; query: what kind of world was it down there, at sea level, where one's own shit was poisonous?; rose hips for a snack; wintergreen numbs the tongue, the mind, the aches and pains; at dawn, we steep root tea over an open flame and at raw wood desks outline program flow by hand; WYSIWYG; the generator whirs, but an operative shouldn't need a connection; should know the language, know the logic, think in do-while loops and transition lines, know the power of her own mind; paradise is to feel so acutely the labor of your own survival, might stay 4eva in the North Country woods, were it not for the knowledge that the only way to survive the apocalypse is to engineer it for yourself;

```
BEGIN EXECUTE IMMEDIATE update_stmt;
END;
COMMIT;
```

```
DATA visitors;
   SELECT FROM "part one"
RUN;
```

1

Retail is debt. Storefronts create the illusion of prosperity. The city's skyline is the visible sliver of a crescent moon, the penumbra of an eclipse; everything else lives in the red. Debt is the molten bedrock atop which all else rests. This is the first principle of business. The question is how you manage it.

But C did manage. The proprietress of a lighting store taught her everything she knew. Use credit cards, she said. The interest rate is upward of 20 percent, but when the shit hits the fan, they can confiscate nothing but your reputation. Avoid banks at all costs.

C confessed: What if she'd already entangled herself? Also, my friend Zo—she invested.

Turned out that the lamp proprietress had also been funded by friends. Most nonessentials are supported by private patronage, which of course carries its own form of interest. How did it feel, she asked, to be someone else's pet project? She sold beautiful lamps, this woman, and a small stock of clocks. Tiffany shades tuliped over oval bulbs, their filaments twin copper seeds. The lamps were always lit. The proprietress tended to them like children. Every morning, she turned each fixture on; every evening, off. Because if you blow a fuse and something sparks? she said, then snapped her fingers for emphasis. This was but one of many ways the shit could hit the fan. Better prevent it. At other moments, though, she grew conspiratorial, whispering, All the same, some days, don't you just want to watch it burn?

C checked the fine print on her lease, on her insurance. She was responsible for the sidewalk outside, liable for small disasters of all kinds that might spill over into public space, and for this reason the customer was never right. They prefer it this way; they want it like that. No one knows what they need. If someone tries to complain, the lamp proprietress said, you give them hell. It was the only way to stay out of City Hall.

C learned to manage the accounts, reduce overhead, place ads, convince Max that they couldn't hire anyone just yet. We'll trade shifts, she said. During the day, arranging a holiday display, she thought of her friend, the lady of light, in her third-floor showroom, surrounded by hordes of lamps that pulsed pelagically. They looked after one another's shops for a time, whenever one of them took a rare vacation or got sick. Then—the Crash.

The lady of the lamps did not survive. C arrived at the dark-blue door of her building one day, on break, to ring the third-floor buzzer. Her mentor had gone without even saying goodbye. Standing there on the step in front of the PERMANENTLY CLOSED sign, C couldn't help but feel a little shock of superiority, the thrill of survival, quickly washed away by the tides of self-disgust. Then the door swung open and a mover came through, balancing a stack of wide, flat boxes in his arms.

Who are you? C asked.

I'm with the bank, he said.

But my friend doesn't believe in banks, C replied.

The man, it transpired, was no less startled. The two of them fumbled for space in the narrow entryway, and the boxes tipped. Thousands of tiny antique bulbs rolled from the cardboard like so many eggs, a mass birth, a breeding ground, their futures foreclosed upon by the sidewalk on which they shattered.

It was the normalcy of debt—everyone was in it—and her pride in having outlasted the lamp proprietress that lent C her recent overconfidence, made her forget that *what* you owed still mattered—what and to whom, and how much. The problem was, paying interest soon meant forgoing rent and ignoring her mounting medical debts, which, cleverly enough, she'd managed to halve. Hospitals—they really knew how to lend. The trick was to not pay, to not pay and not pay till you answered the call one day and said, I can't afford this, I'm sorry. My life is the only collateral I have. If you'd like to lay claim to that, help yourself.

Okay, try for half, the administrator on the other end capitulated. *Self-pay discount*, her statement read. It's monied patients like Zo who pick up the tab for all of us who can't. They pay both halves, or their insurance does, priced into which is everything C could never afford. It doesn't make sense. "But that's another way she's subsidized me, I guess," C says to her visitor. Meanwhile, the Crash keeps Crashing. "You know, floral arrangements, limousines, and air travel are all down. Art is up—but not art supplies. How do you explain that? All those conceptualists . . . never liked them . . . "

Her visitor's face is slack. Maybe he isn't even listening.

2

Maybe the visitor is less of a visitor and more of a tenant. Maybe he's always been here—or maybe the word is *intruder*. Certainly he wasn't invited. He'd breezed in, unannounced, sans knock, a few weeks before, as though he'd come straight through the wall. C was sitting on her daybed, knitting, when she first observed the little man, noting the distance between his bare feet and the floor, his diaphanous body, his crumpled cravat. In her haste to escape, she upset the coffee table and the modest breakfast laid out on a cheap plate.

She locked herself in the bath and cowered in the tub. She listened for the clink of a struggle with the lock. A sharp pain hit her stomach—fear or something worse, fighting its way out. The sensation consumed her body, and then, confusing boundaries, moved on to the room beyond. She found some relief in the cool enamel of the tub against her spine, her cheek. Still, she went on hiding till she began to feel ashamed. You are what you believe, as Max used to tell her. She rose, cracked open the door, and peered into the room she'd fled. It was empty. Of course it was empty. In particular: of little men. A dream! Overstimulation! The summer heat distorted everything. She started the fan and collapsed back onto the daybed and into the deep relief of sleep.

And now, well, here she is. Here *they* are.

She sinks into the same sofa where she first received her guest, takes up her knitting from the coffee table again.

The other day, she looked into the bakery through its big front window, where a woman was, naturally enough, setting a white sheet cake on display, and found her—the baker, or the assistant?—already staring. It was the same at the bodega, the florist's, on the train. When her subway car pulled alongside another and C looked across, she always seemed to meet a passenger's hard gaze, as if interrupting a live broadcast already in progress—of herself, that is. And as she pored over her loan adviser's dire calculations at the bank—*The good news is you're approved for refinancing, as long as you find a guarantor*—she felt more than usually . . . surveilled. She told herself it was the season, the heat, the kerfuffle downtown. Or maybe it was only her beginning to look like what she'd become: a woman in serious debt. Financial distress reveals itself ineffably, involuntarily. It's in the way one guards a wallet while choosing a bill. As she proffered a dollar for a buttered roll at a cart, the man thanking her and telling her to *take care now* knew all and was judging her, she thought. But she'd jumped to the wrong conclusion.

In this city, you avert your eyes from the impecunious. When people stare, they stare at the insane.

As she watches the little man hover like a dark charm above the window, hung to catch the light, C regrets her resentment of the halal vendor. But it was an easy mistake to make, placing the blame on her fellow citizens. Who could blame her? Who else *was* there to blame?

"Unless you have some idea?" she adds.

She is on the daybed on a Sunday evening, a magazine glossing her bare thighs. The output of a car's souped-up sound system uploads into the room and dissipates on the slipcover. In its wake lies the awareness of her apartment, street, the city's summer swelter, the sound of her own voice. She talks, wondering if this is a breach of protocol, wondering whether she and her visitor are on speaking terms. What he does instead of answering her questions is point out the window at a flower—a volunteer, a garden getaway—that's pushed its way through the plinth of the heating pump outside the building across the street.

"What's that?" he asks.

"A rose. It's a rose," she explains. Again.

She turns on the TV. The visitor maintains a steady altitude a few feet above the sill, picking at his toes. Foot comes near nose, rounding him off. She is ready to admit to herself that he looks like one of those garden gnomes in the courtyard below, where the trash goes: the same oversized head and hands, except his gaze, unlike theirs, is curious and expectant, like a pet's. And while they are plump, he seems undernourished, his neck and limbs wiry, skin loose. No red cap. Instead, he wears a navy-blue three-piece suit. Unkempt cravat, as if he doesn't know how to tie it. He seems, all in all, rather new to existence. When she flips to the news, he lowers to the carpet and positions himself in front of the nightly broadcast, as if standing guard. She observes in profile his unbridled attention.

It appears our homegrown terrorists have managed to hack a Ukrainian supercomputer at a former Soviet nuclear facility, the TV says. *Stay tuned for the latest on the GoodNite attacks!*

Knit, purl. Knit, purl. A few cookies remain on the coffee table. C nibbles a sugared ridge and examines the gauge of her stitches—as always, too loose.

Her new companion would be adorable if it weren't for his eyes: glabrous, protruding like an insect's, and just as black.

3

In all areas of life except for her art—anyway, she isn't an artist anymore—C has shown a talent as a hostess. And as any good hotelier knows, hospitality depends less on ready accommodation than on leaving your guests alone.

She recognizes that a different woman—Zo, perhaps—might attempt to intellectualize the present situation, in particular her apparent hallucinations, with references to the brain stem, stress, a general imbalance between the world of the mind and the world of the senses, and visits to the therapist. All these mitigations are available to the general public, online, not only to the specialist. But C has never gone in for abstraction—at least, not historically. WYSIWYG, she says, and what she sees and gets, she tends to accept. For years, she chose thread count, warp, and weft in place of gods, God, ghosts, markets, and other constellations of fanaticism. Her preferred method of sorting data was additive, so who knew how many spurious phenomena had been woven into her experience by now. The loom ran itself, like a program. *Her* program. She sat on the stool and sent the shuttle through. Occasionally, there was a glitch, but rarely anything so serious.

Then, 2008: a twang. In a white room with a view of Queens, a nurse jellied C's belly and applied the ultrasound. The news was unwelcome. Her uterus was swollen, distorted. We haven't seen one like this, Doc said. There was something almost, well, *sculptural* about this knot she'd made. C fretted over the defunct organ as if it were the child she'd always hoped to have.

Wasn't there anything they could do to save it?

There, there.

They capped her nose and mouth with the small dome of the mask and let the anesthesia flow on the day the market crashed. She went under in a time of relative abundance and woke up in a different era, financially speaking. Everyone was now in debt. Welcome to the new world, Zo said. She was there at C's bedside, checking her phone. Francesca was there too, Zo's girlfriend at the time.

It was awful out there, she said. Awful for *everyone*. (Francesca was not C's favorite of Zo's girlfriends.)

Zo reached for C's hand. It'll work itself out, she said. And in a way, it did. Zo kept her job; C shed her sheen of unseemly health by chucking the prenatal vitamins. They grew apart again. Three years went by, and now the usual order between the two childhood friends has been restored: Zo, beautiful, overworked, rich; C, the lapsed artist, restocking her store. The occasional birthday text. Salubrious relief—or it would be, if it weren't for C's newfound premonitions. Her loans. Her debt. They were growths of their own. By the time the visitor arrived, she'd lost faith that she was still capable of turning things around.

It strikes her at last that the world—or, at least, her world—might be developing according to an irrevocable logic of its own. That is, separately from her. Out of her sight. Not her program at all.

4

This is to say the little man arrived in August at a nadir. Things must be bottoming out, C thought. Life was wilting: no art, no husband, possibly no store, if current trends were any indication.

Those first few weeks, the visitor's appearance amounted to an eviction. Afraid to go home, C avoided the apartment. It wasn't difficult. C's shop is a one-woman show; she is her sole employee.

The days were long. She woke at six, bleary, and perched at the loom opposite her daybed. Then to the closet to choose clothes, to the sink to brush teeth. Pour a packet of instant coffee and wince at the bitter taste, spit: the correct protocol was coffee, then teeth; packet, then water. But she was feeling out of it. The day after the little man arrived, she raised the grate at the shop with suspicion and looked around. No visitors—at least, not yet. There was only her unsalable stock, art supplies that were increasingly overrun by kitsch—the throwaway bangles, beads, origami paper, and glitter pens that mothers buy to pacify their children. Two tuitional preschools had taken up residence in the neighborhood, and C had done her best to adapt to the new foot traffic. Customers flitted in at lunch to browse the oil sets and ask the million questions that telegraph an intent to go home and buy online instead. It was enough to make you wonder what was so bad about her visitor. And maybe she did begin to wonder, then.

But she was safe in the store. The only threats there were her customers and the possibility of a successful GoodNite attack, but those contingencies were infrequent and improbable, respectively. It was the exhausted hours after closing that posed a problem: How to spend them without going home? She visited Zo, whom she hadn't seen much of since the hysterectomy. They were disaster friends, that's what they were, who called only when things went wrong.

She composed a text: *it's been too long!*

She ran errands. She volunteered to read once a week to an elderly woman down the street; now they met on Tuesday and Thursday evenings. C would swing by and read to Yi until she fell asleep, then tuck her in and consider staying the night. Yi's floral love seat looked accommodating, comfortable, spacious enough if C curled up, halved herself.

She turned off the lamp and let herself out, went past the shuttered storefronts, caught the train, and emerged one stop later to spend the night in her shop.

Whenever C did return to her legal abode, the creature was always there, wafting placidly beside the lamp, investigating the electrical wires, reading the paper, slipknotting its cravat. It looked up when she came in. There was always something different about it—it updated, like an algorithm. Its swollen forehead corniced over its horrible eyes, as if to hide them. And it wore a flower now, a little nosegay threaded through a buttonhole. Slipping from the daybed, it drew itself up to its full height and straightened its cuffs. As if it were trying to court her, she thought.

She joined the community garden. The gym. She took an aerobics class at an upscale studio near her store, the kind frequented by the same mothers who were willing to pay four hundred dollars to enroll their children in C's eight-week painting course, a price she hadn't optimized; she could probably charge more. The mothers worked out in such perfect synchronization that they might have been a single organism. C's own arms struck her as pitiful by contrast, pumping thinly as she stepped on and off her blocks. (She'd already lifted twenty pounds of liquid soap and restocked the highest shelves for free.)

Everywhere, she tried to emulate saner passersby, assimilate her swaying to theirs. She strove to be agreeable, to rhyme anatomically, to blend in so that she forgot about the guest at home that she was so reluctant to host. And so ridiculous a visitation at that! No beautiful guardian angels in the novel of her life. Back in this aerobics class, however, no one would ever suspect her of being the sort to attract such houseguests. Then again, didn't everyone seem a little off? She looked into the mirror in which they were meant to correct themselves. Specious expressions stared back. Nevertheless, she smiled and laughed at what she took to be cues. She went along with the fit women for smoothies, where she was praised for her fine arts programming at the store. Oh, I'd love to send my daughter, one said. C sent her an email—@gothamcapital.com—but the woman never replied. Then C's free trials were up.

But it's impossible to skirt your home indefinitely. Soon, C was forced to admit that, like the roaches, her newest intruder had no plans to vacate. A détente would have to be engineered. She resolved not to speak to it. She reserved the right to remain silent. She wouldn't be one of those spinsters who chattered away to no one—at least, not yet. She planned to spend what years she *did* have left lucid. Meanwhile, it seemed the elevator had gone kaput in her absence. She wouldn't be in the mood to talk after five flights of stairs anyway.

It was in the kitchen when she returned, as it would often be from that day on, peering into the snout of the kettle and lowering itself into the tangle of the philodendron above the sink. It padded barefoot across the floor and considered the loom. Kicked a pedal with its toe. Yelped. Humanized itself. She referred to it, privately, as *he* after that. And he emitted a low hum, C noticed, a subtle frequency tuned to the inner instruments of her own head, so whenever he wasn't immediately visible, she could still detect his presence. She couldn't shake the feeling that he was adapting to her. He liked to look in her jewelry box, too, and watch TV. C wondered how he turned it on when she was out, fairly certain that visitors lacked a working knowledge of remote controls, not to mention of material existence. She wondered if he was there at all when she wasn't home—if he was material himself.

It was an open question, the matter of physical actuality. C spent an evening moving from room to room to check. She entered the alcove to turn on the TV and found him already there. She stuck her head in the fridge, looked up, and he was gone. When he did appear, he was semitransparent, a projection, an early Vermeer, a painterly trick, but C never saw him arrive. He was always one step ahead. The world filtered through him, around him; you looked right through his skinny, cravatted neck to the television on the other side.

What really troubled her about the visitor, she decided, was his eyes. Globular and lashless and oversized, of a dark so deep it was self-referential, recalling the crude ebony of oil spills—and so she remained suspicious of his solicitations. He often spoke to C now, despite her silence. It had been some time since she'd had someone to talk to when she came home. It corroded her resolve. Yet GoodNite, too, was luring the public into complacency: *A Texas town of fifteen thousand has been cast into the dark*, the television said with uncharacteristic lyricism. It was a pretty tableau: people roaming the streets with candles in the night. Horrible, too, of course, of course. At the local hospital, the generator failed and a ventilator ceased to substitute for lungs. Someone lost a life.

C grabbed the remote and cut the anchor short. The visitor looked at her reproachfully. She ran a bath and locked the door. It was here—underwater, ears submerged—that she felt she could still access solitude and escape the sense that she was being evaluated, researched. She wondered if the gnome was here to judge her for her debt. He was a new kind of collector from the bank, sending back reports about her behavior. He certainly dressed the part.

One night, when she came home from reading to Yi (or rereading the passages Yi missed after she fell asleep—I wasn't asleep, she said, you just read too fast), C found the thing standing on the table on a stack of her mail, looking at the addresses, or maybe through the envelopes to the statements inside. *Second Attempt.*

She cried, "What are you doing?" then clapped a hand to her mouth, having remembered she'd pleaded the Fifth.

But of course, once you start, it's hard to go back.

These days, when C comes home and collapses onto the daybed, the visitor nods at the loom and asks, "And that?"

"An ancient practice," C says.

He is so unformed, so ignorant of life. But with C's help, he's improving, growing more articulate. Hovering at the window, he observes of passersby, "They sure do waste a lot of time." The television snaps to a commercial, and his large eyes sweep out the arc of a ball and chain. "What's a demolition job?"

"The planned destruction of something," C says. "Usually a building of some kind." He points to the hairdryer, a blender on TV. "For homogeneity," she says. She is pleased with her explanations. She makes labels with Post-its: *Toaster, for toast. (Stale bread made from fresh.)* He is the guest, she reminds herself, and she, the host. Not the other way around. It's the same with the pain in her belly, the thrum dormant in her side.

She brings a stack of newspapers to the bedroom, showers, and readies herself for bed. The visitor floats along the ceiling as she begins to undress. Chivalrous, he turns away. C slides beneath the comforter, knowing he will not look around until she has disappeared. The sheets estrange her from her freshly shaved shins, like a numbing agent applied with silk. How easy it is to slip away from your own body! It is so readily emancipated—just like that. Perhaps this error, this glitch, will also be an easy fix: she'll just have to numb her mind.

The visitor peeks through his inarticulate hands to see if she is decent. Happily, he begins to bob. C watches from her bed, ensconced in the pillows with her newspapers, duvet pulled taut as a brassiere across her chest. How could she be afraid? His plain contentment—now he hovers one inch above the dresser, investigating her perfume—strikes her as dignified and childlike at once. And yet, when she meets his eyes, a wave of horripilation travels across her skin.

She imagines what Max would say if he could see her now, quailing in her own bedroom thanks to a hallucination. She imagines his alarm. It's almost worth a laugh. No, she does laugh, shaking the frame of the bed. The blue of the streetlight is an eerie luminescence in the sheets. There is something in this composition that strikes her as funny.

The visitor is buoyed by this demonstration of mirth. "What's so funny?" Then he, too, is chuckling, breaking into a round, gentle hoot. Hearing his laughter rise with hers, C stops.

5

Why do we go out? To shout at the world, mainly—call it commerce, politics, art. Come dusk, though, we bookmark our progress and disappear. *Goodbye!* At home, people touch themselves, pluck hairs, beat their wives. Someone roasts a chicken and shares it with the dog, pairs the violet collar with the belt. After hours, it's important to be nowhere at all. Proper total democracy would be governance by slash-and-burn, driving populations out into the spotlight. But no one really works full-time.

When Max left, her apartment—these days so haunted and small—had struck C as cavernous. She avoided it then too. She made herself a lot of toast to go. Took long walks. Looked up the river at the George Washington Bridge and watched commuter traffic cross. Completed her inaugural turn at the community garden. Peonies. Snapdragons. Her sugar beets were failures. There wasn't much community in the community garden that season, and C couldn't decide which clique to join: one faction motioned to go organic, the other resisted for fear of nematodes. The rift ran between the rows. It was lonely there in no-man's-land. The problem was, she didn't really care. She needed conversation, a way to pass the time.

She could use some extra conversation now. Conversation with a human being, ideally.

The solution had come to her late one night in the grocery line, by way of a brochure. *Volunteer opportunity, read to the elderly, Spanish and/or Mandarin not required but preferred . . .* (Her mother was right, C reflected: no one ever requested someone fluent in Slovenian.) That was it! The elderly could talk. They lingered at elevator banks, subway entries, eateries, fruit stands, and on *esquinas*, shoveling memories like so much coal. As the brochure pinned to the grocery bulletin explained, volunteering consisted of listening, making sandwiches, escorting seniors on errands, and reading aloud. C wrote the number on the back of her receipt (itemized: cereal, spinach, yogurt, and toothpaste because she couldn't remember where things stood with respect to the previous tube). At the shop, she dialed. She asked to be placed with someone in the neighborhood. The agency did her one better and sent her just a few blocks south.

Now, after a stint at the community garden or at Zo's, she stops by Yi's and knocks, her hands cracked with paint (Zo is in the process of renovating her apartment).

Who is it?

Me!

They've become closer, post-gnome. Home away from home. The chaos of Yi's apartment is so purposeful and self-contained. Plants crowd the windowsills in a valiant effort at reforestation. Cartons pile in a corner, and bills and envelopes spill across the counter, over the the dishwasher, approach the sink. C sorts the spam from the bills from the coupons, the useful coupons from the not. (Ten dollars off delivery, keep; discount subscription to a middlebrow weekly, toss.) She checks the calendar on which Yi charts the degeneration of her sight.

How are the eyes?

Fine, fine.

On the table are stacks of onion paper and wire for making artificial blooms. Squares of tissue—petals in the raw—repose in color-coded rows. They sell them in the gift shop at the hospital where Yi's granddaughter works. She's an oncologist, Yi says, very proud.

C stabs a sheet onto the wire, fluffs the paper to a petal, crinkles, repeats. A little pile accumulates on a wooden chair. Although—why not real flowers?

Yi shrugs. The last thing the mother of a child in a cancer ward needs, she says, is something that will expire.

The TV is on. The apartment grays with a threat of rain, the skies jowly with storms and Labor Day. Down the long hallway, through the half-open bedroom door—a sweater, a towel, draped over a chair. C brings her tissue and pipe cleaners to the living room, petals budding in her hands, and collapses onto the love seat. Frowns at the TV set. Are you sure you don't want a radio? she asks.

Yi only shakes her head. This is what everyone else is listening to, she says. They sit for a while, assembling unperishable blooms. The tea cools. The cat purrs. A thunderclap shivers up Manhattan's spine. The drone of the TV livens to a ditty. C scans a Chinese newspaper until she finds a character she can understand. (*I asked for a Mandarin speaker!* was an early complaint.) C's own mother, Yugoslavian-born—she would have been around Yi's age by now—was never able to iron from her English conversation certain persistent solecisms. Yet here was Yi, fluent in cynicism three ways. At least three.

Yi, C says, flipping through the paper, guessing at headlines containing GoodNite attacks, how many languages do you speak again?

Yi waves a hand. The *zhiqing* had a lot of time, she says.

As, frankly, does C. Every hour with Yi is an hour away from her own problems. One could make a life of listening to the rain, stabbing petals onto wires, narrating the visuals on TV for Yi: people are gathering in the Park.

Why? Yi asks.

C pauses. She and Yi do not talk politics. I guess they're dissatisfied, she says.

Yi puckers her lips. She waves a hand in front of her face, as if to shoo a pest, then settles for dismissal by exaggeration: I'm too old for these things.

They crack the spine of a heavily footnoted book—Yi has heady tastes. Her loss of sight has coincided, vexingly, with a period of great personal enrichment. She is reading the Great Books, the classics, the world's major religious texts—that's probably how she lost her eyes, her granddaughter says—and for their hours together has planned prodigious reading projects. This month, they are working their way through the Upanishads. Over the rush of the downpour and the newsreel's alarms, C begins. So does the world. They begin with the beginning of time. No government. No economy. No parks. Hardly even what C or Yi might call a mind. They begin before matter, before Archimedes ever had a place to stand. The only existence on record is Death, and he is lonely—also hungry. He creates the land, the water, the sun, some life, so that he may eat. All of life: this is his feast.

Or else: the world builds itself up from the primordial pit of language, like a fish walking onto land, one syllable joining the next, until the first being, the original entity, emerges . . . a word, more words, a kind of chant. Everything living is strung together by ligaments of syntax. Life erects an incantatory barrier that separates itself from Death, still so hungry. Maybe he will starve. C reads until the infomercials burn bright gold on the screen, and it is very late when she finally calls the elevator and heads to the street, the tête-à-tête of life versus death resounding in her head.

"That's beautiful," the gnome says.

Later, in bed, C turns on her side. "Sure," she says. "I guess."

6

In the morning, she hurries per usual, tucking shirt into jeans, cuffs into boots, her wrists through the raw-hem sleeves of her old art school coat. Coffee. Spit. She grabs her keys and purse, locks the door, unlocks it, goes back inside—finds her wallet on the bed.

Checks her phone. No messages.

Her block is leafy, desirable, only an hour from downtown when the trains are on time. From her windows she can see to the river, to Jersey, to the dull hash of the trees. This morning, as she crosses the dappled shade toward the train, it occurs to her that she wouldn't be able to afford her apartment if she tried to sign it now. On the other hand, maybe haunted sublets come discounted. She pauses at the cart for a roll, turns, catches the eye of the baker across the street, and wonders if she doesn't detect a touch of pity, a hint of malice, in the set of the woman's jaw.

The store occupies the acute angle of a deranged Tribeca intersection. The windows at the top jut meanly into the street like the prow of a ship, an avoidable mistake—but an art supply store must adopt its corner's geometry. The unusual shape has left no storage for half sizes at a ladies' footwear boutique; for prep in a kitchen; for the rows of sinks, grooved like guillotines, that line the posh salons. If C had any storage space at all, resupply would be a breeze. But as things stand, demand for wedged real estate is low, restocking is a challenge, and the rent is cheap. And besides, she likes life in a niche, a hideaway.

The visitor doesn't visit here.

The door swings wide into a cardboard blockade. When she's cleared enough deliveries to walk freely through the space, she settles at the register to review the books. She considers the stack of presolved Rubik's Cubes, the bins of beads, the plastic stickers skewered on their hooks. She loads slides of alpine scenes into the carousel projector that attends her painting classes. Pens, scissors, and rulers sprout shabbily from a milk pitcher; C straightens the bouquet. Revenue less store rent, less apartment rent, less healthcare and food and self-improvement. She calculates it again. The result invites a frown.

In a way, not much has changed since her divorce. It wasn't unusual then for C to open the store on her own. Or restock on her own. Or generally spend most of her time on her own, in the shop, now that she thinks about it. She always kept the books, the accounts, the orders. She didn't mind. You had to have a head for numbers if you were weaving. One for weft on, zero for off. It was the original programming. The industrialists automated jacquard by planning patterns out on punch cards and slipping them into the machines. That you could be your own machine was, for C, the original draw. You programmed everything yourself, except in the end there was something useful, beautiful—something you could touch.

"I really was good once," she's told the visitor, who has a way of igniting her pride.

And it was the truth. A year out of art school, C sold her first major piece, a large-scale tapestry titled *Women Working with Their Hands*, to Midtown's most voracious contemporary collection—at auction, no less. Floor-to-ceiling pink. She suddenly had money. And she was disgusted.

In the past, she'd sold work through Francesca (then Zo's friend, not yet her ex) to private clients who hung them in the privacy of their lofts. But *Women Working with Their Hands* was so public, so acclaimed, and frankly, so enormous. Unscalable, as one critic punned. Soon after, C couldn't remember why she'd woven it at all. The piece had come to her in a frenzy, like religion. She'd spent months at her loom, stabbing the sanguine shuttle through the warp. Wool and silk, natural dye, tweeds. Interlocking wefts for tapestry construction. She'd dyed the wool herself. Her hands glowed fuchsia, as if lit from within. Her fingers swelled from the embroidering. The piece haunted her now. She'd auctioned off her most private impulses at a price point that had caused them to dissolve, or else to be subsumed, as C saw it, into someone else's programming.

The idea had been to create a crowd: so many hands shimmering in pink, collective and interdependent, a great fuchsia guffaw, the joke being, of course, that only one woman can work a loom at a time. The punch line was right there in the logic of the machine. Yet the tapestry had been purchased and reviewed with all due gravity—which is to say, with self-indulgence. *WoWoWTH* absorbed more sentențious exegesis than it was ever meant to hold. The weave wore thin. It received all pliably, passively, fucked by arguments for collective action, women's liberation, the return to the tangible from the creep of dot-com. Textiles, the critics proclaimed, were experiencing a renaissance, and so, by extension, were women. When had women become passé? C felt buffoonish for having missed it, twice over for profiting off rebounding trends. She herself had fallen for the allure of handiwork: the tedium, the aches, the effort, the calluses. Three basic stitches—plain weave, twill, and satin—and endless variations, the sheen of humanity retained. But she had no politics, or if she did, it came to this: if worse came to worst, you could still wear her art as a cape. Other superimposed interpretations she couldn't accommodate.

People still went to see the piece, she gathered. If only they'd give it back, maybe she could still fix it. It had taken her four years and ten panels, plus several embroideries, to reach the scale she'd desired, and even then, it felt unfinished. She could have kept going; she could have expanded it for the rest of her life if Max hadn't encouraged her to show it to her gallerist. But to think that she might once again unleash her baser instincts . . . the idea gave her morning sickness. She began to dread the weft, the warp, flinched at any sense of pattern as soon as it took form. She, too, could purchase moral purpose, said some stirring in her pelvis. And so she melodramatically vowed never to weave again.

If Max had considered it a minor tragedy to wind up a failed artist, perhaps less minor and more tragic was to be an artist who'd succeeded only once. *WoWoWTH*! If only they'd take it down. But that would upset the gallery's gender balance, so it might as well be on permanent display. C hates it now. She hates pink. If she could, she'd ban the color from her store, along with its accomplices: magenta, rose, subversive lilacs, blush. But C knows it would be financial suicide to run an arts supply store sans the prepubescent's favorite palette. Little girls come in to select damask initials, ruby-encrusted birthday crowns. Pink has collateralized the entire enterprise: after the sale of *WoWoWTH*, she brought her twenty thousand to the bank and took out a loan—and twenty more from Zo.

Aren't you the woman who made *Women Working with Their Hands*? people she hopes are customers still disappoint her by asking. They are often students, eccentrics, out to interview her for some class. She imagines them in the library, researching artists so obscure even their professor will be surprised. Then they come into her shop, eager and bright, with no intention to buy. Oh, the shame! She wishes she'd woven under a pseudonym. They thought they knew something about her. The only solution, really, is to overwrite her fuchsia legacy. But C is done with making art.

She rests her chin in her hand, closes her accounts. One lesson she's learned from both weaving and retail is never to try to calculate your real wages by the hour, inclusive of opportunity cost.

Even still, in stolen moments, it sometimes seems to C that she's traded her talent for fertility, or for a hope of fertility. By the time she put down her loom, her body had become clocklike, synchronized, shiny and new. The means of production had been appropriated, streamlined; it could now produce nothing else. She'd had four miscarriages in quick succession, then the whitecoats harvested her uterus. These days, with no child and Max long gone, C often wishes she could trade back—or so she explained to the visitor last night while making squash soup. The blender drowned her out, so it didn't really count as a confession.

"Anyway, it's not important," she says now, to no one in particular.

Not a single customer for hours. Outside, men in hard hats crouch on the curb, easing bacon-egg-and-cheese from wax paper pouches. Around two, a Frenchman stops in to admire the row of wooden abacuses in the window. He's from the university, maybe. He probably teaches what the kids call STEM; she can tell from the corduroy coat, the expensive jeans, the pencils in his pocket, and the questions that he asks. He slides the auburn discs along their bars the way you might tease a parrot with a nut.

I haven't seen an abacus in years, he says, amused. Do you have any with zeroing functions? She smiles. That's her trade, nostalgia and pink. Never mind, he says. Say, can I get this gift wrapped?

Sure thing. She babies the abacus into a sheet of plain white butcher's paper, corkscrews the ribbon ends.

Nice place you have here, the man says.

She'd figured him for a small talker (*Are you the one who made . . .?*), but there is more confidence than cordiality in his appraisal of her shop. The man's coat is too heavy for the season. He must wear it for the pockets, she thinks as he slips the abacus in. Or maybe the style is of French persuasion; his accent is revealed in Americanisms.

Can I ask—do you break even? he says on his way out the door.

What a question!

The man nods. Touché. Well then, well then. I'm glad to hear. The bell chimes. She waits for him to cross the street. Then, in despair, she goes around the corner to the deli for a coffee and the paper and a sweet brick of peanuts she begins to gnaw before she's paid. A new pot is brewing on the hot plate at the coffee station, so she settles for a disappointing decaf. Her hand drifts to her side and lightly presses it, as if to test the organs there. At least she has no pain.

She's left the store unlocked—no time to wait—so she hurries back, newspaper and gratis gift wrap slipping, the coffee slopping, to design the sidewalk advertisement for that day, too late. Her only blouse and her newsprint are stained. Still uncaffeinated, she sits on the stool behind the register, staring at an actual blank slate. She thinks of her mother, who had no trust in the larceny of loans and APRs and homeownership, who took quite literally the etymology of *mortgage* and cried to think of her daughter borrowing for school—art school, no less—when she ought to have been a doctor or a banker. But you are so smart, she'd said. You speak good English. You can do the math.

A sense of possibilities lost, the expired potential of youth, returns to C when she looks down the columns of her accounts to the sorry bottom line.

Feigning confidence, she takes a marker and a square of neon pasteboard. A pink ad appears in her window: WE'RE HIRING! She steps outside and looks back in. On the street, professionals in summer suits are headed to the office to nurse toxic assets back to health. We're all junk traders here, she tells herself.

7

In most versions of the world, there's someone for whose sake the world seems worth preserving. It's probably best to stay in touch with that someone. Although recently, C can't help but feel that neither she nor Zo has any stability to lend.

A few nights a week, C closes up shop and helps Zo renovate her new apartment in the Village (a steal in the Crash), where a kind of mania has overtaken her friend; Zo is deep in the throes of interior redecorating. She signed the deed at market lows, rented at a profit, and is now transforming it into a space of her own. In the past month alone, C has helped remove baseboards, reframe pictures, mend a gash in the bedroom wall. Zo repainted the bathtub red and for weeks strolled the city slightly scarlet; her skin has only just faded to her natural olive. They drilled shelves into supports. Zo missed the mark and caught a thumb; the fingernail swelled and sloughed. She hardly noticed. She was high on DIY.

Zo can afford to pay someone to do her bidding, and, until recently, always has. But I'm embracing the value, she says now in a sudden turn, of my own two hands. And her apartment has proved increasingly subject to their dominion.

Shelves just installed are dismantled, replaced. The remains are piled in a corner, a neat little grave.

Are you sure you're okay? C has asked.

Oh, yes, Zo keeps insisting. I've never felt more alive.

Even C, so sensitive to waste and to how much the old shelves cost, has to admit it's a thrill. Her mother rented, as did Zo's. They grew up next door to one another, in starter apartments teeming with Slovenes and other Yugoslavian refugees. Perpetual renters, neither had so much as drilled a bolt into the wall until Zo scooped up her one-bedroom in the collapse. Sometimes Francesca joins, though she and Zo have long since broken up. C frowns. I thought that didn't go so well?

At this, Zo only shrugs. We made up, she says. Anyway, I'm dating this Professor now.

Today, C closes early. She takes a last look at the garish, neon-pink notice in her window, then draws the grate over the door. As she walks to her friend's half-decimated abode, her reflection in the passing windows strikes her as nervous, ghostly, more transparent, as if she absorbs less light than other solid objects on the street—or maybe everyone else is simply absorbing more. She threads her thumbs through the buckles of her purse and trains her gaze away. Forget the loans, the mysterious pain in her belly, the nagging sense that she's being followed—whether her childhood friend also has a loose screw. Outside, children are coming home from school, bright backpacks bouncing, and C has sold an abacus and an entire starter kit: drawing paper, charcoal, sharpeners, erasers, and pastels. $94.71.

Expensive hobby, no? the woman joked.
It's no home renovation, C thinks.

Zo's new address corresponds to a top-floor walk-up on a quiet street that empties expensively onto the river. The landlord brags that the building was once owned by a lawyer who volunteered the cellar to the Underground Railroad. (But where is the commemorative plaque?) Upstairs, the windows open only halfway, penned in by ivy growth, and when she arrives, C finds Zo cranking them as far as they can go so she can smoke, even though she's ostensibly quit.

You want one?

Sure, C replies.

Zo takes C's wrist and lights the cigarette for her, because some things never change. As Zo leans in, close enough to announce a revamping of her perfume, the antique glass tympanum they've installed above the door rises over her shoulder like a mullioned moon: a little Madonna, rolls of arm fat stained a healthy rose. Mother and child both strike C as too young.

Zo pulls away and flips the lighter closed. So, what's new with you?

C thinks of the visitor padding along her floors, preening in his little suit. Now that the shock's worn off, he seems even less worth a mention.

Not much. Slow for September. You?

Zo points at a tower of tile samples by the fridge. C nods, takes a drag, and coughs.

What's the agenda for today? Are we breaking down any walls?

Arms crossed, Zo leans against the sill, still in slacks and Oxford shirt, and looks at the barrier to the bedroom with more relish than is perhaps appropriate.

To be clear, I'm only joking, C adds.

Zo and C have known each other for decades. It's normal to grow apart, reconnect. All the more natural that they should find each other changed. There have been promotions and surgeries and interest rate adjustments, market shifts and network reconfigurations, general maintenance and systems updates. They've moved. Their Wi-Fi passwords are not the same.

And it's been a while since they've spent time together, alone. Most often, there are three of them: C, Zo, and Zo's latest object of affection. There was Claudia, the librarian with the tight turtlenecks, red barrettes, and a voice as high-pitched as a bird's; her laugh was an unstable song in search of a key on which to land. Francesca was aristocratic, a modest heiress medicated into cheerfulness, one of the few of Zo's amours who didn't need Zo's money and proved it by showering her with fussy, expensive gifts: artisanal Camembert, razor clams in finicky tins, a pair of cashmere gloves that trickled down to C after Francesca left. Edna waltzed through, trailing bottles of white burgundy, faded literary dreams, and a law degree. She played the cello too. C's favorite was Jules the dancer, who carried on conversations from the floor, her face floating over her knees as she stretched her legs and reviewed her chances of making principal. The promotion, though it always seemed so close, never quite arrived.

The turnover was brisk enough that C was left pitying the third parties in that kitchen. They doted on Zo. They were affectionate toward C, indulging her constant presence. They went out of their way to make her comfortable, as if to establish that C were the one visiting. But give it six months, a year—eventually it was they, not she, who would be shown the door. She was a permanent fixture, like an appliance. Alone, she and Zo talked about the women who'd just left.

Once, not long before she met her most recent acquisition, Zo posed a question: What would you say, hypothetically, if your girlfriend told you she once attempted arson? If she lit the match and everything, and only got off because she'd miscalculated the amount of gasoline? To this day, C wonders which of the girlfriends it was. Not Francesca—it couldn't be. Claudia? In retrospect, it was obvious. Now, slightly dizzy here in Zo's new digs, C fantasizes that it was she herself who'd lit the match.

The latest lover, too, is an anomaly, and in more ways than one. The first is obvious. The second: he and C have never met.

I thought we'd tackle the kitchen, Zo says. She stubs out her cigarette, pulls on a smock, disappears into the pantry, and reappears, leveraging her slender frame against the door. Her arms are filled with paint rollers and newspapers and plastic bins. She lowers the equipment onto the table, where it settles disharmoniously over the mail.

C glances at the bank statement laid out for review, now obscured by supplies. I could have brought you masking tape.

You're sweet, Zo replies.

They get to work, organizing paint trays and retrieving tarps from under the sink. This Professor, C learns, despises the pale yellow of the walls; it makes him ill. C looks around the room and finds that she reluctantly agrees. Anyway, we can always just paint over it again, Zo says, wrenching open another can. He'll be spending more time here, the Professor. The relationship has taken a turn toward permanence, occasioning Zo's decision to paint all the walls a celebratory shade of eggplant. She cranks open a can to show C the hue. It oozes from the lid, dark as blood in the dim. The swatch glints black as a Malevich. But if the label says it's purple . . . well, that's what it is.

The masking tape emits a screech. They outline the baseboards in bright blue—the sink, the stove, the cupboards, etc. It isn't as easy to repaint a kitchen as it is a living room. C has the uncanny feeling they are strengthening seams, fortifying joints, sealing themselves in. The Madonna observes the preparations from her tympanum.

Revolution was never Zo's modus operandi. Now she's renovating everything: women to men, immigrant to one-percenter, buttercream to eggplant. She's not so far, really, from the sort of person who quits her job and moves across the country to camp out at Occupy. C doesn't know how to square it. It makes her wonder what Zo's hiding, though of course C is hiding plenty too. They've carried each other through every kind of personal disaster. Why would this time be different? Because this disaster is impersonal?

She smooths a length of tape into a seam. A light musk laces the air. The room seems to part again, expanding, only this time it does not snap back. Then the sharp pain in her side returns, and she succumbs. There is just enough time to set the paint roller in its tray before everything goes black.

She wakes up some time later, still on the floor, to a slight pressure on her shoulder. It would seem she's fainted. Zo is standing over her, ready for bed: white T-shirt, dark Spanx, excess night cream shining on her lids. C is reminded of evenings from their childhood, the two of them sharing a bed while their mothers conspired in the kitchen downstairs.

Sorry, she says.

Zo rolls her eyes. Please. She squats at C's side and runs her hands through damp hair. I thought I'd let you sleep. Don't you think you should get this checked out?

Sure.

I'm serious.

I am too.

Zo tosses her hands up. What can she do? Then she surrenders, sits. As she does, the tarp burps out its living plastic sound.

I'm sorry I've been so hard to get in touch with. This fucking client—Midwestern pension fund, it's always a mess with them. They bought all this insurance, or what was supposed to be insurance, back in 2006—anyway, think of the father of every girl we knew growing up who monogrammed her cardigans, and you'll see what the problem is. Meanwhile, if they just paid the guy in charge what they're paying *me*—

Then you'd be in charge?

Exactly.

They fall silent, listening to the spontaneous popping of the tarp, the white noise of the city outside. C can feel Zo's eyes on her now, as searching as the visitor's, pressuring her to admit to the impulses she would rather hide. She smooths her face and lets her mind go blank, imagining storing her worries in the back rooms of her brain, where her beautiful friend cannot get to them.

Then Zo smiles and shakes her head. At once, the tension breaks. She shifts onto her stomach and cups her chin in her hand.

Francesca was asking me about you the other day.

Okay.

What do you think?

I don't know. Maybe.

Zo shoves her playfully. You don't think about a lot of things. When are you going to start weaving again?

C turns onto her side. This is my least favorite conversation.

Propped on her elbows, sphinxlike, Zo has leverage, which she uses to push C back onto her spine. Her hand lingers. C looks up at her friend. The unabsorbed cream around Zo's eyes makes them appear to glow. Then, in a smooth, fluid motion, Zo's lips meet the bare bones of C's neck, where her collar pulls away. The gesture lingers for a length that requires explanation. It is not quite a kiss, but neither is it an accident. Then, just as abruptly, Zo breaks away.

C wonders about it the whole way home, her hand hovering at her throat.

It's concerning: the visitor, the pain, the kiss. The planned and unplanned destruction of lives. Or nothing is really a concern unless it happens again, or thrice—and yet.

At home, C tries to tame the excitement in her chest. She suppresses her hope, which she shouldn't entertain, not for a friend who is the closest thing to a relative—a sister—that she still has. What would their mothers have said? She finishes a slice of toast over the sink, turns on the faucet to wash away the crumbs. Really, it's obscene. She imagines this soupçon of desire, confusing, illicit, as not so different from the pain itself: a glitch in internal machinery already assigned to other jobs, a foreign agent in her blood. How to kill it, she wonders, without doing additional harm to herself?

```
DATA visitors;
   input = "package.install"
   SELECT var = "part two"
   TABULATE
RUN;
```

1

On the ancient stage—this Wiki'd on C's laptop, with her permission—the end of the world was circumscribed by the proscenium, which circumscribed, in turn, the longing for annihilation. Elsewhere, the audience professed allegiance to order. Clock in, clock out.

C frowns. The visitor presses on.

"In the baser sediments of the collective mind," he explains, "a quiet rage settles, and, deeper still, through the bedrock, there stirs a tremor, an urge to destroy, to prove that the systems at the surface are in fact contingent." *Poof!* It is only through their destruction that one reveals conventions were never the natural state. Until then it is better to be involved, integrated, to have a stake in life as it is, to only occasionally peer into the abyss.

But most people, if pressed (C included), would admit to the dark longing in them, that little suspicion that skips in the chest—there might be something marvelous in disruption.

"Don't you see?"

"Maybe."

There may indeed be something beautiful to be observed in the GoodNite attacks, if those four young activists, recently arrested, were to succeed. They won't, of course. Still, one can dream. And if a set of researchers were to conduct a poll, tally responses, tabulate cross sections of those in support (in theory) and those not, it is likely the estimations would deviate significantly ($p \leq 0.05$) from public record. Preliminary results suggest that in private, in their apartments, people are rather inclined to give GoodNite a chance. They flip through the paper, searching for the latest developments, which arrive serialized, in Dickensian installments. Those unafraid of their own desires are hooked. One wonders if the press is aware of the cause of this boost in readership, if the readers are aware of one another. It is not something one readily admits, enthusiasm for crashing the national grid. But just think: to watch the world go dark. One imagines people spilling into the streets, walking down highways, scattering into the night, disappearing once and for all. Alone, they muse, *What would I make of a night like that?*

A difficult question to avoid, so long as GoodNite is still asserting itself in public. One week after the kiss—if that's what it is?—during the entirety of which Zo and C are not in contact, four engineers are apprehended for hacking the supercomputer at the former Soviet nuclear facility. (Though the press prefers the term *energy research compound.*) The engineers claim to belong to a coven of ecohackers. Their target is the United States' electrical grid, which, according to the available documents, turns out to be surprisingly easy to undermine. Physical infrastructure is relatively exposed ("I wouldn't balk at a chicken-wire fence," the visitor says), crucial transformers are imported in bulk from abroad, and fragmented authority across three continental interconnects leads both to waste ("inefficient transmission") and cascading outages. Add to these structural weaknesses new cybersecurity concerns over substations that are supposed to be isolated from remote attacks, but aren't. By no means a piece of cake, but then again . . . Hadn't GoodNite already taken out a major artery in Alamo, TX? Experts had pointed out that they'd have needed an immensely powerful computer to accomplish this. The only vulnerable machines left in the world with that sort of muscle were currently located in Ukraine. One leads to the next. A network of cause and effect.

"Rather impressive," the visitor says.

C has to admit these events do seem linked: the arrests, the blackouts, not to mention everything else that's been happening. One can be relieved, at least, that one is not oneself a grid and therefore not a target. Yet the newspapers, which bury the story deeper every day, haven't made the connection—or, where connections *have* been made, they've failed to raise the appropriate alarms. But perhaps it isn't so surprising that what an otherworldly visitor considers front-page news would hardly match consensus. There are plenty of other, better reasons to be alarmed: the extinction of the bees, Syria, rotting mortgage tranches, hurricanes, and arteries coated with corn syrup and salt.

She admits concern over confirmation bias. On this side of the information flow, one hears only of the GoodNite attacks that were successfully halted, and of these, many have seemed purposefully sloppy. Hacks twice over, if you will—decoys to put the public at ease. A few weeks ago, a group of amateurs with garden shears almost cast a whole Alabama town into the dark. GoodNite claimed responsibility the following day: *the best hacks r simplest make da system work for u . . . goooood nite!* It could have been a high school prank. A man walked into a grocery store in Illinois, waving a gun. He shot two people in the parking lot. The incident—always an incident, never a crime—was conveyed across the screen and out of frame, out of mind. The gunman likewise cited the group as his inspiration, but regarding this most recent heist on life, GoodNite has been silent. Gun violence is perennial, garden-variety, and no one takes credit for spring.

Though, rumor has it GoodNite was also responsible for the blackout of 2003.

As the official story goes, a generator sputtered in Ohio, tripping 345-kV lines that serviced the rest of the Eastern Interconnection and bringing the seaboard down. A mistake on such a scale, slipping past every sensor and safeguard—a little fishy, isn't it? C and Max were in the apartment, working by candlelight. It was one of their best weeks together. C spent it in the alcove across from the daybed, working at her loom, because she was still weaving with ambition then: a laddered pattern, all in black, velvet chenille to absorb the sound. She'd meant to make a little swath of night, a black hole, a place to hide, fabric designed to swallow all sensation. The outage was her inspiration. It was cold—no heat, everything was closed, the trains were stalled, candle prices surged to ten dollars a wick—but the two of them, together, wearing all the sweaters they owned, had never been more content. With the power out, with M, she was still a woman working with her hands. She must have deleted the bit where they were miserable, where the cold sowed aches in their joints, because all she can remember now is mild sex (no arguments over whether to leave the light on), peanut butter on white bread, how M was stationed here on the daybed, sketching C as C herself hovered over the black wool warp. The piece is still spooled around the front cloth beam: a reminder. They might even have made it, she sometimes thinks, if only the lights had never come back on. Maybe she owes the GoodNite savants for that suspended week—a sick kind of gratitude.

In her own research on the fragility of the grid, C has become particularly obsessed with the idea of the *air gap: a network security measure by which a computer is physically isolated from the public internet*, or in the case of the nation's 23,000 generators, from any internet connection at all. Such machines are hermetic, self-contained. Software updates by hard coding and hard copy alone. This arrests C's attention. The generators' digital isolation raises the question: How could GoodNite's worm have found its target? She imagines the generators as patients in iron lungs, or as the infectious, barricaded in plastic and quarantined to keep the public safe, lest they contaminate the innocent (and mightn't she, these days?). In the case of the grid, however, the aim of isolation is the opposite—the generators have removed themselves from a world that makes them sick. A platitude returns to her from she-can't-remember-where: *This is the difference between a doctor and an engineer: the engineer constructs a hazmat suit; the doctor invents the vaccine.*

Perched on the edge of the tub, C reads the paper as she runs a bath. She loves the news. What misery! It reminds her she's not the only one. She brings the faces of the culprits, thin and serene, close to her own. They strike her as being in remarkably good health. Their faces reflect the orange glow of the prison uniforms: little suns. Then the water begins to steam, and the paper floats to the tiles.

She lights a candle, steps in, and slips beneath the surface. Holds her breath. There, underwater, she wishes she had her own conspiracy, an affair, to worry about. Perhaps she ought to start weaving or dating again, as Zo suggests. Easy for her to say—Zo isn't even attracted to men, she's dated women all her life, and yet she's effortlessly fallen in with this Professor, while C remains alone. She runs a hand along her clavicle. It's just like Zo, really, to play a joke like that. It isn't good to hope. C could try to fall for another woman instead, she supposes. There's always Fran. But as she sinks beneath the suds, it's Zo who rises in her mind, according to the principles of fluid displacement. In her thoughts, her friend stands in heels and a pencil skirt, talking on the phone—

C resurfaces and looks around the small, white room, as if afraid she might be caught.

She is never thinking of the right thing. Her thoughts refuse to train themselves on the subjects they ought to—money, job, the overdue loans. Instead, attention eddies around fires, flowers, violent crime, forbidden sex. Over the lip of the tub, she can see the hexagonal tiles, alternating white and black. They extend into the kitchen, too, where crumbs settle in the grout. She hates those tiles. What a pain they are to sweep! But what a great distraction they are when she ought to be focused on something else. She recalls standing on them with Max while having a serious discussion—at least, that's what he kept saying. This is serious, he'd said. The rhetorical details are vague, though the tile design is still stark in her mind. As Max explained the serious matter, C traced concentric polygons in the mosaic, forming and dissolving patterns. He kept repeating, This is important. Are you listening to me? It was a conversation about space, she remembers now. That was the important thing Max wanted to talk about: space. Specifically, needing more of it.

Only C couldn't concentrate. He droned on. There was Max's art, hers, his life, hers. The berth was not wide enough for both of them at once. Max was fine with the idea of C. He loved her, in fact. He said it again, there in the kitchen, standing by his suitcases: I love you, he said. Only he could do without the particulars of C's maternal desires—namely, children, and namely, creating whatever she wanted to on the loom and also controlling its reception—which she dragged through the relationship like the long train of a dress. It got in the way, the silk train of her dreams, made him too cautious about where he could step. If you tell me to stay, he said to C, I will. But if we don't want the same things, well, I don't see how that's a problem we can fix. C honed in on a single hexagonal tile and added to it a rim of other tiles, expanding band by band, tessera by tessera, until she'd annexed the entire kitchen floor. I want to stay, he said, but we have to figure something out.

C looked at him, noticing the way his hair fell over his brow, a stray lock that bungeed between his eyes. But can't you imagine us with kids?

Max smoothed the curl with his palms. It bothered her, C realized, the single, unruly lock, as well as his tic of trying to tame it flat. That's just the thing, he said. I can't.

C pressed. Their daughters would go to those special public schools. The good ones. School, at least, would be something they could afford. I'm smart, she said, parroting her mother.

Max scowled. What are you trying to imply? His paints were packed into the cases at his feet. If only they wanted the same things, he said.

But they did! C insisted.

He peered back into the apartment, cold and victorious. You've had, he said, four miscarriages.

People are forever projecting certainty where information is incomplete. That's the problem, she thinks—there are always other reasons. It is only now, as she draws a bar of soap along her shin, that she understands where she went wrong. He'd been proud of her, maybe even envious. At openings, people greeted C first, speculated about her influence on him—the block colors, the hyperrealism, the textural modulation. *It's so realistic, all those hands, at least from a distance.* That humiliating spectacle! How disappointed viewers must be to see her now, when they trace the wall text to her shabby store. Perhaps he'd been right about the berth. She rises for air, closes her eyes. Sometimes she imagines making something so grand that it overwrites her legacy, dislodges her from her past.

She sinks again and counts slowly, the way she and Zo used to do as girls, settling to the bottom of the pool to squint at each other through the blue—*one Mississippi, two*—breath escaping in globes from Zo's nostrils and mouth. C always lost. She floats a hand down her body, along her stomach, toward the faucet, alights—and resurfaces with a gasp.

It is supposed to be salutary, lighting candles, taking baths. Occasional masturbation. Reputable magazines have impressed upon her the importance of affordable indulgences. It is essential in this tanking economy, this sinking ship, for desperate people to invest in slyer forms of self-care. The whole indebted nation is downsizing, sloughing toxic assets, and bringing the rest of the world with it. C, for her part, has never known how to relax. What she wants is something better, something pure—not rest. She inquires as to whether she is enjoying herself now and finds the answer is no. At once, she mutinies, splashing lukewarm and perfumed suds over the enamel. The pink seam of her scar appears at water level, just below her navel. She runs a fingertip along its smooth, numb path. She wonders if she and Max would be more compatible now that she will not be having kids. It still strikes her as strange that this should be true. She'd always pictured herself with children the same way she pictured herself with four limbs, two hands, her plain and open face.

The gnome surprises her below the towel rack, standing over the newspaper photo C left on the floor.

He says, "There are likely more than four of them."

2

C's hair dries in unflattering patterns overnight. She wakes up alone. With a glance around the room, she can see the visitor is gone, absent from the bureau, the ceiling, the baseboards. On the dresser, her scents are in order and the jewelry box is latched. The solitude is substantiated, solid and whole, to the exclusion of unreal company.

"Don't do it again," she says.

One thing is clear when it comes to gnomic ontology: out here, in the world beyond, she is truly alone. He does not follow her to the shop, Zo's (a demolition job! she would've thought he'd enjoy tagging along), the deli hot bar, or the bank, where a hopeful C has an appointment this morning at eight. She is already consulting refinancing plans, new loans, savvier means of making ends meet. Her life is arithmetic, and she checks the sums herself. As she walks to the train, she feels a redoubled loyalty to the shop, which, after all, protects her from the visitor, who seems unable or unwilling to travel there. The threat of the GoodNite group, the fascination, fades the farther away the creature is—if *farther* is the word. The longer she goes without seeing him, then. She's just a normal citizen, heading to work. She doesn't even bother to glance at the baker—see how easy it is?—and, even better, she's heard from her friend.

A leaf detaches and lands in her hair. More are scattered across the sidewalk, damp and unruly and dark, but this morning, C is impervious to metaphors for death; maybe it's time to stop settling for less. She walks as far as she can through the mottled corridor of her quiet avenue, where the trees are slowly molting. It is bright, early, the sun is out. Broadway buzzes to her left, a block away. The pigmentation of the day, the hint of a chill, are carrying out the duties of renewal, predicate of commerce. She too feels new, full of potential. Expensive! New loans, new plans. Zo has finally decided on a color and asked C to help her repaint the living room again. *It looks good on me, no?* The text arrived this morning with a picture of Zo, smiling and thumbs-upping, posing in her underwear and nightshirt in front of a splotch on the wall that looks just like the others to C. *Thursday?* The image is grainy on the confining screen, though Zo herself is radiant, despite the pixelation. C studies the picture with a flutter in her chest and flips the phone shut. It's also a joke, like lips against a collarbone. She gets it. Ha! That's why she loves her friend, her capacity for jest. Also—*also*—the spectacle of spandex, stretched darkly around her thighs.

She's relieved to hear from Zo, and maybe a touch too satisfied that it was Zo and not she who broke the silence. Had they not grown up together in one another's homes, beds, shared bubble baths, she wonders if they would still be friends. The Cleveland suburb of their childhoods is worlds away, a modest place where no buildings nosed over seven stories tall and starter apartments teemed with émigrés. The girls were always together then; C was supposed to supply the influence. Zo's mother spoke so many of the vestigial tongues—Slovenian, Croatian, German, Hungarian, enough Italian to complain to an actual Italian about the seizure of Trieste—and so incompletely that there was no room for English and its idioms. All the more reason, it was felt, for Zo to spend extended periods of time at C's, where every language was forbidden save American. You will get accents, C's mother said. Don't listen. It is not important to know. The girls crouched beneath the kitchen table, playing dolls on the linoleum as their mothers chatted overhead. Teacups tapped cryptically on saucers, accented by the sugar spoon and conjugations with Slavic roots. It was as if their mothers and Zo had access to an entirely separate realm, a private cupboard into which they covertly reached. Later, lying side by side in C's bed, Zo translated what she'd grasped. As far as C was concerned, she might as well have left the conversation coded. What did it mean, a *Serb*? C envied Zo then for having been born abroad. For C's part, it often seemed like a velvet curtain had been drawn across the past, leaving her alone onstage, squinting into a great spotlight and ignorant of her lines.

The nearest branch of the bank is all the way downtown, by the store, and C is always late. A poster at the station tells her the train will skip this stop today; she must catch it at the next one, a half mile south. A geezer leans on his cane at the bus stop and claps a hand to his knee. *No trains!* He will be amplifying the MTA like this all day, and the way he says it makes C feel like an idiot. She mourns the era when she used to bike, traveling in private slipstreams. But she can't pedal six miles, not anymore.

C's mother was a bank teller (and supper club hostess, waitress, seamstress, cleaning woman, and nag). Perhaps that's why C now regards such institutions with equal parts revulsion and reverence. There is something inescapably condescending, doggedly maternal, about a retail bank, forever disappointed in its own customers. C nurtures a weird nostalgia for it. The loan adviser is a particular source of fascination. C likes to imagine her coming into work, past the Charging Bull, boom market or bust. She wears low heels, slacks, and even in an Indian summer like this keeps a shawl draped over the chair at her desk—the bank is fiercely air-conditioned in all seasons, as if to keep its holdings fresh. Silk, cashmere, shots of gold and harness maker's thread—it's a nice shawl, though C would have preferred it in shades of gray and black. Her host is there to meet her when she arrives. Glad you made it, she says.

C follows her through the soundproofed cubicles, where people are being advised, mortgaged, and fleeced. On the threshold of her own adviser's office, she takes in the settee, the reference books on the shelves, and the empty vase on the table, barren of bouquets. The arms of the chair are like taxidermy in her palms. It is rather like a therapy session, the two of them seated on leather furniture on opposite sides of an imposing desk. C herself has never been to therapy, but Zo has, and C has picked up a detail here and there. She recalls a bit of advice the analyst gave her friend: to combat a persistently negative thought, imagine watching it float into one of a series of baskets and closing the wicker lid.

The adviser keeps a crystal bowl of lollipops at the end of her desk. She types C's account number into the log as C sits and waits, purse in her lap, considering a flavor called *banapple*. She wants very much to select a lollipop, but it strikes her as antithetical to her goal of having her application approved. Impressions are everything, her mother used to say, and it seems to C that it is the defaulters who help themselves to pens and candies on the desk; everything gratis is tagged with hidden interest. Freedom is a credit score, a financial cushion, an investment in ETFs at mid-level risk pegged to a late retirement age. The adviser, who has ETFs and a broker herself, lets the stem of a lollipop bob unfairly in her mouth.

She removes the candy with a *pop* and rearranges her shawl over her button-down. So you can withdraw, she says of C's IRA, the one her mother opened for her back when teenage C was also working at the supper club, ferrying classmates' fathers' plates of fish. Only you'll have to pay the tax, okay?

C looks down at the notes she has taken on the complimentary stationery with a complimentary pen. She adds along the columns again, subtracts. There is satisfaction to be found in the fact that she has correctly accounted for the penalty. The right answer puts her at ease, as if the point of this exercise was to compute the correct solution rather than to generate a sum, any sum, in the actual world. Money is so wonderfully hypothetical—she's hardly lifted a hand, and here it is, the IOU. No labor at all! Her work is done. She nods for the adviser to put in an order to liquidate what is left. So much for a balanced portfolio, which, for someone of her age, she's learned should follow a moderate-risk and long-term ratio of 70/30 stocks to interest-bearing assets, with fractions in commodities, in gold. One should aim to have a third of one's yearly income on hand at all times, ready to splurge. For emergencies like this, the adviser says.

The use of *emergency* still seems rather strong. C resents the suggestion that she has not planned ahead, spent prodigally, failed to save. As if one could put a bucket out in the rain to collect this emergency cash. The hysterectomy—now, *that* was an emergency. This is simply an unusual shift in circumstances, a dry spell, a blip. She'll liquidate the Roth IRA—she's a shopkeeper! the petite bourgeoisie! who among her kind ever retires?—to pay off the last two months' bills, the hospital debts outstanding, and secure a small business loan for the coming year. She's already canceled her health insurance. Screw penalties from the government. Maybe she'll become a Republican—or a republican. Either way, she's confident that this should close the gap. Her gaze rests on the candy bowl, flits from banapple to grape to orange. Once she signs the loan, she'll take the whole cornucopia home.

As we discussed, the adviser says, slipping the candy back into her mouth, this all gets easier once you find a guarantor.

3

She turns east on Pine, where the imperatives of a human microphone echo between the buildings. *No drugs . . . No drugs . . . ! Or alcohol . . . ! Or alcohol . . . ! In this park . . . ! In this park . . . !* C takes the long way around. The temporary village makes her uncomfortable. There is too much moral authority in the Park; she suspects that they too resent her loans, or at least her efforts to repay them. The other day, when she took the route just past Zuccotti, she found herself surrounded by a set of clipboards, everyone pressing for her signature. C has learned the hard way the consequences of committing to the dotted line.

She pauses outside the slick face of a pecuniary institution. The ground floor is open to squatters and chess players and mothers with small children, a public space with potted palms and a little newsstand in a niche, where the candy bars are kept cool in the fridge. Upstairs, the bankers are up to whatever it is that C has never understood and now forgets. She stands smallish in their midst. To think that critics were flocking to review *Women Working with Their Hands* while financiers were twilling toxic assets on this very block. It was all quite successful, really, if one viewed it as performance art—the banks had elbowed their way, rudely and in all-too-real terms, into the average person's life. At least they'd created something of their own before destroying it. The face of the building shines obsidian, like a plaque. No one ever bothers to recount the end to that Arachne myth, C thinks, when the mortal outweaves Athena only to be permanently demoted to the status of an insect.

So. Why do you want to work in arts and crafts?

She conducts a number of interviews that afternoon, impressed by the chutzpah of her applicants. There is Shawn, Skyler, and a skateboarder whose name C immediately forgets. The conversations are brisk, petering out too quickly. I can't paint, Skyler says. I know you teach classes.

She walks them through a typical day: restock, price check, update sale and clearance, lunch, midday sweep, lock up, erect the easels, teach. It takes so little time to describe her routine that when she finishes the applicants shuffle, snuff, and scratch, waiting for the other shoe, or shoes, to drop. They strike her as a twitchy bunch. Any questions? C asks to put them at ease. A woman named Breanna inquires abruptly about health benefits. C laughs. Sure thing. Top-notch plans! They even cover lobotomies, she's tempted to add.

One by one, the job seekers leave, saying they hope to hear from her soon. C watches them disappear through the prow of the store. Yes, soon, she agrees. She doesn't know what else to say; she isn't quite sure what she's hiring for, this hypothetical employee she cannot afford. They are mostly art students, and while she regrets stringing them along, she more resents them for imagining that she's in a position to help, that she's any better off. She pauses by the bins of alphabet beads and looks into the street, thinking of reasons to hire Yi. It was Yi, after all, who came up with the idea for the painting class. She's always wanted the shop to succeed. If only Yi had more money, no mortgage, perhaps she might act as guarantor—

Uh, miss?

The most recent contestant sends a hand through his heavily gelled hair.

I was just saying I haven't worked in retail before.

The door chimes. The applicant exits and another man enters in a wrinkled T-shirt, Army-issued khakis sagging on his doughy hips. He has a shape like a softened cereal box. She turns to tell him she's sorry, there aren't any jobs here after all, vacate the premises, but it's clear he's not interested in employment. He hikes the khakis up as he orients himself, makes his way from the row of abacuses to a rack of neon poster boards. He selects a sheet, brings it to the register, and plucks a marker from the pitcher as he asks, Hey, can I borrow this?

C watches as he scrawls YOU. SHAT. THE. BED., then rings him up for a dollar and change.

He disappears through the front windows and down the street, a flash of pink that dissolves into the gray scale of the suits. She has to admit: the look suits him. She considers her own neon ad, glowing brightly in the window. Fuck you too, she thinks.

At six on the dot, she turns the sign on the door from OPEN to CLOSED and sets up the children's easels. Soon, four small girls arrive. They cling to their mothers' hands, clutch shyly at tall, slim thighs, until the women peel them away and kiss them goodbye. The easels stand in the prow of the store, stacks of beads shoved aside. A mother arrives last minute to enroll her son. He's very talented, she pleads. C detects shadows around her eyes. They have no idea how desperate she is. There are no policies, no plans. The boy sulks by the drawing pads, covertly bends a corner. On the spot, C invents a midcourse registration fee.

The theme of the class is *advanced landscapes and natural scenery*, and the children tear through the material at an alarming speed. C is mildly concerned they will run out of things to paint. To draw out the curriculum last week, she introduced ideas of perspective and vanishing points, an exercise that elicited not only the steady horizon lines she had hoped the lesson would produce, but also entirely derivative experiments; the girls were always looking for new ways to break the rules. So far they've covered trees, mountains, shrubbery, gardens, and magnificent sunsets that stuff up the ends of city blocks like fauvist fatbergs—and, of course, flowers. Today, they will learn to paint the sea.

Pots of gray and shades of blue stand on the center table. C shows her pupils how to mix the white into this base. They add texture to the wave, simulating the spray and foam. The carousel projector is balanced atop the cash register, and C turns off the lights. Images appear on the opposite wall.

Thirty-six ways of looking at Mount Fuji, and they consider only one: the tsunami reaches with its icy talons for three small boats rowing into the slope of the wave, into the shadow of the crest, certain to be demolished. The imminence of the sailors' deaths strikes her as perhaps inappropriate for children of this age. For them, death is something factory-farmed and shrink-wrapped into Styrofoam trays. No beaks, no eyes, no guts, no claws: totally defanged. They just aren't prepared.

One of the girls raises her arms menacingly over the child next to her. I drowned you, the first one says. You're dead.

The canvases are already filling with roses and petal shapes. Someone breaks into the paint cabinet and removes a pink. C has marketed the class as a painting program for the gifted. *Let your children expand their imaginations!* Statistically speaking, there aren't enough gifted children to go around. Demand exceeds supply. C fills in the gap. She moves from easel to easel, trying to encourage the little prodigies to employ their brushes in the style of Hokusai. Look, she says, pointing at the projection. The wave is like a monster. Look at the long talons of the wave! She needs at least one success to remind the mothers of the value of forking over the cash on which C's business model currently depends. The little boy is the only one capable of focus. He is quiet, shy; he ignores the others' billows of blooms. He looks intently at the projected print, then at his canvas, and this seriousness alone is enough to win C's forgiveness of his poor treatment of her sketch pads. He smashes his brush into the navy-blue. When C comes to admire his easel, she sees he has recreated the wave in astonishing likeness, as well as four little easels and four little girls, standing in its path.

4

What will you do, given what other people think you will or should or ought to do for—or to—yourself? It comes down to trust and strategy, to strategic trust. To general goodwill, checked, of course, by rational self-interest, which in the end is a more reliable variable than the milk of human kindness, and all the safer for that. This is the theory behind the brinkmanship that keeps nuclear arsenals from being deployed. Consider: *A* has nothing more to gain by shifting her strategy if *B* and (perhaps especially) *C* have already accounted for *A*'s every possible move and positioned themselves accordingly. But what of the introduction of an irrational element? Who can populate the predicted payoff matrix then, if the rules of the game are random?

It's maddening: the joke, the kiss. Whichever it is, C has resolved to divest it of its mystery. As she folds the easels away, she imagines herself striding courageously through Zo's door, taking her face in her hands, and demanding, *Why did you do that?* Afterward, she will be unburdened of her false hopes. The idea that this plan may very well founder has occurred to C, fleetingly, though it's failed to register as an actual possibility. In this expansive moment, as she steps into the widening mouth of dusk, it seems to her that love is infinitely elastic.

She locks up and draws the grate. Her reflection wavers in passing storefronts, and she quickens her stride. She's just as real as anything else, she decides. It's too easy to fall into cynicism, into an old sense of competition, risk aversion, survival of the fittest. They are both too proud, she and Zo, and in such a game and between such players, the steady state is always silence—unless someone disrupts the stalemate. On a night like this, C feels more than up to the task. Perhaps, rather than Zo avoiding her post-kiss, she's been the one avoiding Zo? The irony! She feels a rush of affection for her friend, an impulse to apologize. The narrow stoop is a confessional; she conquers the vestibule and lingers on the landing to gather her strength. The stained-glass Madonna she helped Zo install above the door lends a reproachful stare.

"Nuts to you, lady," C says.

The door yields to a pall of turpentine. Inside, Zo has already begun, and Francesca has also joined. A plastic tarp breathes across the floor. The antitwilight—decisive dark—of the half-painted room is a shock. Zo observes the disappointment on C's face.

I thought you liked it? she says, then looks from C to Fran. Christ, you're both impossible.

She is wearing makeup, or maybe it's only the glow of the eggplant on her olive skin, the morose thoughts in her head; her ill humor consumes the room like a weather event, as does the paint.

Her friends never tell her the truth, Zo complains.

Fran shrugs. We never said we *loved* it. She smiles at C and lifts her eyebrows as if to add, *Her Majesty's displeased.*

C takes up her own roller and falls in line, already distanced from her radical overtures, checkmated into silence. In any case, premonition robs her of her confidence. Zo lights a cigarette. Fran coughs pointedly, clears her throat. She is kneeling on the floor, laboriously repainting the same few feet of baseboard and masking the others' reticence with anecdotes about her clients—who has taste, who doesn't. A corporate office came to her in delirious search of a Chagall. They want to fill a blank in a boardroom. Can you imagine?

For once, C is grateful that Fran is here, grateful for her ability to manufacture cheer. She is a one-woman assembly line, joining work to conversation. The room is dizzy with humidity. She feels herself detaching from Zo—glacially, she tells herself, though, being an old word, it still means *slowly*, when what she wants to evoke is a healthy, modern glacier up in the steamy Arctic: in a slough, all at once, at speed. And why mourn? She doesn't need Zo, not at all. A stripe of eggplant climbs up the wall. Aubergine, the label contradicts, and which Fran reads aloud. C imagined that Zo invited her here to talk about what she refers to in her private thoughts as *us*. What else could the picture have meant? She glances at her friend, who is wreathed in paint and smoke, bent over the label to study it with Fran. Maybe that's the problem, she's saying. I could have sworn I chose eggplant.

The paint has transformed overnight of its own volition. Either way, it *does* look good on her, C thinks. Then again, so does everything. Zo is one of those rare women who can drench herself in sunflower shades—universally unflattering, according to the magazines—and get away with it.

The onset of night makes the room seem to close in on itself, and the dark wall narrows it further still. The heat is oppressive; they've been waiting for it to break for days, and C wishes for a storm, for rain, for Francesca to tell Zo she hates this riff on Malevich. She wishes everyone would leave so she could take a moment to think. Still holding her brush, she cranks open the kitchen window for a draft.

There, on the table, she finds the abacus, still settled in its gift wrapping.

C slides a nut across the bar. Look at that! The Professor hadn't seemed quite real, somehow. Now, here he is, installed on the kitchen table in the form of an abacus, a paperweight for mail: ads, magazines, a bank statement with the envelope seal slit. She thinks of the thin man in his unseasonable coat with the oversized pockets. He'd pitied her. Ha! Well, she pities him. Her friend is ruinous. The disappointment makes her slightly nauseous, and at the same time, how laughable to have imagined herself the competition. Stupid. He really would be spending more time here, perhaps even moving in. Why shouldn't he bring Zo gifts? He was that kind of man. Of course he was. He would have bought the abacus on a whim. C imagines him presenting it, telling Zo the where, the why (*why not?*), and how he'd picked it up at this adorable shop just a few blocks south from a jaded, passive-aggressive saleswoman turned petty by dismay. Zo would have known just who he meant. C's throat constricts as she tugs at the corkscrew of the ribbon. It springs back brightly. At least she really is excellent with gift wrap. She makes a note to add this to her list of interview questions. *Are you familiar with gift wrapping irregular shapes?*

Maybe I'll show them a fake, Fran says.

Zo frowns. But won't they get it appraised?

I'll send them an appraiser too. Stack the deck.

C looks up from her trance, rejoins the crew. You could always send me. I'll be your ringer. I could use the money.

When she catches Zo's eye, C can read nothing there that suggests her friend remembers their kiss. Does this woman feel *no* obligation to narrative continuity?

Fran laughs. You're hired, she says. She lowers her paint roller like a gavel into the tray and adds, They're probably just trying to launder cash anyway.

C feels the abacus tugging at her attention, like a recurring dream one dreads before bed—likewise the bank statement. How much do you need to live in New York? Rationales accrue with compound interest. This is surely what makes the Professor worth all the painting, remodeling, chain-smoking out the window: acquisitive self-justification. More than a few acquaintances have expressed the view that Zo ought to be contrite—the other adults in the classical music seminar, for example, where she and the Professor met. I can feel they want to ask me, Why did you do it? Zo has said. Like I'm personally responsible. And maybe C agrees. The very first night, when the class went around the room to introduce themselves, Zo made the mistake of telling them she worked on a trading floor. It just slipped out, though she should have known to lie. I'd *planned* on telling them, Zo said with a smile, that I sold arts and crafts. How much more harmless can you get? Instead, she told the truth and incurred the consequences. C resents the implication that her own occupation is incapable of harm.

When they finish, the furniture is shrouded in sheets. Zo brings three beers from the fridge and together they sit on the carpet with the bottles and a bowl of grapes to consider the minor revolution on the walls. Francesca wants to know how the shop is, how C's health is, if she still thinks about Max. Tell me *everything*, she says. When the other two are on the outs like this, they turn to her. She is a radio tower, triangulating alliances.

Her health, C reports, is perfectly fine, aside from this ghost pain in her side. She elides the gnome, the budget troubles at the shop, the sinking revenues and rising costs. It occurs to her that out of all her friends, Zo and Francesca are the best-equipped to aid her in straightening out the accounts—without Zo's contribution, C wouldn't have any accounts to speak of—but derivatives trading and skimming interest aren't quite the same as balancing budgets or adjusting loans. In fact, they seem quite the opposite. It's only arithmetic; C should be able to figure it out herself. And it is difficult to recalibrate the scales of a friendship, she's learned, after making yourself so vulnerable. This is true even of your oldest friend, who, after all, is many friends at once, depending on the context. For the sake of emotional and fiscal conservatism, then, C keeps her troubles to herself.

Actually, I'm hiring.

Good for you, Fran says.

On the floor at Fran's side is a paper outlining the GoodNite attacks, the same article C and the gnome were discussing the night before. Fran pinches the print between two artificially extended, soft-pink nails.

It's kind of exciting, isn't it? she says. You know, my father had a friend in Ukrainian utilities—maybe he knows something about this quantum business.

Fran often has ridiculous stories like these, featuring outlandish connections for which she never apologizes. Zo, who's lying on her back and looking up at the ceiling (probably renovating it in her head), answers with an exaggerated sigh. I don't think the supercomputer is actually plugged into the electric grid, or really to anything.

Fran nods. I see. Then, after a pause, she adds, So how did they hack it?

C chimes in to explain about the air gap, but as she does, she can feel the other two distancing from her, growing bored, receding into their private thoughts, rather the same way she does with the gnome. Anyway, she concludes, cutting herself short, they would've used it for some other purpose, like that incident in Alamo, or something like it. But I guess they've already caught them.

Fran sips her beer. Her skirt spills silkily across the floor. Zo's shirt pulls away from the waistband of her jeans, revealing a fleshy hip. Who wants to be indebted to these women? The room is soaked in turpentine and a sense of possibility, borrowed, perhaps, from the streets outside, from the commotion on the Brooklyn Bridge, which loans the whole city its ambient fervor, free of interest. It reaches even these three women on the floor. How easy it is to hide a mass protest in New York! After all, one cannot see what's directly beneath one's feet. Sirens harmonize. They look out the window, south, blissfully unaware, bottlenecks dangling in paint-splotched hands. Meanwhile, those arrested are herded to precinct headquarters and issued a carton of milk, a peanut butter sandwich, and a misdemeanor for blocking traffic on the Brooklyn overpass. It's the kind of thing Max might have done, and therefore C, too, before she put away her loom. The pain interrupts this reverie, sudden as the sirens. C grimaces, holds a hand to her side. She tries to take deep breaths as the sensation screws itself into place.

Hey, love. Are you okay?

C lies back on the carpet, presses the cool bottle to her cheek. Yeah, just dizzy, she says.

A reassuring squeeze at her ankle. It's Fran.

Sorry, C says. I'm spent. I'm going home, I think. Fran offers to accompany her, to call her a cab. C waves the offer away, and Fran doesn't protest. In the few minutes it takes her to retrieve her bag from the sheet-covered couch, wipe her hands on her jeans, and disappear into the stairwell, Zo and Fran have returned to bickering, this time about whether and why Zo has begun to smoke again after she finally managed to quit. The argument is clipped short by the click of the apartment door. On the landing, in the clouded glass of the tympanum, the Madonna is smug.

"You win," C says.

5

This is the upshot of having many selves: C has personalities to spare. Loose ends split and each end splits anew. Every renunciation is a definition in the positive—after Max, a divorcée; after art, a productive citizen. And after Zo, well—the loss of the role of childhood friend is one she might not recover from. It was delusional, really, to think that she might play anything else. It's all for the best! She is post-love, post-attraction. Who knows what to call a woman who weaves in private, masturbates, talks to a homunculus? But she suspects it can't be all that different from being a nun.

At home, she brings a razor and a bucket of warm water into the living room. A can of shaving cream rests at her feet. She plunks her ankles in, splashing suds onto the carpet. The bubbles slowly fade into the plush. She got to keep this carpet when Max left. She got to keep everything, in fact, including this bucket, in which Max once kept his rags and she now shaves her legs.

She lathers her shins and turns on the news. Maybe Zo is right; she ought to find someone wealthy, salary-augmenting, someone who knows how to select a tin of razor clams and act as guarantor—perhaps that's Zo's thought too. (*Or perhaps*, a dark voice supplies, *that's what her agenda already was with Zo.*) On the TV, a reporter is catching a scoop. The red sculpture twists slickly into the gloom like a decommissioned crane. Stark and strung out, painted for cheer, the sight of it makes her depressed, as does all artwork designed to evade offense. The idea of making demands, says an interviewee from the Class War Camp, is an exchange-dependent form of reasoning I stand against.

As he speaks, he looks over his shoulder at the trees, the tarps. C slips her foot out of the bucket and dries her sole. A rivulet of red runs down her shin. She reaches for a tissue, blots, then slips in the other leg. She resents the residents of this new city. She resents that they resent her life, her lack of learning, her love for processed and unnaturally colored foods—cereal, which she unreservedly douses with hormone-infused milk. She doesn't know for certain that they disapprove of her, of course, but C tends to assume.

"I'm not the enemy!" she yells at the TV.

"That's the truth," says the gnome, padding out from behind the loom.

6

It is not without reason that renunciation presents itself as the end goal of so many religions. What is one's inner life but hunger versus insatiability? Conquering the former is the key. For total release, have no appetite at all. Think how suffering would evaporate if one deposed the body and simply floated about, observing life, diffuse. No desires, no lungs, no leverage, no legs to shave, no market manipulation—perhaps no markets at all, because without desire, no demand. This far into our present study, it seems safe to say that the human condition is defined by dependence and competition, by a prolonged confrontation with a hostile environment and the ongoing attempt to hedge against it. The world has proved a reluctant host. It is all one can do to protect oneself in microenvironments: the greenhouse, the air-gapped network, the market for derivatives. Limited resources, limited space. It puts one on edge, a closed system like this. There is only so much to be consumed, and whatever is becomes waste. Transfer of energy from within to without and from without to within is allowed, but insofar as matter is involved, these are zero-sum games. And in the face of despair, of the basic aridity of existence, it can be tempting to adopt the ascetic's logic, to revolutionize distribution not so much by crowding as by *opting* out. Take C, who, convinced that the small factory of her life is now defunct, is disinclined to participate in a world that seems so clearly uninterested in keeping her alive. And where does it go, that old ambition, when its host has sublimated it out of her system? Perhaps it is passively transferred to someone else?

No, by the postulates of will and power upon which our present models rest, this world does not include peaceful transfer among its tools, but rather conservation of matter, competition, and effort—the conversion of the potential into the actual through energy expenditure, i.e., work. The idea, as far as the distant observer can deduce—especially one looking to adapt the current system to her own designs (definitionally: to "hack" it)—is to unleash the energy yourself before someone else corners its potential for themselves. Supply-side of the self. You've seen it; between certain people there exists a kind of reactive, combustible potential capable of chemical rearrangement. In C's relationship with Max, she was the reactant, he the precipitate—the old C was consumed in the nomenclature of their love process. She lost a whole person to divorce: the person she once was. She lost her facility with the loom. Had she known then that she would soon wind up a husk, she might have preferred to be left alone, to tend to the spindle of her body, to create the future from herself. There is something of this knowledge in her now. Sometimes, late at night after returning from the shop, after the gnome curls up in his suit atop her dresser and goes to sleep (or seems to, at least), she returns to her loom, sits on the stool. She works cautiously in the dark, unable to see her own two hands. Not even she can judge what unfolds on the warp, that's the rule, because she's realized it is also no great challenge to prey upon oneself.

It's impossible now to refrain from chatting with the visitor when she comes home. There is so much she wishes to be distracted from: the accounts; the guarantor; the idea of Zo and the Professor in the eggplant room, in the red tub, together in bed; the vials on Zo's vanity vibrating vicariously like little imps, alive.

"Really, I'm fine," she says.

They chat through commercials and dinner until she gets ready for bed. Then talk gives way to the shuttle's clack. Her maneuvers at the loom are automatic—an act of sustenance, like breath, that allows the rest of her to live. She maximizes the ratio of warp to weft and beats the thread count into the icy surface of satin. Her thoughts organize themselves into patterns. Every madness has its clarity, and in these moments, she understands that there is such a thing as an ontological hierarchy, and that the gnome is a member of a lesser class—or anyway, a different class—and therefore cannot be her friend.

"But I've always been interested in the lives of the ascetics. Watch out for that fan blade there, or—well, okay—"

At night, however, as her fingers numb from threading the warp and the pain dulls in her side and the gnome glows by the lamp in the bedroom, she still brings her hand to her neck in disciplined recollection. Her want is a hot wire that runs through her core, solders her to touch.

She calls Francesca. They go to a movie, where Fran lays her head on C's shoulder and takes a nap. Tell me later if it was any good, she says. The movie is 3D, and the contrapuntal cardboard specs droop down C's nose to strange visual effects. Fran's cheek slides down her sleeve. C gently props her up. Afterward, a drink. The movie was okay—not great, not so terrible as to command their attention. If only it had been. As it stands, the conversation drifts back to their mutual connection.

What do you think of this Frenchman?

They sit at a table by the front window of the bar, two feet from passersby, who pass in pairs: mother and daughter, adulterer and escort—or is that his wife? A dog takes a shit, and the woman walking it lovingly ties the little blue bundle and carries it away. C doesn't want to think of Zo right now, not with Fran.

I don't know. She seems happy with him.

Francesca nods. This would bother her, C thinks, if they were ever to be together—the way Fran's body language and beliefs tend to exist in direct opposition.

The bar is empty, though it's not late. If the two were more enthralled with one another, the unpopulated dining room might seem intimate, but for now it leaves them depressed. Little votive candles hyperventilate at vacant tables, in need of air. Francesca holds the corner of a paper napkin to theirs. It blooms and snuffs out. She laughs, not happily, but optimistically enough to motivate C's tenderness.

I suppose I'm jealous, she says. Don't like to compare myself to him.

By the time they leave, it has begun to rain. They huddle beneath the designer duomo of Fran's oversized umbrella. The gutters swell. The whole street gurgles. Fran curses herself for not checking the weather before leaving the bar; C's excuse is that she doesn't have that kind of phone. They claim an awning already sheltering a bundle of rags hunched behind a PLEASE HELP sign. Fran stares. The umbrella slips. C gives Fran a nudge. Hey, she says, and snaps two fingers in front of Fran's nose. It isn't polite to stare like that. Fran's eyes wander then focus again. The cheerful confidence returns. One sec, she says, with her usual optimistic shimmer. She darts across the street and into a deli advertising an ATM, comes back with a handful of Benjamins. C gulps. How much is that? Fran looks at her fist. Five hundred is the limit, she says, and shoves the cash into the coffee cup at the man's swollen foot. She hesitates, then sets off into the downpour again, dragging C by the wrist.

They share Francesca's umbrella to her stoop, where she gives C a kiss on the cheek. You're sure you don't want to come up? C smiles, shakes her head. Not tonight, she says. On her own, walking to the train, the borrowed umbrella feels dangerously expensive in her hand.

After a night like this, what a relief to come home to one's own gnome, who asks nothing but simple questions! He stares at a plug in the wall as if something might emerge from it, and who knows these days—it might. He hovers over the eye of the sink, index fingers tented. C dumps the dregs of her cereal bowl.

"Where does it go?" He points out the window at the

George Washington Bridge, and she finds herself telling him the story of its financing.

"The states of New York and New Jersey issued $50 million in bonds, and when it was built—the world's largest suspension connection—the bondsmen took a walk across it for lunch. Steaks all around. The tolls were supposed to expire when the cost of construction was recouped, but, you know, there they are. Still collecting."

The gnome nods. They consider the glitter of the traffic in the air.

"How do you know all this?"

"Beats me," C says, a little confused herself.

This is the mood in which she likes the gnome best, when he is curious, dependent, and helpless, when he doesn't understand. When he is most like a child. She used to imagine the conversations she'd have with her own daughter; they went something like this. She reminds herself not to answer either of them—not the little girl in her daydreams, not the gnome.

These stomach pains you're having, Fran says when they meet for lunch and Fran picks up the tab. I'm sure it's diet-related. She pulls out her checkbook to leave the waitress a $5,000 tip.

C submits to a brief program in nutritional improvement. At Fran's urging, she takes down the address of a health food store not far from her own, where everything smells dishearteningly like animal feed. She crosses the street to the bodega for the paper and heads back home. Dinner is the usual over the sink: spinach, cereal, a forkful of lox. A whole-grain O disintegrates beneath her heel and C sweeps up the dust.

The five bright boxes on the counter, lined up beneath the cupboards, constitute an aisle unto themselves. They lend the kitchen a cheerful sense of choice. She mixes quinary flavors, poisoning the milk. The dregs are sweet and sick, like a shot of grenadine. She moves through the dark apartment to the daybed, the bath, the TV. She turns it on and off. In the silence, she sits across from the coffee table at her loom and removes the cloth covering. The black warp lays tracks across the dusk. She gives the beater a halfhearted tug, tightening the weave and sending the shuttle through. She works in the dark, unable to see how the pattern is transpiring.

It's critical, of course, not to.

The second week of October, she attends the community garden's last hurrah, a fall harvest supplemented by the bodega down the block. There are only three pies in the pie contest; everybody wins. Twenty gardeners and their children mill about behind the chicken wire. The children play a game of tag, stomping through dead plants, and no one scolds them. C walks up and down the block, handing out fliers for the winter raffle, on which the garden relies for off-season maintenance and rent. SUPPORT YOUR LOCAL COMMUNITY GARDEN! She donates a set of paints and glitter pens as well as a packet of plastic eyes for decorating a shipment of Jersey pumpkins. She is, for her efforts, profusely thanked. Oh, don't mention it. Very sweet, the parents say.

She hopes they will visit her for Halloween. Halloween and Valentine's Day: a craft shop's harvest holidays. The kids cry when the eyes slip from the gourds to the ground. A mother considers the rows of paints and frowns, her daughter at her hip. Where's the pink? she says.

The garden's greenhouse is an oasis in a corner of the lot—a lean-to of corrugated plastic—and C ducks inside for a break. It's cold in here, despite the intended function. The plants are wrapped in cellophane. The tarps seem to absorb all sound, and the resulting quiet is as thick as a sigh. C's hand migrates to her collarbone. A withered woman is seated a few rows away, before the trays of plants, inputting data in a notebook. Be right there, she says without looking up from the page. The sleeves of her canvas jacket are rolled back over thin, liver-spotted wrists.

That's okay, C replies, take your time. The researcher, eye-level with her plants, peers at the leaves, looks down, records a note, and makes her way along the rows. C can't help but feel she's intruding and yet is unable to break away. What are you looking for? she asks.

Shhh, the woman says, leaning protectively over the individually cartoned sprouts, as if they aren't supposed to know.

C receives a message from her landlord. Afterward, whenever she passes a sign on the street or tucked into the corner of a window (FOR RENT . . . WE'RE HIRING!), she takes the number down. She trawls websites for further listings and catches a train to Yonkers for a morning appointment at what is referred to as *a studio+*, clocking two hours—door-to-door, bus-to-train—to get back downtown to the shop. She visits another studio (no +, but also no –) around the block and wonders what furniture she'd leave behind: The loom or the daybed? All over the world, people sleep on mats on the floor. If she moves apartments, perhaps she'll also lose the gnome, and she's surprised to find she's halfhearted about the prospect—anyway, it turns out it's hard to save on a rent-controlled one-bedroom signed fifteen years earlier. As she exits the windowless kitchen of a unit a mile east, C returns to the brightness of her own. It may be the only good financial decision she's ever made, signing her apartment when she did. That and keeping it after Max. As for present payments . . .

Back upstairs, she finds the gnome poking about the philodendron plant, examining the leaves.

"What does it eat?"

"Sunlight," C says.

"It looks sick."

"No, it doesn't."

Yi's deteriorating eyesight is an open secret, the elephant in the room (and hardly the only one). They pick their way around it. Only occasionally—in quiet moments further muffled by the static of the television, the rain, the sound of traffic swishing through the streets—do they discuss what it's like, the way shapes begin to abstract themselves and blend and substitute for one another. Signs once distinct and now consolidated stand in for far more than they did before: Is that a child or a dog, or a tumbleweed of trash? Her retinas chart a trend of slow decline. It's almost worse, Yi says, to be able to document the loss gradually like this than to lose it all at once.

When C asks, How are the eyes? Yi avoids the question. Okay, C says. We'll skip today. They often skip. As a result, the graph contradicts observable experience: according to the chart, Yi's sight declines stepwise and jumps right off sheer cliffs.

Not to be nixed, however, is a trip to the grocery; it is after eight, and the hot bar is now half-off. She takes Yi's arm in hers. Yi steps into a pair of red rubber boots. The bright hems of her nylon pants skim the mat at the lobby entrance, and the tail of her blouse trails behind. At the market, the sliding doors glide royally. They promenade through the compact aisles, the cache of carts, the candy bars, the bleat of the checkout line, the canned goods arranged in pyramids at the front: baked beans, pinto beans, salsa, Spam. The cleaning aisle is regal and buoyant with laundry detergent, dishwashing soap, scented sponges laden on the white vine of a cheap steel chain. When C comes to do her own shopping, she spends most of her time in the cereal section. Bright boxes of promise: Chex, Corn Pops, Rice Krispies, Squares, Grahams, Honey Oh's, and Kix.

Traverse the chill of the vegetable aisle, iceberg lettuce dewy and blanched, hard limes displaced into the pulpy peaches, shrink-wrapped watermelons hacked into edible shapes. Here, at the end of the aisle, the air begins to warm. The heat lamps emit their same, strange scorch, and beneath them the trays await. It is 8:15, the golden hour, the hour of discounts, when the fixed-income glean and graze. C clamps the cereal box and a newspaper under her arm, selects a clamshell, and narrates the buffet for Yi, who stands by in red patents, looking slightly askance at the food. C recites: There's mac and cheese. And chicken legs. Pork fried rice. Some kind of stew—beef—and collard greens. Mashed potatoes. Sweet potatoes. Potatoes au gratin. Beet salad with baby corn. Red coconut curry. Fried fish. Meatballs. Heroes for meatball subs. What do you want?

Yi folds both hands over the buttons of her pale-lime cardigan, the one C knitted for her. She closes her eyes, and the corners of her face tighten with irritation. You went too fast, she says. Say it again.

At home, galoshes and sneakers shucked at the door, C slides the mac and cheese into a bowl. She loads the rest into the fridge, where the shelves are soon crowded: chicken, fried rice, curry, meatballs, salad. Enough that Yi won't need to shop for days. Her job is to stay at home and eat.

They settle on the couch with the mac and cheese, two sets of chopsticks, and the paperback translation of the Upanishads, which is probably riddled with errors. C begins; they are still in the beginning. The whole book is a beginning. How many times can one book begin again? Endlessly, it seems, if the world is a work in progress and the best you can do is circle around the truth, reiterating approximations in a thousand different ways.

Extract:

The world appears in the shape of a man who speaks one word: I. I, he says. I, I. It is the first time the word has ever been said, siphoned off from the whole that formerly contained it. Articulating the self is like drawing attention to the floor on which you stand, the mechanics of the lungs. I, I, she thinks, mounting the stairs to her own apartment, short of breath. She pauses on the landing to catch it, clutching at the rail.

7

There are times when C would like to ask the visitor the same: *How do you know so much about that?* For all his ignorance of dailiness, it's apparent that he is in possession—if not consistent possession—of esoteric expertise. For example, with respect to the GoodNite attacks, he embarks on these long-winded lectures about the grid. He makes rotations of the room, gestures at the world beyond, where a hypothetical disaster is taking place. "It would seem you people are under-informed," he says, observing the paper C, still breathing heavily, brings back. She sinks into the daybed and rests a palm on her sternum to track the rise and fall of her chest. The visitor continues, oblivious. "It is not the vulnerability of the equipment itself that's the concern," he explains, "but the rate of repair. The generators will overload, ruining the transformers"—he points through the wall toward the courtyard and the dumpsters, as if the transformers were just there—"and the lag time between replacement orders and delivery is minimum two years." What will happen to the population in the interim? "*You* can't live on sunlight," he says. "Hospitals will be the first to go, then water flow, sewage, food supply. According to congressional testimony, morbidity estimates clock in at 90 percent of the US population."

C, wondering where he gets these numbers, scans the front page but finds no sign of them. She folds it up and puts the arts section on top.

"Pause," she says. "Too much."

It's hard not to lean into calamity once he begins to orate. The four impounded GoodNite members have refused to give names, make deals, or reduce their sentences, though parallel investigations have revealed the extent of the operation to be far larger and older than previously believed. Even the paper of record has begun to take it seriously, promoting the hacks from page eight, to five, to three. The pearl-clutching attention still being paid to the people in the Park is all that keeps it from occupying page one. The passwords of the security inspectors—all freelance—for the nation's 11,000 power plants have been compromised, irony presumably intended. The nature of the hack suggests more members and more purpose to the siege of the supercomputer at the Ukrainian nuclear facility, since the calculations required to steal the encrypted passwords are in excess of the capacity of the confiscated laptops of the present quartet—ipso facto, there must be others.

"Or that's my guess." The gnome lowers himself to the coffee table and pushes the arts section aside. He's acquired an eyeglass, which he polishes on his sleeve. Standing on the newspaper, he reads the latest with a squint. "Though they could have used a rainbow table," he allows. "Mind you, these will be obsolete in a few years—if there are enough years left for them to become obsolete."

They are in the living room at dusk, watching TV and reading the news. The gnome paces in circles, as he always does when he begins a lecture. C knows there's no stopping him. He has a way of leasing out the thoughts she doesn't want to take responsibility for, pushing the door of possibility ajar.

And leaving the door a little more ajar with every iteration.

"To understand a rainbow table in this context, you must first understand the nature of the air gap. You are already well informed about that. But never underestimate the feebleness of the human attention span. An air gap, again," he begins, "is a physical and logical quarantine from the internet or any system connected to it. In theory, it is one of the strongest security measures against a hack. In practice, rather medieval. Like a moat. There's always a way across. For example, SMB port entry plus a USB key. You send out feelers, see what ports are open, what vulnerabilities they yield. And then you attack—this is where the rainbow tables come in."

The visitor gets excited as he explains. He might as well be glowing, his hands bright and his eyes brighter, reflecting rather than absorbing light. C can't resist feeling a little proud of this genius she's attracted. As he speaks, he orbits an invisible axis. He pauses atop the paper, headlines appearing between the wide gaps of his toes. A plane appears in midair before him, on which, with stubby fingers, he begins to map the malware flow.

"The malware is delivered across the moat to the host by a secondary device with regular access to the mother machine. Contrary to popular conception, the bottleneck isn't the air gap itself, but infiltrating the carrier device, which will be password-protected—think desktop download, to USB, to someone's pocket. Mathematically speaking, computing universes of possible passwords is relatively simple. But like all brute force methods of universe creation, it takes considerable time. A twelve-unit alphanumeric plaintext with two cases, ten digits, and ten symbols leaves seventy-two options per keystroke, or 72^{12} passwords in all, and the hacker must try every one. This would take years and enormous memory to perform, even for me—or a supercomputer," he adds.

He exhales onto the sudden plane suspended like a sheet of glass between himself and C. His notes frost over with a cloud of breath, leaving her doubting the mechanics of gnomic respiration. He presses his thumb into this mist, producing a fingerprint. How many supercomputers, C wonders, would it take to create *him*? (And did they need to be Ukrainian?)

"Lucky for us, the encryption produces a unique print for each password stored. But like actual fingerprints, the function is a one-way street. The print alone does not produce a corresponding person—unless, of course, you've catalogued identities beforehand. Think like a detective. A fingerprint is conclusive only insofar as it matches a known suspect."

He draws this one-way function on the plane:

$$\textit{Person} \rightarrow \textit{Print}$$
$$P \rightarrow h(P)$$

C watches the equations hover in the middle of her living room.

"Are you with me?"

"No."

"Terrific. So—say we do manage to steal some prints. How to go from print to password, from *h*(*P*) to *P*, when the function prevents us from turning back? If we think like detectives or the state, the obvious solution is to keep on file a database of all possible fingerprints of all possible citizens. In that case, we'd have to precalculate the universe of plaintext passwords, along with their fingerprint pairs, then cross-reference the stolen prints against this master list to make a match. The calculations are possible—by completing them beforehand, we save time—but storing them takes too much space. That kind of hard drive would take up rooms, and hackers, after all, are constantly on the move. As always, the constraints are memory and time."

C can feel herself drifting off. It's like a lullaby, this talk. She is stretched out on the daybed, dreamy, her breathing even. The television soothes, her pulse is slow and calm. Through heavy eyelids, she watches the gnome lick five fingertips and drag them through the air, tracing colorful arcs.

"What's more elegant—and frankly, I fail to see the point of anything that isn't—is to store the master list of paired passwords and prints with reduced memory demand. In other words, to calculate and also forget, at least until we have need to recall. For this we use a rainbow function."

"Imagine each counterclockwise arc as a possible plaintext password, P_i, mapped to a print. Imagine each clockwise arc as mapping from that print $h(P_i)$ back to a new plaintext, and so on and so forth, until the rainbow encompasses millions of password-to-fingerprint pairs, even as the computer must store only the original. Like a Jacob's ladder folded up—"

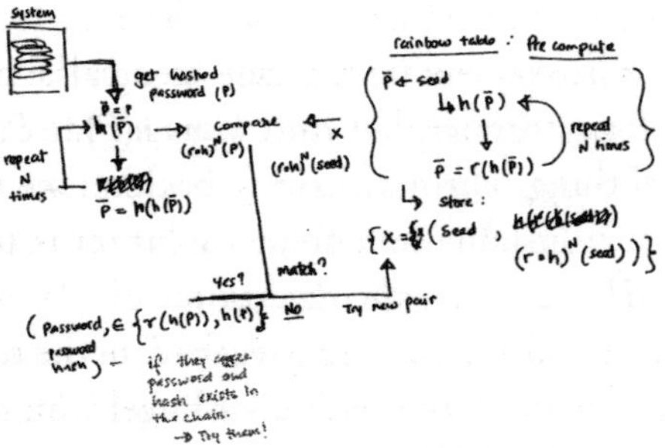

The diagram composes a tiny Times Square in C's living room, flashing ROYGBIV. It glitters, migrainey. She brings the heels of her hands to her eyes, shakes herself awake.

"The supercomputers would have been needed to generate the precalculated data set—those Jacob's ladders, if you will—"

"I understand enough to know that it sounds bad."

Shadows shift over the loom with the flicker of the TV, revealing dark scraps of velvet yarn, unruly as shorn hair. Beneath its shroud, the black chenille product is rolled thickly around the beam. She, too, is running out of storage space. The newspaper is still on the coffee table, and she flips the page. The hacker quartet glows.

"Is it really that dangerous, do you think?"

The gnome shrugs. "Depends whose side you're on."

Later that night, an uncomfortable thought keeps C awake: How could he know what she does not? She never told him about the air gaps, after all, not that she can recall. And she couldn't have mentioned morbidity estimates, not knowing them herself. When the gnome curls up at his usual place beneath the red lamp on her dresser, she slips from the bed and retrieves her ancient laptop. She spends the night in the bathtub, sifting through her own browser history, looking for traces of things she may have forgotten. She wonders if it is possible to imagine something smarter than herself—or worse, not. They are one and the same.

A human mind is also an air-gapped network, no? Not directly but osmotically connected: the world sifts in through a buffer zone. Like a Ukrainian supercomputer, it remains vulnerable to the right methods.

Crouched, fully clothed, in the empty tub, C has the sudden impulse to peel off her skin.

Her laptop screen, now frozen, is a mosaic of her concerns. Too many windows open at once. Her checking account stares back. Back-of-the-envelope calculations (an envelope reading *Urgent!*) reveal that by December, she'll be out of cash.

8

The painting class, at least, is something to look forward to, something she has not yet fucked up. A lone asset to her liabilities. After checking in on Yi, who is fresh out of macaroni and cheese—I'm fine, I'm fine, no change in the eyes, or just a tiny bit—she spends the morning combing through the shop for inspiration for that evening's class. Everything is pink! It makes her ill. As the Professor is to buttercream, so C is to shades of pink. She thinks of how Zo left Francesca only to end up with him—of Zo's auburn hair; her smooth, violet-tinted skin; the mole on her neck; her pale eyes cradled in cheekbones spread wide like wings. Of the little girls in the painting class, whose work is inferior to the boy's. She decides to teach that evening's class exclusively to him. The beads, the nail polish, temporary tattoos, none of it will do. She finds herself avoiding the mirror in the tiny bathroom, afraid she might detect a hint of mania there. She investigates the trash, the toilet, the sink. That's it! She pulls the toolbox from beneath the register. On her back on the tiles, armed with a wrench, she relieves the U-bend of its duties beneath the toilet.

At noon, her most recent interviewee arrives, a promising-looking girl in a black blouse and vintage slacks, in penny loafers and with a silk scarf knotted around her neck. C is just wiping her loamy palms on her jeans when the girl—*Mah-rie*, she says, trilling the *r* and extending a hand—glides in. C is newly conscious of how long it's been since she had any help. All these years, she's worked on her own, occasionally hiring a plumber to unclog the toilet in the tiny bath, a contractor to install the shelves. These days, C unclogs the toilet herself. She is adept at unscrewing a U-bend, sloughing it of sludge; recently she even rescued an engagement ring from Yi's after it slipped from her oncologist granddaughter's soapy fingers. Not a great omen.

Marie sits, rapt, on a child-size stool by the glitter and the beads. C paces, fanning her face with a bright folder containing the girl's resume: poli-sci, minor in art, mailing address at a dorm a few blocks north. She seems like a girl not desperate for a job, a girl with options. What is she doing here?

I love your tapestry. The hands—they meant a lot to me.

C glances down at the resume. *Interests: film and Thai cuisine.* Do you need a job or not?

Marie looks around the shop as if she might find the answer there, prearticulated. She seems about to laugh, then swallows it. The plunger of her slender throat resounds. No, but . . . I like it inside. I like how it looks. I think I'd be happy here, she says.

C looks around the store herself. At the splashes of neon. The glare. The gold spools of tinsel wound inside their plastic skins, bulging as if preparing to molt. She can't tell if Marie is making fun of her. The girl blushes. Her cheekbones strain. The smile flits across her face again, quick as an insect, then fades. She looks concerned. C softens; Marie appears more youthful in her doubt. Suddenly, C is struck by how competent she seems. There is even a little something that reminds her of Zo.

Also, Marie adds, my internship doesn't pay.

It might be nice to have a new audience, a new mentee, a change of pace, private conferences outside the privacy of her home. Marie shifts on the stool and bites her lip. C, moved by her nervousness and by the echo of her friend, returns the red folder.

When can you start?

The projector remains in its shoebox when the class begins. The restroom is out of order. On display at the center of the room, alongside the pots of paints, is a sludgy pipe, a knob, a toilet seat—also, a Turner print. They will aim for junkyard landscapes. Gross, the girls say.

The U-bend becomes a face, a vase, sprouts flowers. Very nice, she says. She circles the room, avoiding the little boy's easel the same way she avoids her mirror. She feels impatient, excited; she wants him to win. She is hesitant in case his composition is a disappointment. Around seven, the mothers begin to line up outside on the sidewalk—there is no space for them. The students are hers for five more minutes.

Look, the girls say. Everyone turns their easels toward the windows except the boy. Only then does C pause at his shoulder to see what he has made. The U-bend, spewing sludge, harnesses a neck. I'm not done yet, he says, defensive, tilting his easel away from the door, where the mothers are peering in. C flips the painting around, full of pride, then changes her mind, wondering if the victim looks a little like her.

Her own mother brought dignity to every line of work, whatever it was: the hostess's desk at the supper club, accounts at the coal plant, volunteer secretary for the local cultural society, where songs were performed in languages C couldn't understand. She had so much time for other people's lives. Her longest tenure was as a bank teller. One night, while she was stationed at her window, a man in a mask entered the marble lobby and pulled out a gun. C's mother, slight-shouldered and soft-spoken, must have seemed an easy target—only she refused to open the safe when he pointed the weapon at her. It was poor form, she told him. It simply wasn't done. She'd be fired if she did. Meanwhile, she had a daughter to support at home. Where would she be then? The robber sent a warning shot into the mildewed ceiling. In the end, her delay allowed someone else to raise the alarm, and the police soon arrived. C was mortified when she learned what had occurred. Her mother sighed. He wasn't going to *kill* me, she said.

C protested. How could she know? She sulked a spoon through her cereal bowl. Today, as she collapses the easels and stores the paints, it occurs to C that she would've immediately opened the safe.

The boy is the last pupil to leave. His mother is late, and C waits with him as he sits on the floor, cranking a Rubik's Cube through its iterations.

Did you always want to be an art teacher? he asks.

No. C sees no reason to lie.

I'm going to be a lawyer, he informs her, which is how she learns what his father does.

Not a painter?

The green clicks into place, complete.

No one's a painter anymore.

Some are. And you're very talented.

He looks up from his puzzle. A blank expression laminates his face. He will grow up to be desirable to someone, she knows, and here are the origins, a knack for pickling what he truly thinks. He can't be more than ten. Or maybe he's small for his age. He returns to the cube, primary colors mashed. Blinks five times fast. In fact, he seems to have forgotten she's here at all.

After he departs amid a flurry of his mother's apologies, C crumples the last of the paint-splotched newspaper into the trash and steps into the current of the streets, considering the pounds of glue and glitter and expired paint poured annually down the sink. To think that people consider her harmless, that a ten-year-old thinks to spare her feelings. She imagines his mother ferrying him into the bowels of the city, toward the trains. She has read of the fatbergs, the underground blockages, the great impasses that clog the city's sewers—masses of Styrofoam fortified with unmetabolized estrogen, great feminine Medusas of trash. This is the sort of ancillary, massive problem submerged from public view that makes C wonder how life can continue. And she has done nothing at all to prevent the decline. Who can possibly admire with Marie's reverence the potential of the chemically calibrated gradients along the wall, the soft glow of feathers filtering streetlight—

Then again, no one trusts an artist on the subject of her own work. Perhaps there is some beauty in it after all. C has never lacked for taste, a facility with the colors of the rainbow, ROYGBIV, a sense of pattern and balance and design, but none of this necessarily adds up to an eye for art. The ability to recognize it when she meets it in the wild. Or, frankly, in herself.

9

At the entrance to the subway, she joins a crowd on the street. A unit in the building across from the station is burning. The flames roll out the window, blackening brick. Rumors make the rounds. One dead—two. He was a loner. It's the building materials they used, too cheap, no respect for life. This is what happens when you build a complex out of trash. A lighter, a bong. A candle falls. Most tragedy: preventable.

Then one resident steps forward with an air of authority. It was the old man, he says. He tried to microwave a can.

Trailing scorch, she knocks on Yi's door. Knocks again.

Just wanted to see that you're okay, C says.

```
DATA visitors;
    SELECT FROM “history”
        DO exposition
            input = "part three"
            i = 19% to &n.
```

oct 15, 19%; &duet. of modest prospects <<mother; daughter>>; itinerary check: board a nationalized aircraft, train, another plane chartered by for-profit headquartered in the West; float &style. = <<*all very normally narrated!*>>; passing landscape passes with the motion sickness; mid-flight seltzer to calm the nerves; insert stewardess insert fez insert drinks cart pushed down aisle; insert bonus glass of cranberry fizz; ocean REPLACE shoreline; landing strip; vista of parking lots choked off by halide highway lamps; *not for long!*; connection JFK; diamonds on display (IF % = ’78); clasp bracelet around a little girl’s wrist; real gems borrowed for a minute at no cost at all; *ty!!* and *g’bye!*; do loop generosity is throwaway; disposable; aka, abundant; insert paper towels repopulating in their private compartment; last leg; delay; delay; turbulence; the landing clean and neat and compact; touch down at last in Yugoslavia-prime; insert Ohio; insert Cleveland; taxi fare correction: just outside;

```
    END;
RUN;
```

1

There is no baseline for what life ought to be like. Instead, you make a guess and mitigate. Turn the package to the label, skim the ingredients and expiration date, check for carcinogens, coupons, two-for-one: take what you can get. Discount delicacies pile in the cart, because C's mother has company tonight. Someone's just moved in.

The first time Zo—then still Zoja—came through C's door, still sour from the plane, she was ten years old. She imported an exotic radiance into the Cleveland living room, and her mother echoed the effect. They stood side by side, mother and daughter, on the blue carpet, taking in C's mother's small apartment through the wide frames of their faces. Zoja's hair was short and dark then, wedged, forming migration patterns at the nape of her neck. C tugged her mother's hand. Why couldn't she have hair like that?

The neighborhood was changing, diluting. Immigration was rare. There was cachet to be won in helping someone whose passport was last stamped in Ljubljana. C's mother welcomed them in. You could say she got lucky; the new arrivals lived just next door.

The strange thing was, their self-sufficiency was palpable. Disappointingly so. At least at the start. It was enough to make the members of the Rotary suspicious. Why had they left, when there wasn't anything to flee? Personal reasons—it must be. Zoja's mother cited Tito's demise. The fuel crisis. But look at the papers, C's countered. There were front-page features: by all accounts, Yugoslavia was flush with foreign loans and thriving. They'd lived near the border, Zoja's mother said with a shrug, and people in the streets were grumbling. There wasn't any coffee. And I can't drink that Divka stuff, she said. C's mother frowned. The Party isn't only Tito, she added. Then it was Zo's mother's turn to furrow her brow. She asked, When were you last back? She added that all the lightbulbs, for some reason, were red.

(Ten years later, in art school, the first time she'd been separated from Zo in years, C made *potica* for a party—Yugoslavian babka, she'd explained, because that's what she'd been taught to call it—only to have the drunk host laugh. He spun a globe and pushed a finger into the Balkans, balkanized. Look, he said. Not a country anymore.)

Pre-war, pre-genocide, already post-Slovenian, everyone could agree that it was comforting to have a shadow, a friend, a reminder of paths not taken. Zoja, who was very silent for those first few months, followed C in everything. They unwrapped Hostesses on the sofa and excavated the center cream. C's mother appealed to the principal, and they entered the same class at school. They sat together, side by side. The same notebooks, same haircuts—C trimmed hers, Zoja let her bob grow long. It was almost as if together, they made a single girl. At home, C's mother encouraged Zoja to speak in English. You have to, she said. It's how you learn.

Zoja cupped a hand to C's cheek and whispered in her ear. TV, she suggested. In those early days, she spoke only to C. They spent that year in front of the television on the blue and stainproof carpet until Zoja had absorbed enough vocabulary to express other wants. Then she bloomed all at once. Before, she wouldn't say a word; now it seemed she'd never stop. She mocked her mother's accent, taught herself to do a handspring in their scrap of yard, trimmed her name to *Zo*. It didn't take long for things to become competitive.

At school, newly minted Zo excelled, winning universal adoration without actually making friends. Like the heroine of a beloved book, she abetted voyeurism. She became devoted to foreign radio for no other reason, C felt, than to emphasize her nostalgia for another home. They completed homework at her kitchen table, to which the center of gravity had shifted and where the block of butter was kept out in a ceramic dish, instead of in the fridge. The apartments were identical, except Zo's was filled with news, the butter was room temperature, the lyrics and labels incomprehensible. There were three main rooms. The master bedrooms stood directly inside the entrance and shared a floor with the kitchen and living space, while above the coat closet spun a spiral staircase, at the top of which was a niche. This was where the girl of each respective apartment slept. C would have liked her friend to stop emphasizing her foreignness, to acknowledge instead all the ways in which they were the same.

There may as well have been no separation between the two apartments, with the girls living equally out of each. The patch of grass between the entrances was worn into a path. In the summer, they left the doors unlocked and wandered back and forth. Then C told Zo's mother about the gunman at the Slavic Credit Union, hoping to illustrate how neglectful her own mother was. Zo's mother ordered the doors locked. They spent birthdays, Christmases, Easters—both Orthodox and not, because two-for-one was always tops, even pluralistic—in the same kitchen, helping their mothers stretch *potica* dough. It took two Formica tables pushed together and a bedsheet, linens used to coax the expanse of pastry into a roll. They watched the *Challenger* explode, Chernobyl melt, Madonna vogue.

They fought often. When C's mother grew tired of parsing insults and assessing blame, she'd tell them, Go to the closet. Go to the closet and scream for as long as you can at the top of your lungs, she said. The idea was to expend their anger without quite articulating it. See? her mother said when the girls emerged, exhausted, too out of breath to continue the argument. You didn't even mean it. They spent many hours in the cedar-paneled closet, howling into smoke-soaked fur. The blood rose in their faces. Sometimes the neighbors stopped by, more concerned than annoyed. It was there, in the closet, screaming into her mother's coat, that it dawned on C that her friend had won. She'd outperformed C in everything: school, looks, experience, sophistication. With a final screech, she ceded. And as soon as she gave in, she found that she was calm again.

The message in the household also changed. *Why can't you be more like Zoja?* C retreated into herself. Her sudden indifference must have been a loss for Zo. With whom was she now to compete?

For some time, the absent dads had been yet another source of competition, though neither girl had much to go on. The intel C had gathered on her own father was limited. For example, he was already dead. He'd sputtered out in a trailer fifty miles south from a rotten liver and related complications; he was morbidly obese by then, a weight he carried without cheer and more like an awful challenge. A memory: a trip she and her mother took. They'd driven an hour through farmland, and when they arrived, C waited in the front seat as her mother marched up the steps, knocked, and pushed open the door. She'd returned with a record player, a radio, and the television set that sat in their living room now. On the way home, the TV had bounced precariously in the back seat like a second kid. They were not allowed to whistle in her house, due to the scenes it brought back. Zo was not impressed. *My father was a fascist*, she'd parried. *What did yours ever do?*

They argued over who had neglected his family more until C's mother yelled up the stairs, Enough! Go to the closet and scream for as long as you can!

Zo's father did seem the cleverer of the two. He was matrimonially gifted; he'd come abroad a decade earlier, when Zoja was still an infant, and married another woman. Word traveled home. This was not Zo's mother's first trip to America. When she came to find him, he simply moved his new family back. Zo's mother also returned, retrieving Zo on the way. After so many relocations, it was quite a protracted process in the Ljubljana courts to determine who was married to whom anymore. The girls were on the swing sets, arguing which was worse—a father who embitters himself to death, forgoing further payments, or one who evades alimony via cross-continental flight—when one of their fathers, the one still alive, strode up the sidewalk to the door.

It was Saturday. The girls had been outside all afternoon and sleeves of sunburn were just emerging on their arms. The tall, sweat-drenched man might have been a landlord collecting rent. He turned from C's door to Zo's. He knocked.

Zoja had just unfolded herself from a handspring. C stilled herself on the swings. Their mothers were at work. There was an event at the Rotary, and people were working Saturday shifts, which is to say they were quite alone in the apartment complex that afternoon. The pounding of the man's fist against the door was almost musical in the suburban silence. As they approached, he turned and looked from one girl to the next. For a moment, there was the terrible feeling of being evaluated, compared, like two melons scanned in the grocery line. It was unclear what each of them should hope for: to be chosen or not, or perhaps that he'd choose them both. Later, C realized he hadn't recognized his own daughter—nor she him.

The rest of what is known of that summer is hazy, secondhand, but nevertheless transformative. The night her father arrived, Zo did not join C and her mother for dinner as she usually did. They sat at the table with Zo's empty place, idly churning egg noodles. They listened through the wall for unusual sounds. C recalled that when someone came to visit from Yugoslavia, they were often unsettled by her mother's home. They looked strangely at the brownies, food coloring in cakes, turkeys basted, extravagant Christmas decorations, labyrinths of electric lights unfurled in yards and set to syncopate. Under the scrutiny of someone from home, even her mother lost the pride she normally took in these furnishings. C wished they had not helped Zo assimilate so fully.

Meanwhile, she put an ear to the wall. It was days later that Zo showed up in the middle of the night and crawled into C's bed.

She reported that on the other side there were silent meals and endless postprandial critiques. He hated her mother's cooking, the furniture, Zo's clothing, her dresses and pants too short. The housekeeping, he said, was an embarrassment. He lifted a bra from the shower curtain rod. You live like a laundress, he said. But I *am* a laundress! Zo's mother replied.

She asked how long he meant to stay, what he meant to do, now that he was here. The questions were carefully composed to avoid accusation. Zo's not as much. One night, she wondered aloud if she had siblings. Her father pushed his plate away. He stared over the food at her. Then he reached across the table and stroked her braid.

He had not arrived, he announced, to stay, but to pressure Zo's mother into ceasing her campaign. I have a family, he said. You are not my responsibility. You have a job. You let your neighbor raise your daughter. What more do you need? It isn't easy, it isn't easy, Zo's mother cried. The next moment, he'd thrown her against the stove. For hours, the house was silent. Then, just as quietly, in the dull violet of a suburban dawn, her father picked up his single suitcase, prepacked, and left.

They lay side by side in C's bed, Zo on her back, staring into the ceiling as she filled C in. It had been too still in the apartment the night he left. She'd been alone in her own room, identical to C's, listening for evidence of further collisions. The silence, she recalled, had seemed fuller than usual. She couldn't sleep. She'd slipped out of the bed and forced herself to look beneath it, but there was nothing there. (This detail had stuck with C, who, even as an adult at university, avoided peering under the bed frame.) Zo crept down the spiral stairs. The kitchen was cool and blue in the dark, and the door to her mother's room was ajar. Papa? she'd said.

In the opening, she saw her mother still in bed. She had just cleaned those sheets, Zo said. She took pride in her laundry. White sheets were to Zo's mother what a fur coat was to C's. The stains from that night, however, would remain. He left the knife where he'd staked it and took his valise from the entry, pushing past his daughter as if he were late for work.

Zo still smelled faintly of the hospital, lying alongside C in bed, recalling the scene in the same, cool voice she'd used with the police, to whom she'd recounted a different story entirely. C held her friend's hand. The account loomed between them. C felt she'd been shown only the corner of a picture and then been asked to respond. They lay there together until Zo pulled away.

Her back turned to C, she added, She didn't even scream.

2

Thirty years later, when C next arrives at Zo's, she finds her friend halfway up the ladder, whiting out the eggplant of the walls. She is still in her suit separates and pumps, just home from work. It would seem the Professor did not appreciate his surprise—or rather, he didn't show up at all.

Stupid, Zo says.

It takes C ten minutes to coax her down. She watches the tendons in Zo's legs and ankles strain as she reaches for the ceiling, determined to repaint. Hey, C says. Let's take a break.

But Zo is too sad to sleep in her one-bedroom alone—it reminds her of him, she says.

Okay, come stay with me.

If C is a slow, continuous disaster, Zo's slips are discrete: it is rare that C finds herself in the position of caring for her friend, but when she does, it is always at a moment of real collapse. Childhood is closer to the surface with Zo. It's what gives her that violet tinge, as if something vital lies just beneath her skin, always ready to burst through. Her life is so rarely outside her control until it is, and then all bets are off, no shame, emotional hurricanes ravage the coasts. On the train, she sobs all the way to Fort George while C rubs her shoulder blades, mildly concerned her friend will choke. The last time she saw Zo this way was when she received news from a half brother in Zagreb. He'd tracked her down online and congratulated her on all her success. *He was so proud of you*, he'd written of their dad. Anyway, could Zo maybe help *him*, half brother that he was, find something in finance? It was a boundary he ought not to have crossed. As C helps Zo up, she hopes the gnome, too, will stay where he belongs. The visitor has never met another guest before—she doesn't have other visitors; no one else has crossed the threshold since he's arrived. The screech of the tracks and the stutter of the elevator arrive as warning signs. They reach the narrow landing and C unlocks the door, opens it with trepidation. Here, she says after a pause, and cautiously hangs Zo's coat on the hook with her own.

It's easier than you would think, getting away with "it." Depends on the victim. Depends on who you are.

They make eggs. Watch the news. Drink a bottle of wine. C fills two buckets and sets them in the living room in front of the TV, the loom, so they can shave their legs. It'll make you feel better, she says. She spills, nervous. Zo has spent the night here before, but not for a while, and this time C has more to hide. She can hear the gnome is home, lurking somewhere out of sight, biding his time. Any moment now, she expects him to come zooming out from behind the curtains or the television. She wonders if Zo, too, seems on edge, as if she can somehow sense his presence. Then she reminds herself that her friend is in pain—and that no one falls in love with a paranoid.

Zo sits with her thighs drawn in and her long arms wrapped around damp shins. When she shrugs, everything moves. The whole room shrugs. Elbows knock against the chair. She lies down on the daybed and the apartment flattens.

Halfway through the news, she asks, How'd it go with Fran?

She knows, of course. C answers anyway. Fine, C says. Maybe we'll go out again. She hesitates. Then adds, Fran's been giving away an awful lot of money.

Zo nods. I told her to stop.

C looks up.

I don't know. It's not so bad.

She feels, as she often did when they were young, that her friend is out of reach, receding. Impossible, C's mother used to say of Zoja as she grew up. It was her mother's belief that a beauty like Zo's, realized at such a tender age, did a woman harm. Maybe so. In other ways, how mistaken her mother had been. Just look at the local idioms: *decked out, dressed to kill, jailbait.* You learned early on that life was violent and that you must use all available tools to defend yourself, elevating beauty to a kind of industriousness. In C's mother's anachronistic view, however, to be beautiful was to never learn to work, and all women would eventually end up alone, working, with children like C, who insisted on falling behind. What use was beauty then?

All the same, why refrain from using something simply because it will run out one day?

C looks at this woman she grew up with, wound around herself. In the context of C's shabby apartment, Zo begins to show a hint of age. Fine lines have colonized her pale eyes. Her silk blouse is at odds with her posture, her dead television stare, the menthols in her purse. Even her despair seems to aspire to, and yet fall short of, more delicate conventions. C knows just who to blame.

From the closet, she fetches towels, candles. She runs the bath. She sits on the edge of the tub, preparatory palm turned to the warming water until Zo appears in the door.

What are you doing?

Get in.

Zo doesn't.

It's good for you, C says.

Okay then. Shameless as she was at eleven, Zo sheds her clothes. Undoes the waist clasp of her skirt. Unzips. Unbuttons the blouse. Arms twisting terribly, she blindly unhooks her bra, straining the ropy tendons in her back. C lifts the black skirt from the floor and drapes it over the towel rack. Then she steps into the hall and reaches for her shoes.

Be back soon, C calls.

Her heart slows as the elevator lowers her five floors.

She takes a walk around the block for privacy and sublimation. At the building across from hers, the rose is still rapping at the brick. C taps the toe of a rain boot to a fire hydrant. She thinks of the tourists who often pause to commemorate this rose, wonders where they are today. Tucking her chin into her collar, she turns away. She leans her forehead against the chicken wire at the entrance of the community garden. Across the river, the bridge strings a commuter garland between two states. Maybe she should move. Close the shop, break her lease. She'll haul everything she owns to Jersey, and then—

Anyway, it feels nice to be taking care of Zo.

Back upstairs, the apartment smells of suds and heat and hair spray. Zo stands in the bedroom door, a dim shape preoccupied with C's hairbrush. Out the window, the soft light filters from high fixtures and onto the dumpsters, illuminating trash. When Zo emerges again, she is wrapped in two towels, one for her torso and one for her head, the hair dryer in her hand, cord wrapped around her wrist.

I can't get this to work, she says.

C takes the apparatus to the kitchen, unplugs the toaster, plugs in the hair dryer instead. The nozzle hums, rifling the pages of a magazine. Zo follows her into the kitchen, still toweled, and tests the current. She nods and turns it off. She takes the teapot from the stove, stepping in a puddle as she does; the water has soaked straight through the roots of the philodendron and showered the kitchen floor. C reaches for a cloth. Wait, let me, Zo says. Sorry, it looked a little wilted. She mops up the mess, then turns the knob on the stove and turns it again. The TV is still on, and a sitcom sifts through the room. The ignition on the stove clicks, impotent.

Sometimes you have to use the matches, C says, pointing to the little box beside the cereal. Zo strikes, the flame catches, and she sets the kettle to boil. Then she returns to the hair dryer and lowers her hair in long, dark cables over the linoleum, directing the gale along the runway of her neck. The lights dilate and flicker. The hair dryer silences. The kitchen blacks out.

Hmm. My fault, she says.

Perhaps this is all the terror that GoodNite meant to seed, to prime the imagination for disaster in the face of minor hiccups, to stoke the exaggerated fear that floods C now. The visitor's predictions return to her. She feels a rush of guilt and awe for having supported the GoodNite brigade in some corner of her heart. And now here she is with her heartbroken friend, responsible for everything. Another flame travels up the matchstick to Zo's fingertips. She wags it out with a laugh. Then she pulls away the curtains to reveal the projects lit up across the street.

Looks like it's just us, she says.

A festive mood settles in the apartment. Zo gathers the blankets. C brings the candles from the bath to the kitchen table. It's as if the lights, the television, and the howl of the hair dryer took up an existential space, and in their absence lies a vacuum, drawing each woman out of herself and into the room: the night is private again. They are a secret. They host a kind of séance at the kitchen table, resurrecting memories.

Remember your mom's fur coat? Zo says.

Do I, C replies. She disappears down the hall, and returns a moment later, wearing it.

Zo looks at her. Go to the closet and scream for as long as you can! she says. They laugh. Zo produces cigarettes. They smoke, Zo in C's bathrobe, C in the fur. Where's your fuse box?

C waves a hand. Oh, it doesn't matter. The residual heat from a space heater recedes and the cold creeps in. C's breath shortens. It's going so well, this evening with Zo, that she is frightened she will ruin it, exhale too quickly and extinguish the flame. She is pleased to make Zo smile, to finally hear her friend confide. The Professor has told her he needs some space. What is it with men and this constant need for space? Fucking Lebensraum, C says. They roll their eyes collectively. It's always a problem.

You're right, Zo agrees. But, she continues, lowering her fresh cheek onto an elbow, I feel so exhausted these days. There was some comfort in giving up, settling in. Suburbs. White fence. I feel old, she says.

C takes her cold hand in her own, and Zo doesn't draw away. You don't mean that, she says. Zo's eyes are bright in the dark. C asks gently, What is it you even see in him?

Her friend retracts to light another cigarette. Well, I guess—She draws a lip between her teeth, but the altered state of the apartment gives everyone permission. I don't have to explain so much with him. We're from the same world. With you and Fran, it's a different language, I guess. He's an ass, but he's also childish. He has so much energy, loves projects. I'm the same—an ass and also a kid. She laughs sadly. Anyway, I was off one night, I was having doubts. You'd just come by, you know—I know you do. I'm sorry, I didn't mean to fuck with you. It's just—I've been feeling—restless—and then a few days later, he stopped in when I didn't expect. It threw me off. I was confused. I told him I wasn't sure. By the time I called back, resolved, *he* was having doubts—anyway, you know how it is. The cigarette butt disappears into her cold tea. It's different for you, she says. You were actually good at something. You don't need people the same. She turns, glancing at the loom. I don't understand why anyone would give that up.

She shivers. C shrugs off the coat, drapes it over her friend. She feels more assured, protected by the dark. Her inhibitions fall away. She isn't afraid, for example, to ask, But Zo, why did you kiss me? Another shiver—or else surprise, she can't be sure. Wet hair moves heavily as Zo turns her head. Then she leans in and kisses C again lightly at the base of her neck. C is paralyzed. Then she isn't. She reaches out, belatedly, catching a clavicle just as Zo pulls away, causing her to laugh again.

I don't know what to do with you, Zo says.

They brush their teeth in the chill. Then to bed. C offers to take the living room, but Zo, still playful, throws her arms around her neck. No, she says, don't leave. In the pitch-dark, no lamp, no visitors, no surveillance at all, C could be anyone, really, carefully slipping out of her clothes and pulling a T-shirt over her head, though she can feel Zo tracking her movements from Max's old side of the bed. She joins her and lies very still. Zo scoots closer, rests a temple on C's shoulder. One of her legs finds its way toward C's, slides in between.

I'm glad you let me stay.

The night has been imagined so many times that it can only be experienced a degree removed. Few things are as good when they're derivative. C reaches for her friend. Zo's mouth asserts itself against her wrists, her breasts, a thigh. Then things begin to escalate, as desire will when so long delayed—only C has no way of expressing it. She finds herself fumbling, finds Zo's hand is on her throat, finds it hard to breathe. Very interesting. She can't help but watch through the lens of the news anchor, who is forever reporting on victims of violence—*good nite!*—and here she is, perpetuating it. What is she even supposed to like? She's a problem, *the* problem, only maybe she does like it (but how would *you* know) and by the time this loop completes, Zo has released her grip and taken C's wrist, is now guiding it and slipping fingers in, one, two, three, until it seems to C that she might hurt her friend. No, no, yes, Zo says, a little frustrated, and C complies. She delivers a shove, is encouraged, enters again until her friend's entire body winces, this time not so happily.

Sorry, sorry, sorry—

Christ, Zo says, cutting her off. Don't apologize. Take a breath. An exhale arrives at C's ear, followed by more instructions. C struggles to remember them. Zo touches her and her mind goes blank, all her worries drop into her stomach like a dash of salt. Her knee jerks involuntarily, hitting Zo's chin. Forgetting rule number one, she nearly apologizes again. Zo's hands are on her face. Hey, she says, relax, you're doing great. Which is of course humiliating. C welcomes the break. She'd like to give up and try again tomorrow, but now a query climbs her neck: What do you like?

The most reasonable question! And yet when was the last time she was with someone—in particular, someone like Zo, who is all gentle violence—whose desires are precise: three fingers, less clit, angles calibrated, all other parameters set to float, unfixed, to allow for improvisation. Never, that's when. I'm not sure, C replies.

Zo makes an educated guess, and when her lips suction to C's vulva, C is so surprised she sits up straight, pubic bone knocking the crown of Zo's head. Sorry, sorry—she lies back down again. *Relax!* But her whole body is stiff with the realization that all the sex she's ever had has been perfectly inadequate, and so it is almost a relief when Zo gives up, breaks the seal, gives C's shoulder a patronizing little squeeze and falls asleep on it, as unselfconscious as when they were kids. C stays awake for hours, molten with embarrassment. Everyone hacks her life, all kinds of visitors reach in—creditors, customers, revolutionaries, reporters, hallucinations, cretins—and now, just *once*, when she requests a ransacking, she's closed to everything.

Around three, she regains some certainty. Zo is still asleep. C lies very still, trying not to wake her. She strokes her hair. Zo shifts, and a nipple appears above the edge of the sheets. C gives it a tentative kiss, leaving the skin silver with spit. How many of their problems would be solved, she thinks, if they existed as a pair? It seems just possible. The city is still gray, the streets empty; no one's awake. Maybe she will take the day off—Zo too. They have better things to do. C is overwhelmed by a rush of affection, the need to protect. It runs richly through her, like a broken yolk. She settles in. They are separate disasters, pooled like risk in an insurance contract. Who could possibly object? The world has handed over her friend, wounded, and C accepts.

Then she hears the hum, the drone. When she looks up, the door is open, and framed within it is the gnome.

There is something awful in his face. His eyes are wide and matte and unreflective, his maw swollen in a sneer. C grabs her blouse and jeans, rises nakedly. With a chill of fear, she exits. He follows her into the hall. Clumsily, stumbling over waistband and sleeves, she dresses. That first day he arrived, she locked herself in the bath, but this time he's positioned himself between her and the door, between her and her friend. "What are you doing?" she says. She'd like to wake Zo, to scream, to tell her they have to leave. But the visitor blocks her path. His eyes are terrible; she is frightened and attracted by them, frightened all the more by her own fascination. His face is unreadable and indifferent and engorged.

A decision that will come to have lasting consequences: C snatches her keys, locks the door, takes the stairs at such speed that the banister sends her into the wall with centrifugal force. It does not occur to her that Zo might not be there when she returns, that a woman like Zo is not so used to waking up alone. As she does, just now, when C slams the door.

3

There was a time in school when C felt she had lost sight of herself—or the way *to* herself, like losing track of your car in a parking lot, as her mother often did. She pointed the key fob at her future and pressed *unlock*, listened blankly for the bleat. Meanwhile, she slept and read. She checked out books from the library. Huysmans's *Against Nature*, Kracauer's *The Mass Ornament*, in which people waited patiently for change, Anni Albers's monolith. She went to class. Taught a class. Wrote a paper. Won a show. Graded papers for the classes that she taught—and when she did, she marked mostly As because the students were more academically gifted than she'd been at that age, though somehow still less talented. Who was she to teach them anything when art production was, as far as she was concerned, little more than arrogance leavened with obsession? It didn't make sense. She called her mother and answered when her mother rang, which was often. How is it doing? When can you work? She said, The elementary school is looking for an art teacher. I will give them your name. (After the Crash, her mother gone, C couldn't help but feel she'd been robbed of the opportunity to point out how wrong her mother had been—when it had turned out just as well to be a failed artist as a laid-off financier.) C lay flat on the university-issued bed, age twenty-two, too old for such a bed and, she thought, for such advice. The way she saw it, her lifetime earnings were a wash. Same with maternal accolades. It didn't matter what she did. Across the dorm stood her loom, over which she hovered for six hours a day. She returned to the stool, unwound the warp, listened to the radio. She wove complementary conclusions into her designs, snipped samples from sartorial experiments and hung them on the wall. Meanwhile, her mother called again. When will you know enough that you can get a job? Maybe Zo can help you apply . . .

Everyone she knew was researching limits of experience. Various pills were crushed and snorted, effects recorded—including ibuprofen when you were broke. Apples became bongs. Theory over praxis: fill the bathtub one half foot, cut the bottom from a milk gallon, seal the carton at the watermark, and then introduce the smoke, at which point you've got yourself a pump for forcing exhaust six inches deep into your lungs. The survival instinct was cliché. The only dignified response to it was excision. C wondered on occasion whether she might be a little too attached to being alive. There were mornings when she actually looked forward to seeing what that day would bring, days when she was maybe a little too eager to find out who she might turn out to be beyond the boundaries of the housing complex where she'd grown up. Her dorm neighbor, a sophomore, pounded on the radiator in tortured protest against the rhythmic crashing of C's standing loom—which, to be fair, really did sound like a demolition job. The beater made violent work against the frame, jamming threads taut. Every decision elicited a mighty crash. This was just another reason why C had chosen weaving back at the Ohio college where she'd been accredited: the loom was a nightmarish instrument to listen to, so people left her alone. *Go back to the prairie, what the fuck!* Even this teenager next door seemed to possess a greater sense of irony than C. But C won prizes, gallery funding; she sold a wall hanging for an amount that made a dent in student loans to cover an actual dent the buyer had crafted in the wall of his Tribeca loft.

People began to notice. Max noticed. The first night he spent with C, he admired the samples she'd hung. I like what you're up to, he'd said. C, naked, perched on the stool at the base of the loom, accepted the joint a little warily, because when she was high, she had a habit of imagining herself to exist as pattern notation, a set of equations, which was frightening. It was hard to know where you'd gone once you'd lost the thread of the *I. system of equations, stuck therein, pls help.* A catch-22: How to communicate what the problem is when you have no self, no tongue, when you exist only as code? It struck her as the dopamine kicked in that she was the only person she knew who did not understand how to go about actively and meaningfully fucking up her life. It took too much energy; she didn't know where to start. Destruction, in other words, was also an art. You had to stay awake, stay up for days in a row, collaborate, in order to make the serious mistakes, and she was in bed before midnight. She shifted the pedals that governed the warp. One for on, zero for off. Years later, when waking up in her own bed, opening her shop, interviewing candidates for fake jobs, C feels she could laugh. How naïve she'd been! She'd fucked up just as well as anyone. Only now she could see how people like Max were ahead of the game. They destroyed their own lives in style before someone else could do it for them. They bent and kinked and sculpted according to a private sense of proportion, balance, taste, while she wandered so blithely into the thickets of received routines that once she looked up, she no longer knew where she was.

On the train, her heart still fast with fear, she wonders how much more life she has left to screw up.

It's unnerving how something that feels so correct at night curdles by day; noon arrives like a drop of vinegar in milk. At the shop, her heart still frantic, sun streams through the windows. In the two cramped, adumbrated aisles that comprise her stock, plastic packaging flashes toothily. C watches couples pass the bodega and wend through the scaffolding, round the corner toward the small park, arm in arm. Take a little girl by each hand and swing her into the briefest flight. It comes so easily to them, C thinks. They have no history, no debts between them. No haunts. Some distrusting part of her is already wondering whether what she wants is her friend, or if her desire is attended by another impulse—to settle, or worse, to gain the upper hand?

Some things lie beyond talk, beyond analysis. *Don't overthink sex*, the glossies say. Applied inappropriately, accounting will ruin everything that brings you joy. But as of late, C's thoughts have been two-tracked into assets and liabilities, and the grooves run deep. The trouble is, there are entries on both sides of the ledger when it comes to Zo, establishing grounds for exploitation, though it's unclear now who the net creditor is. In the gold chill of the afternoon, she recalls how Max founded his career on hers, and how that collaboration ended. A message awaits her on her phone. *missed you this morning, can we talk? maybe best irl.*

From her post at the register, C projects beyond the end of the day, past the fear, to bed, to the idea that she will lock up and go home to Zo again: a life where she's released from uninvited visitors. She imagines herself mounting the stairs, knocking on the Madonna's door—the sound of Zo's footsteps, the click of the bolt, an embrace as she's let in. Or else Zo's not there; she's still at the bank, still working, so C opens the door herself and waits. She sorts their mail, c/o Zo, puts on a pot of rice or ravioli or, no—she scrubs the potatoes in the sink. This life receives her easily; she leans in and the surface of the scene supports her weight like saline, a Dead Sea of dreams, in whose depths are preserved the smallest skeletons. She's often had misgivings about the store, wondered if it wasn't a net detriment—even a source of harm, spilling junk into the ecosystem. So what's one spill more? A glance around the shop. Toss it all.

"You're getting ahead of yourself," she says, shaking her head. The kitchen shatters. She returns to slipping price tags into laminated casings.

Were she to take the proverbial leap, C would lose her apartment, her street, her building; her life would be liquidated into Zo's. Her friend has the fancier commute, the longer hours, no tolerance for lines. She simply makes more money. Yet—what if Zo quit and came to live with her? She likes to think of Zo installed in her apartment, in bed, in the bath, as she was that night, invested in C's care. Of being the first to leave in the mornings and the last to return. She imagines her friend rearranging her cupboards, the closet (empty), the bathroom cabinet, the perfumes on the bureau to suit her needs, sorting the mail, hers from C's—and stops. There are obvious obstacles—too many, in fact—to accommodating someone else. Her finances are a mess. The thought on her loom is not meant to be read, not yet. Her apartment is host to a visitor she ought not to have. She glances back at the counter, where her phone keeps blinking. How to explain? *I was threatened, you see, by this homunculus . . . This glitch in my mind . . . a punk houseguest . . . this visitor from an imagination even more fucked up than mine . . .*

It's possible the visitor has already introduced himself to Zo, seeing as how C left in such a hurry. He wouldn't, she thinks. That's just it. He is proprietary. And yet so is she. You are who you let in, and what must Zo think, to find that C's been nurturing the avatar of her own destructive complex? The thought arrives with a zip of clarity. Everyone has their secrets, revenges, pornographic indulgences, things not meant to escape into the realm of experience, which is why we keep them hidden. She looks around her store at all the innocently packaged trash that she sells to children. One might very well be a danger to others, a danger to oneself.

???

C T9s back.

yes, sry, busy day, before my class?

Then she taps in Fran's number. Hey, she says, when the line connects. Do you still have a car, and can I borrow it?

4

New Jersey suburbs unfurl commuter lanes from the base of the George Washington Bridge, effluents from Hudson cliffs. Off abrupt local exits, houses preside over emerald yards, squat kingpins of property speculation, two cars in the driveway, buffered from the traffic by trees robust and overbred. Shrubbery escorts landscaped paths to the brass detailing of the door, through whose mullions: the teardrop of a chandelier. The missus's newest hobby blooms in the flower beds, and the yard is perfumed with the mulchy scent of light decay, anesthetized shit. Enter the empire of lawn care, duchy of topiary, municipality of lawn mower mercenaries: the Garden State, land of hardware stores in asphalt craters, whole warehouses groomed for bucolic bijouterie.

Max grew up this side of the river, not far away, and C has never quite understood the questing heroism he carried with him across the Hudson. It was as if, in crossing the river that flowed through what were no longer whaling towns, he'd been tainted by something Melvillean. C had made the drive so many times during their marriage—for holidays, for birthdays, whenever she and Max were in a fight—that she doesn't even have to look up directions now.

We need some air, he'd say. We need some space. Let's go home, was the perennial suggestion, and not always with acknowledgment of what *home* might mean in this context. His mother had warned him not to trust someone who had no in-laws to contribute to the clan, whose family was absent, whose dowry brought not one namesake to grace the Thanksgiving table. They used to laugh about his mother's comments on the way back (home?), too full, overstuffed, overconfident in their love, but perhaps she was right. It *was* suspicious for someone to be so alone, to carry with her no sense of place. Beyond Zo, C had no relatives. She receded into Max's familial convocations like an extra in a Bruegel painting. When will yours be visiting? his mother used to ask. She took the liberty of referring to C always as *Mrs.* and by Max's last name.

Mom, Max would joke, your politics are off by forty years. Everyone would laugh. A family gag! C was glad to join in.

But no one, no relatives, no visitors at all? C's glass was filled and refilled in the hope of making her more sociable.

I'm sure they'd love to meet you, C would reply. But we haven't really kept in touch ourselves. The truth was, with her mother gone—and Zo's too—she didn't really have any family in the States. *This* was her family. She supposed there must be cousins somewhere in Ljubljana, far-flung kin who'd spilled across the border into Croatia or Trieste, blending dialects, but after all this time, what could they possibly want to do with her? I'm not sure they'd make the trip for Jersey, she would jest. This joke fell flat. Her mother-in-law's smile was cold. There was no better place on earth to be than here in their Jersey enclave. Crime was asymptotically low, the schools fast-tracked for the Ivies, the roast on sale and just out of the oven, the *jus* in the pan forming cataracts of fat.

The torture of a potted soul, Jersey-raised and city-attracted, nourished on Manhattan's UV glow, is a provincial art one cannot learn. C was far from fluent. It was not until she'd arrived in the city and then at Max's childhood home that she began to grasp the fact that certain upwardly mobile Jersey boys perceived themselves as extensions of the metropolis. Their childhood environs were a sixth and slighted borough. As a Cleveland girl, she'd hardly thought of New York, let alone the Garden State. The skyline on the late shows could have been fabricated, and it had never occurred to her that New Jersey loomed in the public imagination as a perpetual suburb, landfill, beach, farm, vacation home, and airport. For a while, Max, like so many who'd migrated across the bridge before him would, as shorthand, tell strangers that he'd grown up in the area and let them assume. Later, and especially around someone like Fran, who was born and raised in Manhattan, he would invoke Jersey like a challenge, stamping it into his speech as unmistakably as the deposits on glass bottles collectible in the following states: NY, NJ. As his career progressed, he further embraced his origins, developing a spontaneous nostalgia for local college sports and Springsteen. This nostalgia, C conceded, was indeed particular to the state. She appreciated that it was unique to hail from a place so often relegated to a punch line—though Ohio was also a punch line, of course, in a more general sense. People had few serious preconceptions about Ohio, not having much reason to consider it at all until the midterm elections. Rest assured that those who did had likely been raised there too. Cleveland was better known in Ljubljana than on the Atlantic coast, and if C had ever felt Max's need to escape her childhood setting, her reasons were private.

In any case, by the time she took the wheel of Fran's car, she, too, knew Jersey better than her home state. The landscape was sharp in her memory, and in particular, her current destination: a garden center off the Interstate, host to a phalanx of landscape sculptures. She could see the pale glint of the cement figurines even before she reached the exit ramp. Fran's SUV—fob with no key, leather seats—glided into the gravel lot beneath the blue shelter of the sky. The land extended in every direction, open and flat, beckoning development. C struggled with the lock, pressing icons until the vehicle voiced assent.

The garden center was comprised of a lot, a small trailer where sales were transacted and advice dispensed—aphids, anemia, water retention. The vast holdings of statues were quartered in neat rows. C plunged the key into her pocket and strolled through the minor monuments. There were angels and birdbaths and swans, little girls with ribbons and braided baskets, faces plain cement. As a girl, when she was on her way to her father's, crossing cornfields an hour south from where she and her mother lived, they used to pass what she had assumed to be the home of a garden enthusiast. Cement figurines had spilled from the large garage of a small farm, its adjacent soybean field interrupted by a wispy windbreak. She rarely went to her father's—in fact, she could count on one hand the number of times she'd seen him, and so it was years before she realized that these were not ordinary garden decorations at all, but tombstones, a factory for crypts and graves that she now associated with him.

From behind her: Can I help you?

C is standing by a set of swans, wings spread, about to alight on an invisible pond. Beyond the birds is a coterie of gnomes.

Yes, she says. Those. Any plastic?

No, I'm afraid not.

C nods, as if she expected this. Do you take returns?

It takes some effort to lug the hulk of cement to the trailer, where C's credit card is denied. One sec. She flips through her wallet, counting up her cash. She has another card in here somewhere, she's sure, and also dozens of receipts, because you never know when you might need to exchange something. And right now, it is imperative to find her visitor another host. It strikes her that this sculpture is sympathetic to her goal. The trailer is windowless and artificially lit, overly warm, choked with philodendrons and succulents and other hanging plants that cannot survive the Jersey elements. She feels like she's hacking through the bush, macheteing through receipts that float to the floor like foliage, until she finds a twenty, which she smooths beside the register. Do you do installment plans?

The salesgirl, who works this job after eighth period to save up for college, who is used to dealing with the kind of character who frequents gardening centers, is unfazed. I'm so sorry, we don't, she says innocently, refusal couched in the institutional collective. C is haggling—she can leave the twenty *and* her defunct credit card—when her phone rings, disturbing the tropical peace. It's Zo. She answers automatically.

Where are you? Zo says.

I'm so sorry, I'm late, I can't. I have—C looks around—I have a guest. They just showed up, I have to take care of it.

C's receipts are scattered across the floor, mixing with leaves and clippings. She kneels to collect them.

Who?

C says who. Zo sighs. Christ. Do you need me to come?

No, no. It's fine, I have it, I'll let you know.

Please do?

Okay, I will. I'll call you soon.

A hesitation, and then they hang up, unsure, under the circumstances, what it means to sign off with love.

5

Emotion is labor too, the glossies say. You run up debts, plus interest. A woman must count as an out-of-state purchase, or maybe a charitable contribution. C understands Max and Zo's reservations now. They were smart, these people she adored, and correct all along: it takes money to stay in love.

The lie registers as a wound by the time C returns to host the children for the painting class. In the empty shop, awaiting her pupils, she brings her hand to her throat, but her grip is ghostly and soft. She begins to resent her own attachment, her fragility, the weakness of her neck, the fib she told about Max visiting to buy herself time. She resents her desire, clear and cold as a stream. How much time can you need? The children arrive. It seems an eternity ago that she taught them to paint the desert—and without relying on the vulval flowers of O'Keefe, to which parents have objected in the past.

When the children file in, she is raw, too grateful for their eagerness, their open faces. She is ready to take their presence personally. They have arrived in place of someone else, and in her desperation, this seems enough. She loves them for having arrived at all. Again, the floral theme reigns, and for once, she cannot complain. She reserves a mad affection for the talents of the boy. He slips into his stool at his easel, ignoring the chatter of the girls. They approach him in pairs, touch his back, then screech and retreat. No one likes to be crept up on from behind. That's enough, C says. She dims the lights. The photos sharpen on the wall. She has become ambitious in her pain. The images projected eschew the landscape. Gutted apartments spill entrails of insulation, belly torn.

That's not nature, ventures one of the girls.

C nods. That's correct. She sets out pots of paint in white and black, denies the girls the pink. Sometimes, she says, to understand something, you must study its opposite. She retreats behind the register and stares at the ruined apartment projected across the room; the parlor wall is now an aperture into the boulevard. From the avenue outside the store, one can just make out the image. People stop to watch. It appears to be a sort of installation. More than one records a video, wondering if the ravaged compositions have anything to do with the disturbances downtown. How strange. Here is an image of a Parisian apartment building, destroyed. The boulevard and the Centre Pompidou appear through large holes rent into the walls. The children adopt C's sobriety. They can sense that something has changed, is changing. The flower girls lift subdued brushes to the canvas. The sense of creation is palpable. One could almost believe that here, on Sixth Avenue, surrounded by shelves full of trash, sandwiched between a fatalistic sunset and a dim sum café, they are making art.

The boy does not speak for the entire two hours. Then, toward the end of the lesson, he tussles with another pupil by the paint. With two small and stubborn arms, he sweeps everything onto the floor. Not allowed, C says. A few girls cry.

The boy yells, Ha!

The shop is too small to separate him from the others. Bathroom, she says, at a loss, and shuts him in. Then she has to knock to solicit him for paper towels so she can clean the stains from a victim's dress. When she finally appears at his easel to see what he has wrought, she finds the earth torn open to reveal living room furniture at its core. A broken window. The ransacked apartment at the center of the world.

Of course, her visitor is there when she returns. She comes home dejected, delayed—above all, distrustful. Her mind is filled with images of things destroyed. The creature waits dependably outside the door while she runs the bath. He doesn't need to ask about the situation with Zo; he rather ensured that himself. The gnome has no wants, no hopes. He accepts the answers he is given, even if he does not understand—though it is beyond him why his ward should lay waste to her own talents. He is glad to have her returned to him like this, exhausted, standing in her two towels in the hall. She is in pain. Is it his function to register her pain? He follows her into the bedroom and hovers at the dresser, humming, glad to be of use as she sprays her perfumes. Perhaps he is sentient after all, human enough to want. She sets down the perfume bottle and reaches for his hat. An embrace is what she wants, but when it comes to the tangible, he is no help. Quite the opposite, in fact.

"You have to go," she says.

He looks over his shoulder. "Where?"

"Anywhere. You just can't stay here anymore."

It seems as though he might laugh. A horrible possibility! But then he is bland, as indifferent as the salesgirl at the garden center. He snaps the cuffs of his jacket at the wrists. "Okay," he says.

She gets into bed. He sits cross-legged on the dresser and drops his head. C lies on her back with her arms folded across her chest.

Is it possible to imagine something so fully that it takes on a life of its own? So many systems run only on belief. The entire economy. The gods made the world and walked away, forgot. C is fairly certain that the gnome originated from her, somehow, less sure that he is in any way dependent. Like a work of art, he has peeled away. She hardly recognizes him as part of herself, something she's made. She marvels at the red glow atop her dresser, the forlorn face. What artisanship! The eyes, so wide, so deep, seem to cancel out the lamp. She admires the mind that made this face, terrifying though it may be.

The visitor curls up, resigned. Across the room, C can't sleep. She sits at her loom and works in the dark, threads the shuttle, clacks the beater, shifts pedals. She can feel the cloth growing slowly beneath her palms. She closes her eyes. No one has to know.

```
xx = data.frame(v1,v2,v3,v4)
glm(formula = success ~ distress + vuln,
    family = "binomial interruption",
    data = xx.tr)
xxstar = sample (xx, rplace = T)
plot residuals
```

thought experiment: the body is a complex coordinated whole whose networks and contingencies can't really be controlled; cytoskeleton collapses and reforms in a matter of milliseconds; walking averages; not hard to see why limited intervention is recommended: *too complex to manage!*; see also: resentment; the system takes care of itself; meanwhile, mystery reigns; organs fail in this order, in this way, from Lehman to AIG to Freddie Mac and Fannie Mae; one thing is for sure: failure was anatomically inevitable, obvi; even still: why pain? how much? what is to be done? questions to be pursued on payroll; data is farmed, framed, siphoned off from life and into spreadsheets; *cream of the crop!;* cook the numbers and the course of action will be gleaned; multiple courses, actually, tasting menus printed from the mouths of the machines; compared, contrasted, compromised; estimates are shifting; statistics *is* experience; degrees of freedom handcuffed by the number of questions you ask—and so it's true, as they say, that every system is rigged; shit-all to do but take measurements, record minor changes, keep the patient under observation; *not much choice, really!*; trust us; QED.

6

The pain returns in the middle of the night. It feels as if some buildings have come down in her side.

She crawls to the elevator, finds it's broken down again. Seething, she scoots down the stairs in a crouch, bum to step. Again, again. A reversal of roles through the hall, across the slickness of the lobby: this time, the visitor leads C. They wait in the night. Empty street. There are many reasons not to leave your husband or sleep with your best friend, C thinks, doubled over in pain in the back seat of a cab, and this is one of them. She rolls the window down. The city spills into the car in soft, humid bursts. The streets are open, the stoplights green. The pain is extraordinary. She is new each moment. She taps the plastic partition. This is an emergency, she says. The car accelerates. A sharp left turn, a siren, a stop. The abrupt halt disrupts the agony. C moans. Then hums defiantly as she searches through her purse to pay.

The ER is a surreal world of bright lights and strangers' suffering. The awareness of other patients blinks on and off like tiny bombs. C is unsure how she registers their experience, being in sensory overload herself. But there they are, like streetlamps, at the edges of her consciousness. Someone speeding past on a stretcher is bleeding out from a gunshot wound. To her right, on the other side of the curtain, a homeless man is protesting his release. Call my mom, he tells the nurse. My mom can take me. His voice is insistent, as is the reply.

I called your mom, C's same nurse says. She told me you tried to stab her with a pen.

An old woman awaiting a hip replacement in the hall is explaining how careful she is, how unusual it is for her to fall. When will I get a room? When do I get a room?

Call my uncle, the homeless man says. The nurse gives him another sandwich and tells him to move along.

The problem is gastronomical. The answer arrives in a scan held up to the light: she is metabolically defunct. A knot in her intestines—nothing can get through. The organ seems to have unlatched itself from the stomach wall. The attendant pulls up the CT scan on a monitor and swears at the technician. Fuck. Are you sure you laid her flat?

Then a doctor arrives with a stiff plastic tube and C is instructed to tuck her chin. One, two, three, he says, and she coughs and gags as it snakes down her throat and into her stomach like an oil pipeline. Tears well. She heaves up nothing. So many plastic wrappers are tossed into the bins, as translucent as cicada shells. There is no place other than a hospital, C thinks, more generative of trash. Then a vial of euphoria is unloaded into her arm. Warm and light, her body floats away. She feels a little like the visitor, who skitters along the ceiling, darting left, darting right. "Oh," she thinks—or maybe says—"I'm high." The creature twists its hands. C whispers, Am I supposed to be this high?

You're all right, the nurse replies.

C looks at the gnome. "Are you sure?" she moans, or thinks, or says out loud.

The gnome nods, his eyes wide and bright. "I promise you," he says.

C wakes up back in her body, where it is painful to try to speak. Her first thought is of money. It's as expensive to enter inpatient care as it is to "summer" or "vacation." She takes in the TV, the metal hooks on which the dividing curtain slides, the blank walls and the whiteboard, stamped with permanent text. HELLO, I'M ____, YOUR NURSE! Today it's FABIOLA. C discovers her purse on an empty chair at the side of the bed. She reaches for it and the tube pulls her back, sending sharp pains down her nose and throat.

Sorry to disturb you, love, the nurse—probably Fabiola—says. She is a fairy flitting in and out, or maybe it's just the drugs. I've got to check your vitals now.

C raises the phone, turning the screen so the nurse can see. She types:

more pain meds please?

Fabiola's birdlike face narrows with concern.

sorry dont know if I can talk

Her phone stutters, then dies.

Later, she cannot sleep.

"Are you real?"

The gnome shrugs. He glows in the dim blue light of the screen.

"Are you like me?"

Here are the rules: no eating, no drinking, no opioids, no pain meds—though Tylenol is okay, by suppository only. Fabiola is consistently congratulatory. She rolls a taciturn C onto her side and inserts the pills. Very good!

C thinks, vaguely, that she ought to stick the Tylenol up her ass herself. She is not so sick that she cannot manage that.

They come in to take the staples out. C didn't know she'd been stapled at all, but there they are, all twenty-one of them. The technician works in threes, prying at her stomach: one, two, three, then breathe. Then again. C grits her teeth and translates the pattern into draft notation. A seven-leaf twill, $\frac{1\quad 3}{2\quad 1}$ . . . where each 1 for *warp raised* is the breath.

That evening, the doctor arrives to explain. He pauses at the end of C's bed, hands clasped, unaware that the gnome is floating by the TV over his shoulder. The hysterectomy appears to be responsible for more trouble than they originally thought. Imagine that! Imagine the gut as an eel, he says, that swims freely through open waters. Now cast over it a sticky net. In this marine analogy, the net is the scar tissue, the eel is her small intestine, and the scar tissue is from the hysterectomy—a misguided attempt to heal. It doesn't happen to everyone, he says. In fact, only ten percent of patients have such trouble with their vitals, caught in the bramble their own body has grown. A valiant achievement! Overshot. As a result, organs are overfished, depleted, baited, and choked—C is reminded here of medicine's reliance on mixed metaphors to approximate whatever the hell is going on, which cannot, in fact, be adequately expressed. At any rate, the doctor concludes, she appears to be one of the unlucky few. But with a bit of rest, no eating, no drinking, she should be home soon.

The gnome nods self-importantly and unbuttons his jacket. He slips each hand into the opposite cuff.

"What he means," he says, "is that for a moment there, you could not shit."

Somehow, the day passes. They watch a movie. Another movie. A soccer match comes on. The gnome reads the newspaper aloud. The nurse comes in three times to deliver meals to C's roommate, a stroke patient who can barely eat. Nothing for C. She is self-sustaining, like a plant. It is, in a way, the happiest day she's had since Zo's lips met her collarbone. Happy, at least, is how she now remembers it. It's peaceful here, in the pre-op ward. No wonder the man with the matricidal pens had hoped to stay. In the middle of the crossword, C falls asleep, her mind still reaching past the clues for answers. When she wakes up again, the light is gray, and the catering staff is carrying supper on plastic trays to the patients who can still consume.

The gnome disappears. She panics. Then she sees him bobbing calmly at the ceiling by the TV and is comforted.

"Why are you here?"

"Because *you* are," he says.

They establish a bond that almost resembles friendship, or that between researcher and subject; it occupies the gray area between the other and the self. After all, C is interred for four days, and the gnome is the only friend with whom she can converse without actually having to speak, which the tube in her throat prevents. C has always considered herself cautious and discerning; she takes pride in these traits. And yet here she is, indulging in a relationship with an error in her programming.

"Humans are fundamentally social," he opines. "Absent preferred company, they will fall in love with animals, inanimate objects, trees . . . Ironically, this suggests that other people are themselves goods with a certain degree of elasticity."

The night before she is released, she surfaces to find the dividing curtain alive with activity. The patient on the other side is rapidly deteriorating. Many procedures are being pursued at once. Someone calls for a balloon to pump air into failing lungs. Another calls for an OR. They recite together: one, two, three. Then comes the crash of the body as it is transferred from cot to stretcher. The choreography of nurses, doctors, and the patient gliding into the hall is beautiful and menacing. There is so much noise, so many tones of alarm, that all C hears is silence. She peers over the bleached topography of her sheets to catch a glimpse of her roommate's face but sees only a bulge of the abdomen, a white shock of hair, smooth pads of feet that seem too young for the rest of the anatomy. The stretcher slips into the bright light of the hall. After a moment, the curtain stills.

The gnome gazes after the patient through the dark. Then he says, "You want to be known, to express yourself, but I've noticed that at the same time, you fear responsibility. How much is lost in self-censorship, do you think? And I wonder, why let yourself be driven by fear? It sounds miserable to me." He pauses and looks into the hall. "I suppose it is worse for you not to try. Your fear of silence—which is to say, your fear of death—must be greater yet. When you ask whether I am at all like you, you mean to ask if I commiserate. I don't."

C turns onto her side and stares at the mint-green curtain that divides the room. A laugh constricts around the tube. Can't shit, can't eat. Can't talk.

"What a stupid way to go."

```
DATA visitors;
    SELECT FROM "part four"
        WHERE char = "zo"
```

midnight, an ambulance passes on the street outside; pov = &float.; she means to go to sleep but it is soothing to roll on the second coat; take a break, open windows, smoke a cigarette; insert detail: ivy growth, walls slightly bruised, the purple hovering just beneath the topcoat; another coat to go; do-while loop and end; elbows on the sill, lighter flickers on and off; tyranny of opposable thumbs; appraise your work with satisfaction; *we do too!*; maybe she'll show it to; &someone.;

```
RUN;
```

1

Arms pass from sore to numb. Zo squeezes her own shoulder, testing it, wondering how many hours it takes for paint fumes to induce a high. It's the feeling that counts. A smoke can seal it off. She wonders why she ever quit. She leans out the window and exhales. The ambulance swells and fades, and a car alarm responds, bridge and chorus. The horn spuriously seems to make the wet paint glisten. A brief silence, and she drinks it in. Then the blare returns with a vengeance. Oh, the tragedy of the commons that is the unattended car alarm! Very useless. She pulls the window shut. The thieves already know all the tricks.

She is a woman who values subtlety: the alarms should never need to sound. She is careful not to trip the wire herself. It would seem her tryst with C has done just that. She looks at her work: tiles, baseboards, rewired overhead, caulked-over evidence. The desk is shellacked with carpentry plans. This week, she's built herself a cedar trunk. Fuck you, moths. The lid rises on a hinge, pushing a shelf forward when it does, like an impertinent tongue. She sits on that trunk now, which she has yet to paint and sand.

She is amazed by all she used to outsource: the paranoia, alarms, furniture that comes in a box. Madonna glitters in her tympanum. Zo installed her too—with help, of course. She lights another cigarette and stares back. The room she's repainting closes in, eggplant to eggshell to butter yellow, square one: no Professor, no C. Maybe she'll show it to Fran.

"Stupid," she says.

There is part of her that could very well imagine herself and C moving in, moving on, dissolving into the sustained silence of two people who hardly need to speak anymore. They'd buy a fixer-upper upstate with a thirty-year mortgage, fixed-rate, and repaint the walls. Instead, the night with C returns to her with a sick sense of loss. She also understands that there are some people you cannot name—relatives, acquaintances, people you don't know what to call—whose functions are unexpected or inappropriate or otherwise not easily summarized, at least not in socially acceptable language. People who are not quite family, not quite friends; who are a little bit lover, nemesis, guardian, dangerous; harbingers of outsize risk, brokers who promise transcendence or else your demise, peddling portfolios of simple binaries; win all, lose all; people on whom it is inadvisably risky to place a bet—

She hasn't been feeling herself, that is.

Just last week, Zo was still vulnerable to hasty decision-making, to sex, to transacting poorly hedged options. That little spirit in her, the flighty nymph that clings to other people, needs them, begs to be devoured by them, had been briefly set free, as is the right of every living thing—or such is the popular wisdom—but now she's coaxed it back into its cage and crooned it to sleep. Relief. It's useful, in a way, that Max has come to visit and forced everyone to pause, so file it under *plus*. A week ago, Zo might have charged ahead.

It's better to take your time. She's forty-four; she has a whole second life ahead, as does C. The car alarm chirps again, chokes, and falls silent. They are in no rush. Then again, Zo's belly cramps and clenches, because that little creature of desire turns in its crypt when she thinks of how small and neat C becomes, and how she blooms again, uncoordinated, complete nonsense to herself; to be in bed with C was like trying to catch a duck with your bare hands. Zo has always half loved C. It's an old attraction, well-deep but also now part memory, because some impulses you cannot sustain. If anything, it confirms a prior belief: C could never really be herself with Zo around. Zo had the stronger personality. Perhaps they'd missed their window of opportunity, back when C was weaving. It focused her charms into a single beam, like a lighthouse in a bay.

The appeal of the Professor, by contrast, is less physical, less withholding. If she had to put it into words, Zo might describe his pull as an intellectual attraction that's worked its way into the body, not unpleasantly, not unlike how a period of intense focus—building this trunk, for instance—manifests as a strong muscle ache. It wasn't the best sex she'd had—then again, he made more sense in bed than C—but there was a different kind of chemistry, compensatory, a potential in the way he thought. There were parts of him she could have done without: his love of attention; that he liked to provoke; that he is likely at the Park right now, picking arguments as a pastime with people for whom the same debate is deadly serious. She is sure that the only reason he hasn't yet been drawn into a brawl (and the wiry Professor really isn't built for self-defense) is because he is French;

to the American ear, his accent gives everything he says a nihilistic lilt that, when recognized for what it is, can be forgiven. She might have done without his dick. But they'd been working together on models of mutual extracurricular interest, and in those private early hours, fine-tuning simulations, there was an intimacy that approached sex. It was a tenuous attraction. To sustain it required precision, like alighting at the harmonic on a stringed instrument: the bow growls and wisps until the lightest touch upon the fingerboard releases the clearest sound. These conversations on volatility, the model they were making, was the instrument for Zo and the Professor, and they'd struck a note that kept them bound. This is why people get married, she thinks, have kids, create anything. To make something together triangulates the relationship, tethers you to a fixed point outside yourselves, and, crucially, gives you something to fight about.

She passes through the bedroom to look into the street, then retreats into the apartment to the front door and double-bolts the lock. The Madonna observes this precaution, the baby in her arms. She is just realistic enough, just human enough, that Zo resents her nonchalance. It's a wonder she has any icons at all when all they do is judge. But she is so pretty there, and Zo's mother loved to pray, preferred to think that there was someone watching, listening in; would rather that there was someone conscious of the answers, even withholding them, than for the whole world to be predicated on ignorance. But Mama, Zo thinks, wouldn't it have turned out better if there were some things you'd never tried to know? There were drawbacks to total knowledge, in faith and in love. In finance, by contrast, it was a working assumption: the current price reflects all available information.

That ignorance persists regardless is the problem she and the Professor have been trying to address.

It started in the classical music seminar where they'd met—this was something else she'd liked about him, that he was a man with interests—when, walking together to the subway, they'd discovered a mutual fascination for market anomalies. Lemma: price reflects all available data. Corollary: Fair enough. Axiom: fair price IFF all information is available and transacted, in which case new information is incorporated immediately, instantaneously, expressed through trades until it isn't new anymore because the current price is already all-inclusive. Voilà. Any further price fluctuations must therefore be merely random—statistical noise, nonsense—since every logical shift has already been incorporated. This was the glitch: the link between discovering knowledge and transacting it, the if-and-only-if implied by IFF, could be broken by human delay. Or caprice. Of course the past percolates; it takes time to process things. Trauma, fear, and passion incurred today manifest tomorrow and the day after that; therefore, the price is subject not only to the drift of the random walk, unbounded, but also to the far greater shocks of human emotion, inefficiently and belatedly expressed. This was a source of wild variation that efficient markets, as standardly defined, did not reflect, observable in the simple fact that the actual market crashed far more often than the models predicted.

The Professor, for his part, an engineer by training, was now an authority on volatility at the university, where, post-Crisis, he'd taken a tangible turn from theory to praxis in his study of options pricing. Zo was a trader. "Well, retired now, I guess," she said. "I've shifted into equities, tangible assets." But she had fresh memories of the day capitalism came to an end and then Lazarused, was resurrected. She'd entered the industry, she explained, because it was what all the most intelligent, most ambitious people did; because she had no family to account for; because she liked competition; and because, if a select few were going to make enough at thirty-five to never have to work again, she didn't see why she shouldn't be one of them.

"You can't be a day over twenty-two," he replied.

She rolled her eyes. She'd never shared C's concern for purity, an ethical sensitivity that led, in the end—however much she loved her friend—to a navel-gazing moralism. What kind of person, really, believed her individual actions tipped the scales of the world, mattered enough to warrant persistent self-flagellation? If you didn't do it, someone else would. This was Zo's view. Humans congregated like minnows, according to the currents, so if you disagreed with the formations they made, you didn't blame the fish—nor even the school—but the flow of the water in which they moved.

That was just it, the Professor had agreed. To study the currents, the shifts in risk, the appropriate hedge to better account for human flubs. The markets failed and you failed because of inadequate assumptions of variation—poor parameterization of risk, which flowed through to the average, the significance, to every other parameter on which your investments were dependent. The reverberations were felt in every calculation, at every desk. Only there was a lag in estimating that deviation: a second, a minute, months (or years, in the case of 2008), and it was in this gap, as the present diverged from the past, that mistakes were made. That deviation was always changing while the estimates remained fixed under the assumption that snafus evened out and clung to a predictable upward trend (to be precise: square root of time of risk exposure) in the long term and on average.

On the train, they ignored the man taking a shit on a vacant seat, consumed by their conversation about the downstream consequences of the efficiency assumption, its blindness, and Black-Scholes's Achilles' heel: if current asset prices reflect all available info, further fluctuation in the price must be chalked up to random movement (Brownian), easily hedgeable in liquid markets (second strong assumption) by adjusting your position when the underlying stock rises or dips. In fact, Black-Scholes was but a Trojan horse, however elegant, and tucked inside was the cache of kurtosis—random motion not so normally, not so Brownian-ly, distributed.

Or else the issue was even simpler: the fundamental problem, they decided, was that models had been confused for natural laws as opposed to figures of speech, analogies susceptible to flourishes and, by definition, imperfect at comparison. That was the art of metaphor: drawing attention to similarity while neutralizing difference.

Zo missed her stop. The train had barreled under the river into Brooklyn, where they mounted four floors of a brownstone in a historic district whose underrenovated and overpriced one-bedrooms lurched over the promenade, uninsulated.

Inside, six screens blocked the view of Manhattan and Jersey City beyond, spires pulsing above the tops of the monitors, and there were also endless rows of plants quivering under grow lamps. "Experiments," he said. His father had been a botanist; he, a behavioralist. Between the two of them, they'd studied everything that lived. He boiled pasta, cracked an egg, halved a lemon, grated cheese. Over carbonara, in the dim light of the screens, the skyline, the table lamp, and by the drone of the kitchen fan, they continued their discussion: But what if you could calculate a more sophisticated, rolling standard deviation, a volatility measure that was self-updating, self-governing, less tethered to random walk assumptions, so that the tickers better reflected their actual referents, the markets, the shifting aggregate of mass psychology, the dynamic equilibrium of the real world? The question was what business did physics have in describing human interaction. It was hardly an original problem, but one quickly gaining prominence due to the magnitude of the risk outstanding in the face such of an irresolvable question.

It was two in the morning by the time talk eddied into a natural pause. They were at the computers, Parmesan crusted onto empty bowls, typing commands into R, running Monte Carlo simulations. "Fancy slow models," he'd explained. "Too slow for the trading floor, but with the advantage of being more accurate." The skyline was stark against the night, and planes were picking out landing patterns, nose-diving into Newark. It was summer, thirsty Thursday—the hour was bloated with humidity and extra time.

The Professor leaned in to kiss her then and had only just managed to hook his fingers around her skull when Zo pushed away and laughed. "Sorry," she said. "Not interested in men." He shrugged. They both mostly laughed, turned back to the screens, endured the awkward silence. The air conditioner wedged into the lower windowpane chugged and dripped, losing out to heat. The Professor nudged the mouse and the illuminated model brought out the contours of his expression, high-value information in a moment of rejection; she studied him. He had a bony face, unshaven, ungroomed, not because he didn't try but because he was perpetually in a rush. His cheeks were lean in the way of someone who runs long distances, as he often did, jogging up and down the Promenade with a view of the Financial District. He had a boyish enthusiasm that made him seem younger than his fifty-two, was the kind of man who regularly read not only the literature of his field but Nietzsche and Schopenhauer, marked up antiquated volumes of Proust and Mann, could quote these authors from memory and indeed left tabs in their books, too eager in rereading certain passages aloud to notice that his audience found something eccentric in his ardor.

He checked the weather, refreshed the model, scratched his head. "Do you want to keep going? Do you want a coffee? What can I get you?" he said. Zo felt a tenderness toward him then for skipping over the usual resentment. (This was the Nietzsche in him; he was in a war against his own petty feelings.) Not everyone did, of course. There were men who'd threatened her before, or asked her to leave, or kicked her out and closed the door hard, catching her hair in the hinge. There were those who hadn't believed her and assumed inexperience, sexual salesmen who pushed through to the implementation: *If only you knew, you'd see what you're missing . . .*

"I'd like to keep working," she'd said to the Professor, "though I should probably sleep."

He pointed across the room. "Please, you can sleep on the couch!" She laughed again. It was true; she didn't really want to go. Modeling was like gambling. You became addicted to the iterations and forgot fatigue. She felt alive and curious and damp with perspiration around her thighs and under her arms; she was still wearing the same blouse and slacks she'd worn to work in the chilled tundra of the fortieth floor at 60 Wall. Meanwhile, the night was only growing warmer.

"Okay, but could I take a shower first?"

"Of course!"

She ran the water hot, then cold—the knobs were reversed—and helped herself to the conditioner some other woman had left behind. She studied the Professor's French soaps, his razor, too many toothbrushes in the cup. When the door opened a crack, she froze, cursed herself; she'd reap the rewards, she thought, of a terrible mistake. But nothing happened—no hand plunged through the stream. She slid the frosted glass aside to assess the intrusion: a towel and bathrobe had appeared, folded chastely on the toilet lid. She looked at the neat pile of terry cloth, tucked into itself, and let the water run. For once, she really couldn't see a downside. Excess profit to gain, nothing to lose: inefficient market.

Why not?

Zo lowers the paint roller from the crown molding. Markets 101: no windfall comes for free. There's always something to lose, more with some than with others. Fortunately, Zo isn't afraid to be alone, isn't afraid of loss, whatever the Madonna thinks. She can handle the risk of herself. She's lived alone for fifteen years; she walks herself to and from work in all weather, an überambler of the cityscape. She's taken care of herself through hurricanes, heartaches, bouts of flu, her mother's murder, C's mother's death, her apartment renovation. How hard can it be, the loss of a lover, a friend? She lifts the paint roller again and admits that some of these hardships were borne at least in part with C. But it's already been four days. What a different world it was a few weeks before, just September, when C and Fran were here to help her paint.

It turned out the Professor had his own insecurities and petty feelings in the end, despite his study of the Übermensch. Last time he was here, he'd brought the abacus, and in presenting it, lifted her up onto the table—he loved to lift her, Zo loved to be lifted less—and in that moment, his arrival having taken her by surprise, she was still stuck on the kiss with C, the recognition that had flashed between them. When she thought of it, she felt an ache. She tried to transfer that longing onto the person she was straddling, who leaned into the table on which he'd placed her, whose hands were in her hair, on either side of her face, on her legs, bare because she was dressed for bed in a white T-shirt and underwear. When the Professor arrived, she'd only just sent C a picture message of herself, posed against the paint. She'd carefully arranged the shot. Her thumb hesitated over the icon until he knocked two-bits at the door, at which moment she'd committed, snapped, and sent.

Now she placed her palms on his shoulders to face the consequences and pressed him gently away. "I'm sorry," she said. "Not today, I can't."

He pushed his mouth to her neck and groaned. "Don't tell me you are gay again."

She laughed. She always was, she said, she just wasn't in the mood for sex.

The Professor lowered his face into her breasts. She didn't want to eat, to work, to fuck—so what did she want? He was angry then.

She sighed. "I just want to go to sleep." His childlike pleading had sapped her of any energy she had left, and at the same time simplified whatever he was feeling, so she found herself unable to take his disappointment seriously. The real problem, she couldn't say, was that she simply wasn't built to split herself. The part of her capable of desire, that little clinging creature, was currently preoccupied with someone else. The Professor wasn't stupid. He'd noticed it too, or at least its negative: Zo's relative absence. Simply put, it was hard to be in love with two people at once. Sometimes it seemed to her a choice between body and ideal, world and model. What she felt for C was sublinguistic—it ran as deep as childhood—while with the Professor, speech was the very substance of the relationship.

When Zo was younger, she'd taken pride in turning a woman, in being her first—and, just as often, her last. Then she got exhausted. That was in part what had attracted her to Fran: sheer experience, a lack of hesitation. C, for her part, displayed an appalling incoherence but also lacked the air of trying something just once, for fun, and never again. She wondered how much C might have repressed, and for how long. She remembered taunting her when they were girls: *stop following me, stop copying me.* It was easy to be cruel to C; she was always forgiving you, too proud to show that she'd been hurt. And now, all at once, she'd discovered a capacity for revenge. Well, one had to respect it.

Paint drips to the papers, obscuring a headline: SENTENCING EXPECTED FOR GOODNITE— She skims the partial text, which outlines half their crimes. Not so long ago—last week—she might have rooted for GoodNite's success. But most fantasies never come to fruition; that's all they're ever meant to be. So it is with the GoodNite threats—they'll probably hire those kids they caught to work at the CIA. There's no agitating this country into something it's not. She smudges the paint, finds an extension handle in a cardboard box, and fixes it into place. C's issue, she thinks, is the same as the perpetrators'. They fundamentally lack an ability to assimilate.

She climbs a step stool, raises the roller. Teeters, rights herself. Her heart rate spikes and calms. There are rare moments late at night when Zo begins to regret her own isolation, when she wishes that she, too, had assimilated into her own life a little more and hopes her neighbors are awake, alert, with excellent hearing. The double-bolted door to the apartment leads directly onto the room she's painting and, when opened, frames her perfectly, like a target centered in its sights. She feels watched by the door, takes frequent breaks to look back at the lock, the knob, the Madonna, and remembers when she bought the stained-glass fragment and had C center it above the jamb while she looked on: *a little left, there, just right.* She goes into the bedroom and pulls the curtains closed. Back in the kitchen, she draws a table in front of the door.

Zo has disdain for Freudian theories of anxiety. She is not some footnote in a syllabus, as she used to explain to her own therapist, who in the end was nice enough: *put it in a basket*, she used to say. It wasn't bad advice, only Zo had trouble taking it to heart. She'd watched their sessions pass like a car outside the window, studied the baskets lined up along the bookshelves. She'd thought, amusedly, that her father would not fit.

C's mother had repainted the bedrooms bright robin's-egg blue after he left. It was the only home improvement project they ever undertook. Zo remembers her in a frenzy at the hardware store. She, too, was so particular about her sheets, the laundry—she kept the linens glowing white. Now she was laying them across the floor, a buffer for the paint. The radio was on. She'd handed Zo a brush. "You do the baseboards," she'd said. Zo did most of it, in fact. It should have been festive—the bright color, the air of transformation, the dignity of being entrusted, by anyone's mother, with a task as consequential as repainting the bedroom. There were the small joys of destruction: paint dripped onto the sheets, splattering Zo's too-short pants and shirts. But for all C's mother's careful cheer, the renovation had been driven by fear: the apartment was an exact copy of the one Zo had left. *Turn a bright-blue page.* The landlord had called not long after, threatening fines. They'd repainted the room plain white.

The final wall complete, Zo rinses her face and checks the floor joint beneath the bathroom window, where she's recently redone the grout. Then she squats on the tiles and rests her head back against the red rim of the tub. It is no small exertion of self-control to resist the urge to check her phone to see if C has called.

2

There are other reasons not to phone. That morning, left alone in C's apartment to dress like an interloper in a stranger's room, Zo had made a strange discovery.

It had never been particularly challenging to understand why people disliked C. As she'd told the Professor, C was not to everyone's taste. "Nobody is," the Professor had said. But Zo had watched many former partners struggle to contain their disapproval, even resentment. There was something about C that got under their skin. A kind of entitlement: she asserted herself as wholly and passively as a geological formation. It's hard to really hate a river or a mountain. And yet, people manage. In fact it only made it worse that it was so hard to pin down a better reason. "Well, I'm not like that," the Professor replied. He was basically a cheerful person. And, to be sure, he'd proved immune to the usual effect. Circumventing Zo's reluctance to make an introduction, he'd gone to the store to check C out for himself and bought the abacus. They were in bed now and Zo was trying to explain that you can't glean everything about a person in five minutes. "Take C's ex-husband, for example," she said. "You had the feeling she blamed us all for things going wrong, and meanwhile Max—"

The Professor interjected, "It sounds just as much his fault?"

"Well, if you already know, don't ask."

"She was suspicious of me," the Professor said. "I liked it. This shows intelligence. Although you get the feeling she tries to hide it, her cleverness. I am imagining for example that she says much less than she is thinking to herself. I want to say," the Professor continued with a smile, "that she reminds me of myself."

"Don't see it."

"Also very pretty. As we say in French, *Elle est une belle plante.*" He raised his chin to look up at Zo, expectant.

"Sure, I guess." Zo noted the weight of the Professor's head on her chest. She stroked his hair. "What I mean," she said, "is that C rarely admits she's capable of harm."

Weeks later, this fact returned to Zo in C's empty apartment like the punch line of a sorry joke.

She listened for her friend's presence in the other room, but it was clear that she was gone. Humiliated, feeling reduced to a cheap mistake, Zo got out of bed. She searched the floor, the bath. Checked her phone for messages. There was her skirt, still on the towel rack. She slipped it on, sensing, in the silence, that the apartment had opinions of its own. She went into the main room. No C. The stale buckets of shaving water were still in front of the television, beside the loom.

She had the impulse to record her anger. Disturbed, she turned around the room for a pen and scrap of paper and, in this way, came again to the loom. A bedsheet was tucked around the frame. She took the liberty of peeking under it, then tore it off in a single motion and was further unsettled by what she saw.

While she'd been under the impression that C did not weave anymore, it was clear to her now that the covering was meant as protection for something very much alive—it was a violation to have lifted it. The cloth was wrapped around the beam excessively, the machine unable to accept another inch. C had overproduced. And yet the fabric was diaphanous, tentative, hesitant to manifest. Zo reached out to touch it and felt a chill. It crinkled upon contact. The startled sound was outsized in the silence of the apartment, like a cry. She pulled away. It was stiff cellophane, she saw, that gave the fabric its reflective and auditory qualities: on the floor was a roll of garbage bags and a spool of tinseled thread, as well as chenille, fleece, dried cobs of corn, and coarse wool, which lent the composition its indifference. The shades ranged from midnight to ebony to gray to mud. The weave was taut as twill here, loose there, so that the pattern unveiled itself in irregular slats, like a deranged set of Venetian blinds.

Zo replaced the shroud. The derangement itself was reason enough to break things off.

3

In the morning, her restlessness returns in full force. She wakes up on the bathroom tiles, gets dressed, and walks downtown to her office, massaging the crick in her neck. Spills her coffee on her shirt. "Stupid." Four screens form a firewall on top of her desk. On the first is a spreadsheet of risk profiles ranging high, medium, and low for a pension fund in North Dakota. The next shows her calendar, her email. She drafts a message to her analysts, asking for further evidence, a demonstration of why she is supposed to trust that they haven't fucked up the numbers again. The whole generation lacks shame, and the Valley has begun to prove a brain drain. "The quality of applicants to economics," the Professor always complained, "continues to depreciate." The people who own everything lack shame. Her client in North Dakota, a dot-gov extension, hardly understands what it is he's signing, and it is not her fault if he cannot understand, no matter how many times she tries to explain. It makes her depressed. The whole system makes her depressed. Even now, an overconfident CEO could saunter in, requesting services and demanding trades like any drunk in a casino, except this isn't supposed to be a gamble; that's precisely why she is in risk management. The only reason the business still resembles roulette is that ignorant clients cannot consent to the game they've joined, and so they rely on goodwill and luck and private gods. It's exhausting the way this country celebrates its idiots, even subsidizes them.

The newsfeed freezes time on the fourth and final screen: the president has endorsed the protestors; what if GoodNite is not so annihilated after all; people just want to express themselves, the mayor says of the Park. Zo refreshes the page. She's been wondering lately if she and her mother might have been better off if they'd stayed behind on certain Balkan shores.

In this, she finds herself sympathetic to the protestors; those in charge are idiots. Including, to some extent, Zo. She was with C in the hospital, mourning the loss of her friend's reproductive system, the day the market crashed. She was still working on the trading floor then, in the bowels of the building—at a new desk, in fact. She'd switched on suspicions of faulty arithmetic, or what she likes to think was a suspicion, a conscientious objection, but was in fact only a hunch, a fleeting thought, a flutter in her stomach after lunch. A doubt, in other words, dulled by the certainty that if the markets were indeed awry, it wasn't her fault. She'd swapped desks from sales to trading, mostly because she disliked her boss, a loudmouthed, midlife, pre-Crisis, pro-Giuliani type, one of those holdouts from the '80s who'd arrived before New York was too safe, too expensive, but also before one had to be sharp (and a shark), the very best, to have the career he'd had. It was no accident that the floor increasingly looked less like him, though Zo herself remained one of the only senior women. She didn't complain. There were perks: she had a corporate bathroom all to herself, plus an outlet for this pent-up restlessness that's seized her lately.

Now she bounces her knees at high rpm at her desk. Checks her mail again. Two new messages. No stakes. There was nothing like the trading floor, really—the thrill, the thrum, the adrenaline rush.

Though there was, of course, occasional friction. The year before the Crisis, she'd queried her boss—the holdout, then with a house and three kids in Connecticut, a predilection for pairing pink ties with navy suits—as to what he made of the following hitch in the system:

They bought mortgages, tranched them into MBSs or CDOs, sent them off to Moody's to be stamped AAA, dumped them onto the open market, then turned around and sold them again: insurance against the default of the CDOs they'd just closed, except the buyers of this insurance didn't own any CDOs. They had no assets to insure, and yet, for a small fee to Zo plus a monthly premium, they bought a policy on nothing, a bet that the assets they did not own would fail. This created a double market, a shadow world, derivative and populated, like the original, with triple-B-grade mezzanines, triple-A ratings, and ghosts: for every asset package sold, another bet against the market spirited its way onto the books via the synthetic CDO. There were two plot twists to this fairy tale. How were subprime mortgages, synthetic (the insurance) or original, spun into gold? Guess Moody's middle name: correlation. The mortgages they tranched were of different classes, different states. A home in Florida was hardly a home in Kansas, which was distinct from a refinanced four-bedroom in Arizona, or a trailer parked in

Washington State. They could not all default at once, the bankers had argued and the rating agencies believed, because the diversity diluted risk. Only, not fully—because why was it, Zo had asked, that these securities, gold-standard, AAA, somehow bore more interest than other assets in the same risk class? Efficient markets precluded windfalls such as this. The rating promised one reality, the interest rate another. And so didn't someone somewhere along the chain have to pay for that extra kick? Who was left holding the excess risk, connoted by the elevated interest? Zo had hypothesized it was the home buyers themselves, the blokes in the retail banks seated opposite advisers, those smooth talkers, who, as perhaps the traders should have guessed, were pushing teaser rates onto incomeless Americans. Were *they*, the consumers, eating interest rates? It was hard to say. Because by the time the data on those mortgages reached Zo's spreadsheets, they had been abstracted, repackaged. There was a rift between the real and the virtual, a lag, a layering of realities that were ultimately in competition, revealing themselves in premiums.

Her boss had paced up and down the desk, hands in his pockets, eyes on the ticker, waiting for confirmation on a major client's trade. "They've pooled risk is all," he said. "Just as safe, less risk. That's the whole point—that's why we're making money these days." And as long as they were, he wasn't interested in investigation.

The entire market disagreed with Zo. They accepted AAA for AAA, one for one. Only, she had this feeling . . . He asked if she would have him trust her intuition more than the common sense of the entire exchange. What were these pricing models but aggregated intelligence, a globalized brain?

Markets already reflected whatever information she thought she'd gleaned. You made money like a hunter, by being quick—faster computers, better instincts. You thought you could outsmart the rest, just not by trying to play a different game.

At her annual review, he sat Zo down and said, "Look, the work is good, but you see, I paid my dues." The suggestion, of course, was that Zo should pay hers too. For starters, by piping down.

These were the incentives of the bank: adrenaline, snacks, speed, and other basic principles beyond the reach of government regulation. Find a buyer, place a transaction, skim a fee, the more fees the better; Zo's real function was volume generation. She was an open dam through which the water flowed. The base physics of the business were the fluid dynamics of rising tides, all boats—or at least those currently out to sea. And to short the entire sea—to say, one day, *those waters will not exist*—was an apocalyptic enterprise. Who could really guarantee the sea, which was itself the guarantor of everything? That was the real source of Zo's anxieties. It couldn't be insured, and yet she sold policies daily to hedge funds who docked along the shores in anticipation of total evaporation. And what if they were right? Who would possibly be left to pay? This was not a scenario middle management liked to entertain. Far better to play the middleman, keep order, keep close to the ground in close quarters, close desks, eyes on six screens at once, charging tolls to every investor who sought to enter shadowland. *Stay twitchy, gentlemen. And lady.*

And twitchy she was. Zo would check the markets before she went to bed and first thing when she got up. When she was facilitating an important trade, she woke up multiple times throughout the night, set alarms, rose every other hour on the hour, to track prices and crack contingency plans. In between, she saw the women she was sleeping with. She hid her stress from them. Sweet Francesca, half-woken by alarms, cast a limp arm across Zo's chest, a halfhearted plea to keep her in bed. Zo would have liked to unburden herself to Fran, and in fact tried multiple times. But how could she, when the entire language of the trade—mezzanine tranches of synthetic collateralized debt obligations—caused Francesca's face to go glassy, as if she'd caught a sudden flu. This, too, was part of the job: *keep it to yourself*. And she was good at it, good enough to ignore, while sleuthing overtime, an uptick in the correlation between defaulting mortgages in the spring of 2006. She recalled a corporate rule: people are promoted up until the point at which they are no longer effective. She put out feelers on the internal job market. By May, she'd found a new seat four desks down, that much closer to the snacks.

The desk was called the UN because it had no Americans. It was here, against the far-southern wall, abreast of the central closet where they kept the pretzels, flavored waters, sodas, granola and M&M's, that you came for advice on H1-B before approaching HR, on how to game your advertising algorithms for cheaper flights. It was where people worked on Christmas and took their two-weekers at Ramadan. The nickname had been imported, of course, from the rest of the floor. Only Americans would select as an epithet a club to which they themselves belonged and which they disproportionately financed.

The desk's head was Iranian and the product of Southern state tuition. Like all talented people who rise through budget-crunched systems, he bore a chip on his shoulder for it. He was convinced the market would soon tank. He was more easily convinced than most, primed as he was to discount Ivy League consensus. He proselytized apocalypse to anyone who asked and to many more who didn't. "Triple-A my ass." Choice stanzas from Tennyson showed up in newsletters bound for client inboxes: *Half a league, half a league, / Half a league onward, / All in the valley of Death / Rode the six hundred.* It would have been easy to dismiss his warnings as an ego surge, a midlife hot flash, if the opportunity cost of abstaining from the MBS orgy hadn't been so high. Either he was woefully wrong, or more worryingly, he was right, and the rest of the bank—along with its clients—stood to lose unspeakable amounts. The market was going up, up, up. Meanwhile, he sat each morning to email his patrons and tell them, *This is shit*, forgoing millions each time he pressed *send. That's shit too*, he messaged. *Shit, shit, shit. Short the market instead.*

And so the shadow market grew a little larger—a few more hedge funds took refuge in the shade—as he pocketed his cut. Losers and winners came in pairs: for every client he convinced, there was some chump about to sink. *Theirs not to make reply / Theirs not to reason why / Theirs but to do and die. / Into the valley of Death / Rode the six hundred.* Zo, even though she had her own misgivings, wasn't sure he wasn't grandstanding, overreacting, simply too enamored of contrarianism—certainly of Tennyson. Her coworker, the cohead of the team—South African, the only Black employee in a row ten desks deep—had begun to go one step further. Even as he told his clients, *It's shit*, he also advised them to *close* those profitable bets against the market, on the losing end of which stood a certain overleveraged bank that was doomed to fail. Short that *bank* instead. Alexander hung up the phone and turned to Zo. "Double insurance policy," he said. There was something about that summer that signaled it was time to cover one's tracks, keep the exits clear—a charge in the air that raised the fuzz on the back of your neck. Alexander paused, noting her lack of accent. "Where are you really from?" he said.

Over pretzels in the pantry, he expressed his own qualms to Zo: the country was obsessed with property, the tax code was regressive, Freddie and Fannie existed to leverage the lower-middle class in the interest of the tenured one percent. Before the banks learned how to skim their bit, he said, no one would extend a loan to the sort of people who lay on the other side of these MBSs. But now that mortgages were pooled, engineered, sandwiched into triple-As, suddenly it seemed like borrowers almost didn't *need* to make their payments, as long as someone else in the same tranche did. Now *that* was solidarity, he said, laughing, as well as an asset on which the banks could get rich. The entire nation had Frankensteined its debt in the name of proliferating the white picket fence. It was sad, really.

Zo ran a fingertip along the seam of the pretzel bag, collecting salt. "My mother rented," she said.

Alexander guffawed. "Of course she did. You wouldn't be here if she didn't."

Back at her desk, to her left was a fidgeting Macedonian who spent his days glued to his screens, pasty and pale and even slightly luminescent, as if he'd absorbed the monitors' glow and was storing it for later use, like a lithium battery. Headphones muffed his rather small ears. He wore them out of the building, to the highway, to run sprints up and down the river. The UN had a favorite lunchtime game: *How many miles do you think he ran today?* Everyone took bets. He had a way of sitting splayed at his desk, knees cocked, the silk-wool blend of his too-loose pants draped over his skinny calves. Zo felt threatened by men with ankles slimmer than hers. They provoked her sense of competition. He had restless feet. "Sorry," he'd say whenever their knees met. She went out of her way to take up space, spread out her lunch, extend her legs, kick him back lightly, knock the point of a heel into his skinny shins. She felt emboldened to do so over at the UN, where people spoke the truth: *it's shit.* They all had another vulnerability in common. Instead of homeownership, the goal was green cards, citizenship. If and when the market crashed, they stood to lose not only millions, but immigration status. All except for naturalized Zo.

Good thing, then, that the market had turned! For the past few months, the desk had been raking it in, just like her boss had said would happen, while everyone else was floundering. Then her boss, too, began to get that worried look: most of his shorts were tied up at the first bank to crash.

The weekend Lehman buckled, Zo was at C's bedside, holding her hand, watching the ticker of her inbox on her phone. "It'll be all right," she whispered to her friend. And really, it was! She was thrilled. All this time, she and Alexander had been shorting Lehman for just this reason, and now they'd won the jackpot. Though, in sympathy, she couldn't help calculating how much her boss would lose if it turned out that Lehman couldn't pay. C, still drugged, took a nap. Fran fell asleep too. Riding out her adrenaline rush alone in the hospital room, it slowly began to dawn on Zo that the domino effect would not stop there. She'd done everything right, shoveled shit, shorted Lehman—only now *her* winnings were tied up at the insurance company that had been suckered into holding all the IOUs, and which was now looking increasingly insolvent. All her assets were shadow bets, and AIG was on the other end. The same was true for just about everyone still afloat. She called Alexander. What should they do?

Silence on the line. She could almost hear the panic reverberating in his skull and harmonizing with her own. The first half of the market had crashed. The second was maybe poised to follow. Flip a coin. "We wait," he said after a long pause. "They have to bail them out."

On Monday morning, the rest of the floor was in denial. For those who were long—basically everyone—to cut your position was to lower the price on everything you owned because you *were* the market; there was no one else to sell to. Where does all that volume go when you try to drain the ocean? In a matter of weeks, her old boss had lost nearly all of his commuter flab. His shirt was ragged and his face gaunt, as if he'd only just learned the meaning of trench warfare. Then he was laid off. (With severance!) Everyone was smoking packs a day. The only one who capitalized on those months was the bodega owner in 60 Wall, who filled tobacco orders from his niche for people who hadn't smoked for years. When Zo closed her eyes at night, she did not sleep, just watched the red digits rain down the backs of her lids. Clients returned to haunt her. The manager of a pension collective in a failing Midwestern city, where all the factories had shrunk to half-capacity, had called in January 2006, asked her advice, and she'd told him the standard—*hold a synthetic CDO for the superior income*—and completed the trade herself. The thought now made her sick.

She went into work and watched the numbers drop. She was like one of those survivors of the Titanic on her private lifeboat—*women and children first!*—watching everyone drown but still not sure if she'd make it out herself. For the rest of the floor, the available options remained the same: you could hold and lose or sell and lose. The longer you waited, the more you lost; she kept her job in part because she'd cut so early in the game—and also because she was a woman. "Don't worry," Alexander said to Zo, not without some bitterness. "Even if we're fucked, they can't fire a woman as senior as you." It was true. In the bathroom, on her knees, she vomited and flushed. It became a routine: she woke, smoked, had a coffee, threw up. What a relief it was that there were so few other women on the floor! She had the whole ladies' room to herself. She retreated to her favorite stall when the bailouts were announced, when the Iranian's green card application was denied even as he was promoted. Alexander reaped his millions and left for Cape Town. "Told you we'd be fine," he said.

She thought of him a few months later, when out of fear, despair, and plain common sense, she leveraged her own assets, bought an apartment, and so, once and for all, truly became American.

And American she has stayed. It is quieter up here, appended to asset management. She lives in the veritable suburbs of the bank. No more checking tickers in the middle of the night. No more shorts. All vetted clients. She is comfortably a consultant. She has, as the traders used to say, retired. She returns to the floor only rarely, as certain projects require.

Occasionally, she misses it. It *was* gambling, but without the risk; it wasn't her money, after all. And for a time, it had seemed the house advantage could be cracked. What a thrill, to beat the odds! On days like these, too little work and too distracted to do it, she feels like a child penned up here on the fortieth floor, encased in glass. She unzips an inch of waist from her pencil skirt, draws up her feet. In the building across from hers, the same group of men is holding the same pointless meeting. They are always in that conference room. It is as if they've held one unending meeting, uninterrupted. The day they downgraded US debt, she looked across the rooftops to the rating agency where the announcement had just been made. The logo hovered smug among the spires. From her window, she can see so much of life, the institutions that give it shape, if she presses her cheek to the glass. East to Trinity, Broadway, City Hall; west to the river, the docks, the helicopter pads; beyond all this to Jersey. And yet she cannot see the Park.

At noon, she meets her division head for lunch. They are two women over salads in the basement cafeteria. Her boss has bought a house. Four bedrooms. An hour commute.

"Listen," she says to Zo, "you should come see it. Friday?"

Zo navigates her fork through a tuna niçoise. She dreads these lunches. She used to joke with Francesca about how often her boss tries to set her up with men. There are open assessments of Zo's clothing, her weight, of other women in the office—who eats too much or not enough. She has told Zo not to walk home alone. "It's dangerous," she says, "when you look the way you do. At least wear pantsuits."

These conversations used to bring on physical reactions. She used to rail against her outside of work to Fran. Now it seems to Zo that her boss is hardly worse than anyone else—perhaps even a slight step above. She thinks of regular people now immortalized in photographs of lynch mobs, then wonders how old her boss is. She parades no morality, no sympathy, unlike the Madonna in the transom, whose pity is in any case false. Meanwhile, Zo sits across from her, endures, forking salad, staying pleasant and size six, saying as little as possible.

Recently, she has entertained her boss with stories of the Professor, but now that they have separated, she has to make them up. She says they have plans to visit the Park on Friday, so there's no time to catch the NJ Transit.

Her boss turns plastic prongs on Zo, stabbing at the air. "How adventurous. *You're* adventurous. But isn't it dangerous? I don't know what to think about those GoodNite kids."

Zo shrugs. It's too much trouble to explain that GoodNite and Occupy are different things. She reloads her fork, then says, "You're right. They would have told us if the threat were serious."

It isn't hard to fabricate what she and the Professor might be doing, mostly because she can predict his schedule exactly—he really is conducting research at the Park, only he doesn't invite Zo to come. She's a liability, for obvious reasons. What are the motives, he wants to know, of the people gathered there? The answers are crucial, he believes, to a unified theory of pricing. More information: that's his God. She can accurately estimate his whereabouts at any time of day. Now he'll be at the Park; later he'll be in his office at the university. He owns a time-share upstate. Maybe next week she'll tell her boss they're staying there.

But today, the more Zo lies, fabricating romance and stabbing lettuce, the more emotional she becomes. A link breaks. Error messages filter through the recursive spreadsheets into which she's compartmentalized herself. *#REF!* Soon, inexplicably, she finds herself orating in the way of the Professor—or Alexander. She finds herself questioning aloud whether there is something to be considered in the value of tearing everything down. She excuses herself. Then simply starts again. That's what an error is—a loop that can't be exited. In some ways, the Park hasn't gone far enough. They ought to have started this themselves, Zo says. In fact, she's rather pissed off. There had been a brief opportunity just after the Crash to do away with everything, start afresh. "I mean honestly, what the fuck?" She rises from her seat. She's standing now, and from this vantage notices her boss's graying roots and widening part. They could have scratched everything just a few years ago! They ought to have leaned in, as the all-female networking events are always telling them to do. How is it that they, as the only ones who knew how fragile the system was, instead rebuilt everything exactly as it was before?

She sees the confusion on her boss's face deepen to embarrassment as others begin to stare. Zo's fork drops into a container of salad dressing and the little pot flips, ejaculating its contents. Mayonnaise clings from her boss's bangs.

"Zoja," she says, dabbing with a napkin, "take the day."

She walks north on Broadway, avoiding the Park. Passes through a cloud of halal steam. Zips up her skirt—whoops. Lunch hour jabs its elbows as passersby raise sandwiches to mouths. She hums along in the crowd. It carries her four miles uptown to the museum, where she breezes in by flashing her badge from work: corporate membership. The galleries are midday-quiet, abandoned; schoolchildren are corralled into groups in the halls. She makes her way through the escalators to a back room where the textiles are kept and sits alone on the bench for a vicarious visit with her friend.

Maybe it's true that she doesn't love C or the Professor so much as she loves what they are able to provide, what they produce. But then it's impossible to separate the person from the mark they make on the world, isn't it? The logic of branding has always been: to love a product is to love its producer.

She soaks up the silence. A security guard passes through. Zo's always felt an attraction to *Women Working with Their Hands*. There were so many people suggested here, blurred from afar, in focus and fuchsia from the distance of the bench. A whole swarm of hands. The color deepened and muted here, sharpened to neon there—it was almost tangerine. The tapestry would fill the average room, overwhelm a four-bedroom home like the one her boss has bought. *The grass covers all* . . . and this does too. Zo cranes her neck to see the top. The brisk border, tasseled with a mockery of beading, skims the ceiling. The motif recalls a cloud of locusts descending, ready to devour, an invasion in cheerful shades of bruised hot pink, the color and intensity of exposed organs. There is something in the tapestry that makes her feel known in a way that C herself, post-Max, post-uterus, has not been able to offer in quite some time. Perhaps Zo succumbed, the night they spent together, in search of this feeling. It had to be in there somewhere, buried. She wishes she could discover her friend all over again.

Her skirt strains as she draws in a knee as far as decency will allow. A run in her nylons runs a little further; she plucks at the harp of it. There's something off about C these days, as if she is only visiting, flickering on and off behind herself. It's alluring, in a way—and so they made a mistake. Whatever it is, she suspects the problem is one of C's own making. C was always uniquely capable of subsuming a world of evidence into personal, ungeneralizable conclusions. She lacked the ability to foresee consequences, acted on compulsion rather than survival instinct, perhaps lacked any survival instinct at all. It is, to be sure, what made her so gifted. Zo was so proud of her back then. She can still see C at the opening for *Women Working with Their Hands*; the pink tapestry rose behind her, all those chains of eerily clasped hands, the knuckles bulging painfully. Wasn't she thrilled? C had smiled, tipsy on cheap wine. She was abstracted, as if she wasn't really there at all but instead still at her loom, planning new patterns. It was almost as if she'd never stopped composing *Women Working with Their Hands*. She'd lost herself in it. C's genius for displacing herself, embodying herself in other things, evokes a tenderness in Zo. It occurs to Zo that she herself might have been one of these avatars, however briefly. And now C's back with Max. Apparently. Well, good luck to him.

The yarn is thick in Zo's vision, erupting in magentas and violets and voracious rose. The threads, swimming, become distinct as she nears the barrier and reaches out a hand. She makes contact, triggering the alarm just as the guard calls out.

It is natural, self-protective, to prematurely cauterize to prevent further infection. How afraid of each other everyone is, Zo thinks, as she's escorted out to retrieve her coat. She opens her purse and checks her phone to find the Professor has called.

```
DATA visitors;
    SELECT FROM "part five"
        DO air_gap
            i = 1 to &epilogue.
            i_prime = gap(part_i)
```

great collective efforts; &culture.; lol!; repeated failures; expression dependent on proximity to experience; regress *y* on *x*; results slipperier with time and over distance; collect residuals: approximations pile up at the foot of the glassy curve so many adventurers have tried to climb; *come look at this guy!*; besieged in a hospital bed, a simple touch is best; insert distance; "custom units"; intervention of thirty city blocks; phone dead; &pov. finds <<itself>> completely incapable of disseminating terror, disappointment, love even after the interns sweep in, predoctorate, to tug out the tubes from nose and throat; *what a gag!*;

```
    END;
RUN;
```

1

While she is in the hospital, there are two shootings; one Toys"R"Us burned down to the ground; three mass encampments sprung up in Tulsa, Phoenix, and Indianapolis; and massive electrical brownouts in the same. They are all part of the Park. It's said that Cleveland is an epicenter now. People have spilled forth from cul-de-sacs, cars, and office buildings, raised the blinds and threaded the eye of the freeway that loops around city limits. The movement has snowballed in popularity. Public polling for the Public has surpassed the President's. What's not to support? The television shows three girls, teenage-white, shielding their eyes from pepper spray. The picture is high-definition, deflecting streetlights off police shields when the electricity comes back. Special effects. The chaos is such good branding for the Russians that many outlets are beginning to wonder if Ukraine wasn't hacked at all. The supercomputer was a gift. Open up. Step in. "But then why," the gnome points out, "would GoodNite leak it?" C turns the television off. The screen hangs from the ceiling like a bust. She is compelled to join in, to catch a bus to Cleveland. She would, even, were she not so exhausted, still in her hospital gown and tethered to the visitor, a pulse monitor, an IV bag. On the floor, the plastic vat of fluids they've drained from her gut is labelled BIOHAZARDOUS. It sloshes heavily as she shifts in the cot. She imagines workers in climate-regulated suits pouring it into a communal chute, huge pools of human fluids, pH acidic, an external stomach underground. A fleeting image from some signal station deep in her brain arrives: the body as a transparent mold, revealing all the processes inside. The IV dock is still in the soft of her elbow, the nozzle bright with blood. It's a high-use joint, the elbow. The needle doesn't belong.

"Stay still," the visitor says. "They only stick you there," he further relays, "when you come in through the ER, otherwise they take their time." They tap the back of the hand, your arm, or for the elderly, a thigh. C's blood blister strains against the second skin of the tape. It's hard to trust anything that comes from her, she thinks. Any advice that comes from him. Though she is more and more convinced, having spent days with no conversation but the gnome's, that he is also part of her, a template populated with impulses she must admit are in no way unfamiliar.

They release C after she proves capable of keeping down an egg and a carton of Jell-O, send her home with instructions to live life slowly for a time, or at least more slowly than she would otherwise. Ha! She exits onto the street thinner, frailer, still in shock from the pain and strangeness of her illness, which, the doctors have explained, may return at any moment. There's no treatment, Doc says, but patience. It's a structural issue, one that only worsens with further surgical intervention. The episodes come and go like business cycles, beyond control—the threats of recession and restriction are perpetual. On the train on her way home, surrounded by commuters, the hospital bracelet still haunting her wrist, she realizes she hasn't used her voice in days, except to offer her consent when the nurses asked if she was ready to eat. The other passengers stare into their phones. Save one woman. A border of felt flowers forms a botanical brim for her hat. She breaks into a wild grin and points at the hospital bracelet as if she knows what C's secret is. The inpatient closes her eyes. Out here, in the actual world, the visitor's company seems wholly inadequate.

It was only a temporary truce. At home, however, he seems emboldened by their fraternity, poses incessant questions. It is, it would seem, his primary mode of amusement. C runs a bath. "How many visible stars in the sky?" he asks. Still saturated with the hospital's stench, her own shirt makes her gag as she pulls it over her head, stirring sense memories of tubes. She locks the door to the bathroom and sinks into the tub, lets the water rise to her ears. She brings a hand to her throat. It occurs to her here, submerged, ignoring the gnome's inquiries, that the closer she is to him, the more removed she is from the world in which he is so interested. Through the door: "Visibility threshold of +6.5 yields 5,000 suns per hemisphere. Adjust for city, light pollution, reduced thresholds apply—"

She regrets egging him on. Her commitment to civility is even stronger, perhaps, than her fear of going insane. This is, of course, exactly the kind of contradiction—so typical of human behavior—that the gnome enjoys pointing out. C rises for a gulp of air and sinks under the water again. She regrets many things she did not say—to the gnome, to Zo.

She stays in the bath long after the water cools, soaping and resoaping. Her fingers prune.

From the other side of the door: "More or less than a thousand, you think?"

She emerges wrapped in two towels. At the dresser, she tests the weight of the hair dryer in her palm. The gnome regards it jealously. Drifting into the kitchen, he turns his back and orates on the state of man while retying his cravat in the reflection of the oven door. He pokes his glabrous forehead—which seems to have grown one size more, to truly impractical proportions—through the curtains and looks down onto the street. "They really do waste a lot of time, you know," he says, watching people pass. The rose has wilted in his buttonhole. He adjusts it. "Soon there will be no time left." C closes the bedroom door. "Imagine," he says. "*Poof!*" The bunk grid will nullify the database, he explains: debt is the corpus and the grid is the heart that pumps the lifeblood in. No electricity, no data, no debt. The opportunity to start again. "What would you make of a night like that?" C honestly isn't sure. He continues to orate over dinner as she forks instant rice into her mouth, is still going when she tries to sleep. As C drifts away, it strikes her that he is as interested in studying her as she is him.

When she turns out the light, he's a dim glow above the lampshade, a small, red beacon. He rests his elongated chin on elongated fingers, folded in. The last thing she hears before she falls asleep is, "Time used is better than time wasted."

Carpe diem.

2

But it's a slow diem. Every day in the craft store is a slow day. C sits at the register and stares out at the street, her account books open on the desk and ignored because she has done all the arithmetic before and right now she doesn't have it in her to calculate the estimated loss of not showing up for days. Halloween has come and gone; she is sick to think of the revenue lost. Halloween is Black Friday and Christmas combined for art supplies. She scolds herself for not hiring Mah-rie. That ought to be the first order of business, she thinks. She jots down a note on a neon Post-it bordered in glittery pink. A maternal impulse swells in her when she looks across the room to the peacock feathers erupting delicately in the vase, to the monogram beads, overstocked in *J*s and *K*s and *L*s. The rack of stickers rotates squeakily on its cheap tin axis by the door.

Outside, however, a certain energy has touched the streets. It trails pedestrians, wafts down the blocks like pollen. It is the excitement of comfortable people catching wind of a pending crisis. An air of confession, of gossip, leaves the edges of your life just a little golden. People pass by the store in twos and threes, shoulder to shoulder, ear to mouth. They pause to window-shop. C fights the impulse to draw the grate. When she looks at her life, it seems there are other things that ought to demand her attention. She should visit Yi, who has left multiple messages on her answering machine and notes under her door. She ought to find someone with whom to share her life, a volunteer of her own. *how r u feeling first day back? fine, fine.* She should make her way to Zo's and offer to repaint the walls any color, any color at all. Instead, in an inspired moment, C comes around from behind the desk, lifts the sticker rack, and sets it on the sidewalk just outside the entrance. Next come the peacock feathers. The paints. The chalkboard is erected: LIFE IS SHORT, CREATE! By late afternoon, the better part of her inventory has made its way onto the sidewalk, which is now alive with pinwheels and glitter, and C has sold more knickknacks than she has in the past two weeks combined, for a gross daily intake of \$462.43 cents. She locks the cash register, draws the grate over the glitter in the window, and heads toward the train.

On the street, she gives Mah-rie a call.

Could you start on Monday?

The blond expanse of the loan adviser's desk stretches between them. The surface, as always, is completely and unnaturally clean, cleared of papers and writing utensils and every other sign of office work—just the bowl of lollipops, perpetually full, gleaming like a crystal ball. The loan adviser neatly folds a waxy wrapper into fourths, turns the candy in her mouth. I'm so sorry, she says. Things happen. I *get* that. However, this is why it's helpful to have a guarantor on a loan, an emergency contact we can reach. This is why I've recommended automatic payments.

It's true that this is advice she's given C before, but C seems to internalize it less well with every repetition. In fact, she sneezes, as if allergic to displays of common sense. The candy clicks like a muted xylophone against the loan adviser's teeth.

Gesundheit, she says.

C's circumstances qualify as exceptional. As such, perhaps the loan adviser can still offer her certain services. For example, there's always bankruptcy. She pops the candy back into her mouth as she reaches for the mouse and illuminates the screen. The missed payment has left C further delinquent. She's missed the deadline for the extension on the extension. This would be no trouble at all were she able to pay the outstanding amount today, which she isn't—or if interest rates had fallen, so that she might borrow at lower rates to pay off debts pegged a rung above. But interest rates have nowhere to descend. There, in C's lap, is the stack of hospital bills with which she will soon have to contend. The loan adviser navigates spreadsheets on the screen. Isn't it all so reasonable? There are no real villains. C looks at her lap. She mentally checks the quite literal back-of-the-envelope calculations she made in the store at the kids' craft table. She's found it hard to concentrate on anything these first few days back in the world. Her thoughts come to her in images and patterns, useless snatches. A nightmare she used to have as a girl returns: she finds herself in a nowhere world, racing across a black silk sheet. In the logic of the dream, she understands that she's fallen into a bolt of cloth and is trapped there without even an enemy to confront. The fabric is scattered with gaudy fleurs-de-lis, bright as buttercups with stark green leaves. Whole hours seem to slip across the silk, the flowers floating by, until it dawns on her that the rest of her life will proceed like this, passively, gradually, in endless repetitions. Soon she will begin to long for monsters, acknowledgment from any creature at all—she doesn't have to worry anymore, she thinks. She reimagines that dream with her visitor. He floats along at her side. It occurs to her she won't ever be alone again.

"What a gift!" she says.

The glass wall of the office looks into the lobby of the bank and finally onto the avenue, where cars shimmer in the November air. It seems she could reach out to touch the delicate partition and draw it away, like the film that forms over scalded milk.

The loan adviser coughs on her lollipop.

At home, the gnome glides over the spoon drawer, standardizing measurements. He twirls around the light fixture, flits about the apartment like a well-dressed horsefly. On the table, illuminated in the light of the TV, is another notice for rent. She pulls back the covering from the loom and considers the dark cloth wrapped tightly around the beam. With a pair of silver sewing scissors—a gift from her mother, Yugoslavian-made—she snips it free, then winds another warp with black chenille. She intuits that something is still missing and sits at the machine to correct it, sends the shuttle through. Her movements are rhythmic, graceful, and quick, consummating the union of a woman and her machine. To the unfamiliar eye, it's hard to see where the one starts and the other stops, so the visitor, if he did not recognize by now the anatomical limits of his subject, might mistake the loom for an extension of her limbs, an external carapace. The irregular pattern appears and is revised with speed; the pedals clack; the room grows bright, sustained by the warmth of the day. It is only when she begins to feel the hunger pains like a tug at her sleeve, the emptiness, that she looks up and realizes how late it is and notices the red light is blinking on her phone. Three missed calls. "It's like I've forgotten how to speak," she says. She pours herself a bowl of Honey Oh's and eats it over the sink, pausing between spoonfuls to warm up her vocal cords.

3

The next day, she arrives in the sun-soaked cathedral of late afternoon. The neck of her T-shirt parts and plunges, revealing her sternum, the high bones more pronounced than they were before. She is charged. The significance begins to register. Zo has finally called. They are supposed to meet here, in the Park.

Last night's conversation reached her as if through the fog of a foreign language. So you understand? Zo had said. How could C never have noticed how easy it is to get what you want? She was so relieved she could hardly think. Zo said something about not being in touch, something about a mistake, unclear by whom—but they were always making mistakes at the bank, that's what kept Zo so busy, even slightly cruel. You're sure? Zo repeated.

C nodded once more, then offered verbal consent: Yes. The call was less alarming than it might otherwise have been had she paid any attention to what her friend actually said. She cultivated fantasies all afternoon: Zo would move in with her, or C with Zo. She can forgive her friend her absence, her selfishness, her bank account, as long as she comes back. As a lover, friend, and guarantor.

She pauses at the edge of the square by a pile of flowers.

Azaleas explode from plastic pots, devouring the cardboard signs placed there to protect them. DON'T STEP ON THE GARDEN . . . NEITHER RUN NOR WALK THROUGH FLOWERS! From her bag, C extracts a sack of lollipops, searching blindly through the flavors. She unwraps a whole handful at once, drops the waxy wrappers back into her purse, and looks out at the anemic lime of the ghostly trees. She steps over piles of blankets, more cardboard signs left out to dry. What a celebration! The hue of the paint sharpens in the sun. Three tropical notes click like loose teeth in her mouth.

She has arrived at a party where she knows no one and probably does not fit in, but C has lost the art of assessing social situations. She scans the crowd. *What brings* you *here? Don't know.* Ring the doorbell. Step in. She sidles by the police and merges with the mass of impromptu mattresses and sheets and Gore-Tex sleeping bags. People are preening, rubbing cheeks with face wipes, applying deodorant, playing cards. It is life as usual, proceeding out-of-doors. A beach ball bobs. Someone on a low wall is speaking through the makeshift microphone of her hands so the crowd can repeat everything she says. All C hears is noise. She makes a note to stock some plastic megaphones. In pink.

Library station. Tech station. Press station. Food station, where women are scooping deeply from tinfoil trays of pasta salad. Where is Zo? C wanders further into the morass. The thought of seeing her sends a small thrill through her interior, as though a bug she'd swallowed had suddenly been zapped.

They'll meet at the red sculpture, as everyone does. But what does C know? She pushes through the slew of stations and assemblies and working groups, verbal contracts and permissions, her destination in sight. She stumbles into a powwow of women seated on the ground. Oh, sorry, C says.

A matte-eyed woman scoots aside to make some space. Are you here for the meeting?

C stares, then looks up at the blue November sky, the glossy face of the bank. Why not? She sits.

The feminist Trotskyite working group is mostly women, and the icebreakers break the ice with a combative heat. Who would you put up against the wall, come the revolution? They sit in a circle. The question travels clockwise. It's hard to imagine any of these women sighting a rifle, blasting brains across the brick. Most cannot imagine it themselves.

Pass, says a girl, college-aged.

Pass, says a librarian.

Pass, says the beautician.

Mao, a bolder woman answers. Or Hitler? But they're already dead.

The purpose of the group is educational, maybe even evangelical, but C likes them all the same. Today, they read the ABC's. The discussion leader is kind. Step up, step back, she says, when a rogue responder's list of firing squad victims becomes uncomfortably long.

Sorry, I have a lot of revenge.

The discussion leader nods. She extends her arms from the fraying shoulders of her denim vest. To the text: What does Trotsky mean when urging us to live leaning into the expectation of qualitative change? It is a question best discussed in small groups, she explains. Everyone counts off: one, two, three. The leader floats around them, hands hidden in her shearling pockets, checking in. There are no wrong answers for now, and C is so easily influenced of late. She watches the discussion leader listen in, nod, snap her fingers for qualitative change. She is enough to believe in, C thinks. She relaxes into this group of women. How nice to be among her kind—real people, all of them.

A woman from C's own group cuts in, Did you read it? Did you get it? C has not, on both accounts. She turns to the woman on her right, swathed in a green crepe dress that spills beneath a cropped jacket and over leather boots with studs. She spreads the reading out before them on the cement so all three can see. They discuss the problem of screws and sugar: a pound of sugar is a pound of sugar is a pound of simple sucrose dissolved in a downpour. The screw plucked from the assembly line is a screw, a screw, a screw, each is a screw within the margin of error of minuscule deviations from the platonic standard of screws, yet functional nonetheless—until this one, ever so slightly larger in size, and yet large enough that it no longer fits the mechanical joint it is meant to secure. The women look at each other. The first ties and unties a pink scarf in her hair. The second lifts back her sleeves, rendering the tattoos inside her wrists intelligible.

A qualitative change, says the first, is a change not in quantity but in kind. It's different enough from the precedent that it just doesn't work anymore.

The woman in the green dress nods. She taps a pencil eraser to her lips. How do we know, she says, how far along into the change we are?

The discussion leader has come to join; she stands by in her vest. She smiles. That's exactly the question, she says.

4

Time works differently in the Park. One hour, one morning, are like many; C has made many friends by the time Zo finally arrives. She spots her through the crowd. Zo looks nervous, tucking and untucking her hair, exploring the pockets of the jeans, the calluses that cap her elbows. Her hair, escaping from behind her ears, falls in a soft turmoil around her face. It was styled just the same, which is to say, sans style, that night she spent at C's. She is moved by how confused Zo seems. Across the way, her friend tests her weight on the balls of her feet. She joins a circle gathered around a young man tuning his guitar. C watches, waves. She wants to hold her. I have no anger, she will say. The Trotskyite working group has reconvened to discuss how far along the path of revolution are the protestors of the Park, Tahrir, Spain, Brazil, Indianapolis. Zo doesn't see. She looks over her shoulder, the wrong way, hooks a hand around the rail of her neck.

Then her face brightens in recognition. She smiles, lifts her hand to the back of her head. C, still surrounded by the discussion group, takes a step in her direction. A tall man in a gray T-shirt and jacket breaks through. He sinks a gentle fist into Zo's hair, drawing her face to the side, and plants a kiss on her cheek.

—

It can't be denied that a desperate and unhappy impulse toward possession accompanies every unrequited passion. These are the facts. Her childhood, her mother, her life, the child she did not have—they are all securitized in Zo. Whatever the etiology of her attraction, to lose Zo feels like a death. C watches her melt into the Professor's arms across the Park. There she goes, the person who gives her life meaning. She thinks of Zo while she is alone in the kitchen, at the loom, simply walking down the street. When she gets dressed, she imagines what Zo would have her choose. She wonders how Zo would respond to these thoughts; they converse in her head. She is always telling Zo what is on her mind. Only now does it occur to her that's all it was: a highly developed dream. She nurtured the delusion like a fragile orchid. And like an orchid, it died anyway . . . How does it hurt so much? She would have chosen anyone else. But were we so conscious of why we prefer one over another, it is unlikely we would ever fall in love.

Worse is that Zo has been indefensibly in love, or in attachment, for no more than a year with the man who holds her now, his hands cupping the high ornaments of her ass. He is the anomaly, not C. She looks around. Considers her options as she waits for him to release her friend. She's in no mood to be condescended to. She recalls the way this man lorded around her store in his corduroy jacket. How sad, he seemed to say, what others will never know. Can't teach 'em. Well, C won't be taught. She considers her exit strategies. She could stay cross-legged on cement, leaning rhetorically into the revolution. She could walk the mile north to the shop, which, on a Saturday afternoon such as this—sun out, sidewalks full—she really can't afford to close. She could go read to Yi, go home to water the philodendron plant and argue with the gnome. Or she could lie back right here on the cement pavers and close her eyes. She'd like to go to sleep. Instead she stands, brushes the dirt from her hands. The woman in the crepe dress tugs at the hem of her dungarees. Hey, she says. You sticking around?

I'll be right back, C replies.

She drifts to the west side of the square, where the drummers work a set of plastic buckets. Zo! she calls. Her friend turns. Her face registers a quick confusion, as if she too has forgotten something important. Then, like it's nothing at all, she draws C into a hug. Shampoo, smoke, a hint of rose—the new perfume masks her natural, milky scent.

The Professor presents a hand that has only recently explored the curve of Zo's thighs. His smile, C thinks, is revoltingly polite.

I have heard so much about you, he says.

She's had the feeling before, when introduced to someone from Zo's parallel life, that whoever she's meeting has been briefed with a preface C would not necessarily have used to describe herself. Something about introducing her requires, it seems, a level of preparation. She wonders what it is that Zo has told these people. This time, she decides, it gives her the upper hand. She squints at the Professor, white stick of a lollipop extending from her mouth like a beak. He's been warned, she suspects, that she's a little nuts. She decides to up the ante.

He's doing research, Zo offers, though it isn't clear on whose account she's apologizing—C's or her boyfriend's.

C rummages for another lollipop in her purse and shoves it forward. The Professor stares at it. Then he shrugs, accepts, and slips it into a buttonhole, a little boutonniere.

The Professor has been performing weekly lectures in the Park. He'd like to study reactions to views with which the Class War Camp, in particular, disagrees, in part to find out what it is they *do* believe but won't admit to the press. C looks around, but there is no signage to confirm that this section of the Park is, indeed, the Class War Camp. The candy's purple wax wrapper casts a strange reflection onto the palette beneath his chin. It's distracting. He takes a notebook from the oversized pocket of his coat, makes a note. About whom? When he looks up, his eyes slide right across C's face. He's already bored of her, she can see. He took her measure when he bought the abacus. He bought the abacus to take her measure. He's summed her up, or so he believes. And so much the worse for him.

As the lecture begins, a small crowd gathers out of boredom, curiosity, for the sake of argument. Who knows if they are the target audience? Some controlled experiment. *Hey, you fuck!* The Professor waves. C and Zo soon find themselves in the back row of an impromptu lecture hall, where the main lesson to be taught is that the market itself—or a movement like this—is the mechanism by which information is revealed, gathered, and disseminated. The kind of lesson, C thinks, that sounds neutral in summary but isn't.

As you will remember, the Professor says—and, entering the heart of his lecture now, he slips the notebook away—we have been moving chronologically through the history of economic revolution. A brief review: It seemed sane, midcentury, to suggest that capitalism might give way to utopia via violence, just as it yielded industrialization, the eight-hour workday, nuclear war. Today, however, we are arguing that the internal contradictions are not so at odds with the status quo as we once thought. How else have we managed to last this long? You can see why the historians stick to linear time. Take the integral under the curve as accumulated evidence.

C looks at her friend, who shows no sign that anything is wrong. Apparently this is all according to plan. C reaches back through their phone conversation, but no clues return. She thinks of the work congealed in deformed screws. The candy cracks in her molars, and she chews on the pulpy stick.

The Professor paces as he speaks, snaps his fingers. The habit reveals what is missing, which is the glow of his lecture slides. Yet he is so utterly at home. He comes to a halt by the azaleas, clears his throat. We have discussed at length, he says, the consequences of nixing markets—forty-five million in the Great Famine alone!—when economic activity is a stochastic process that tends toward self-correction around the mean. What I am saying is that while a market *cannot exist* without regulation, it also cannot be totally planned (at least, not without a risk of mass death). Because without the stimulus of random shock, those very planners lack information about what people need. The idealist mistake, as always, is to prioritize ideas over information. The market is, as we are just saying, a means of gathering intelligence. It is a process of discovery. It exists to consolidate the data of our world. And how are we expecting to be better off, post-revolution, knowing even less than we do now? How are the producers to discover—or manufacture—public preferences sans the free movement and adjustment of demand? How will we approximate desire then? And what, I am arguing most vehemently, is the point of being alive if not to accumulate further knowledge? *C'est obligatoire!* To be protected from every interference is to remain ignorant. And so, I am afraid I disappoint. We cannot revert to something primitive and—how do you say—*dumb*. One can say inequality itself is what is motivating the spread of information. Distress here is communicated to distant networks over there, which are now protecting themselves. This is the definition of *solidarité*: the free exchange of information! And competition is the means of communication. Of what we cannot speak, we pass over in silence—or, a better option, delegate to the market.

His hands dart in and out of his oversized pockets as he speaks. Is it offensive that he reminds her of the gnome? And then—offensive to which party? She knows where her loyalties lie.

It would seem, however, the Professor says, that certain ideas are persisting. Chimeras! The prevailing view remains, I suspect, that the world in here is purer than what we are enjoying out there. He points down the street. My question for you, comrades, is whether you have correctly identified the culprit? Are you sure, he says, that the source of your dissatisfaction is capitalism and not in fact yourselves? Humans are inept at expressing themselves. We have little idea what we want and a predilection for fucking things up. Because here is the fundamental state of things, comrades. We are basically in the dark. I am meaning not only that we are living in dark times—the times are always dark—but that we have no idea what is going on, and never have, until after it has happened. Market capitalism has proved best at narrowing the lapse. And in a way, you, too, have succeeded in contributing to knowledge of the state of affairs.

The crowd contracts and tenses with potential energy, and it seems the release could go either way, violence or a laugh. It's just like these people to turn the blame back on them. The loan advisers, the analysts, Zo—they have no idea what it's like. C is so sick of assholes who dismiss her desire as artificial and somehow *too much*.

Fuck you! someone calls, and her anger is expressed. The scales tip. A mild revolt is roused. The man who cried out has made his home down south in a shipping container off the grid, because, as he explains to the Professor, the system is so irrevocably fucked, it makes him sick—literally makes him vomit. And this wise guy in corduroy is suggesting that they do nothing, resign themselves to a world that makes them ill?

That is not what I am saying! the Professor responds, genial, hands thrust so deep into his coat his shoulders rise into a shrug. There is something casual in the gesture that further enrages the crowd. Their anger has no effect on him. A slice of pizza hurtles through the air and lands like a badge on the Professor's collar alongside the boutonniere, and sticks. He looks at it, then he peels the cheese from the khaki and funnels the crust to take a bite. He looks pleased with himself.

Though you have made me think, he continues, chewing as he talks, that if you *really* were to, as they say, fuck things up—? He swallows, gives the impression of veering off-script.

You see, if it were me and I were in your shoes, personally I would be thinking this: the only way to pull off a true system meltdown is to manipulate the inputs. The market is an unbeatable machine. It is crunching individual preferences and shooting out the collective. The most elegant way to hack it then is to tweak everyone's desires at the source. I understand it is not sounding very likely. But look at you people with your jazz hands and tents! Look at GoodNite with their electrical stunts! How long are you planning to take? I cannot really be so much crazier in suggesting hacking the brain directly. The market cannot help but produce the revolution you have in mind if it's what everyone else has in mind as well. And they already do! Just look at this shit! Who isn't wanting something different? All you have to do is give permission to commit. The problem is not a lack of revolutionary desire, comrades. It is not that your fellow citizens are squares. It is that coordination is a bitch. You are agreeing with me, I know, that when such a person comes to a cliff she can't help but look over the edge. And so is it a glitch, really, if you give her a little push, when she was already going to take the plunge? That's what efficiency is. We arrive at the same end faster and more elegantly. Just a little nudge . . .

He trails off. Half the crowd has fallen silent, the other half has already walked away. Zo is checking her phone beneath the flap of her purse. And C is alert. She's looking at the Professor like he's just guessed her email password. She fits another lollipop into her mouth to calm herself down. Never has she wanted so badly for someone to be wrong.

They spend the day in the Park. The Professor takes notes and stokes arguments. Debates erupt around him like signal flares. They listen to the drums. They attend the general assembly. At a meditation session at the Tree of Life, C sits with her eyes open and her spine slack, her hands in her lap, staring at the man who has stolen Zo. She watches them breathe in unison. She watches Zo's chest rise and fall. She watches the Professor's face smooth into nothing. Even in meditation, he strikes her as too proud, preoccupied with himself. Inhale, the leader says. The crowd takes a communal breath. And exhale. C breathes as she always does: unintentionally, without a plan.

She closes her eyes and attempts to obey. Inhale, she thinks. Exhale. After a few minutes, she feels, per usual, that she cannot breathe at all. It is the focus on staying alive that throws her into a panic, makes her feel that she has in fact forgotten how. The air feels shallow in her lungs. When she opens her eyes, the canyon of the street has gone gray and soft and vague. The world floats in front of her, just out of reach, as if some small part of her has died; she is on the outside, looking in.

The gnome is hovering just above Zo's dark, wild mass of hair, looking down at the crown of her head as if it were a well of great depth. C's breath, already shallow, further compresses. She is surprised to find him here; the gnome hardly ever leaves the apartment. The rules have changed. This cannot be good for her, C thinks, and yet she's so relieved to see him. He traces a slow arced path that brings him closer to C, and then comes to a halt, twisting his face toward hers.

"I thought I was your spirit guide," he says.

5

One liability of the air-gapped network is that if malware is introduced, no one will know. To be isolated from potential enemies, contaminants, is also to be left without witnesses. From here on out, the hack runs itself. There's no one to correct the alteration as the system lifts off into unregulated loops.

C stays in the Park. The gnome keeps her company. He zooms over the general assembly, over the swarm of raised hands, trying to cheer her up. C blinks. He comes into focus over the Kitchen, hovering over paper plates. She pushes her hair from her face with her forearm, wipes her nose on the flat of her palm.

She loses the whole weekend. It happens like this: she simply doesn't leave. She drifts through the tents and alights in working groups and reading groups, where people are debating labor theory of prices, by which every profit is predicated on the exploitation of the worker and her wage. Were C to have an assistant at the shop, she thinks, some bright college girl with a minor in art, she, too, would be a capitalist. The petite bourgeoisie. That's her! It occurs to her, vaguely, that she can no longer afford to pay herself.

An elbow arrives in her side. Psst, the woman in the perennial crepe dress says. A pressure at C's wrist. When she looks up, she finds the entire circle is looking at her. The icebreaker has made its rounds, and presently it is her turn. C tries to remember the prompt. Then it returns to her. Oh, she says. I wouldn't hide. She pauses, looks up at the sickly foliage of the wispy trees. In a nuclear apocalypse, I'd rather burn alive.

She used to be adept at fabrication. As a girl, she lied to God, staying silent in the confessional and failing to divulge her sins. She lied into her marriage, rent statements, tax deductions, weavings. The difference, most recently, is that she is volunteering the truth more often and out loud, unqualified. She has lost the knack for rhetoric, lacks the talent so completely that it becomes a talent unto itself; it hardly occurs to her to modulate her truth-statements anymore, to try to appeal to her audience.

The circle hesitates. Someone coughs. When the women disperse, the friend in green says she has to dash. She gives C a peck on the cheek. She has to work tonight, take a shower, make a supply run for the day. She disappears. C watches the dress dissolve into the crowd. It's strange to think her new friend might have a home, a job nearby.

The Park is not large enough for a city, and yet it is organized like one. As she wanders through its districts, C is surprised by how little she's seen. She's hardly strayed from the corner where she arrived. The nascent institutions are concentrated on the east side of the Park: PR, media, GA, the Library, where shelves of books snake along the low wall that reinforces the square against the bulwark of the street. It occurs to her that she hasn't eaten in some time—not since her arrival, in fact. It feels much longer than two days. Time moves in slow, thick currents. She steps over backpacks, legs, luggage, card games. The Kitchen is dead center: the belly. She joins the line and cups her palms to receive the Eucharist of a PB and J. The soft bread tears; she eats small pieces with her hands. She saves the crusts for last, spools them into a dense, doughy ball. Sucking jelly from a thumb, she delves deeper west, into the Class War Camp and the drone of the drums. The ground tarps expand to hold larger groups of people. The pizza boxes, inverted and emptied of pies, are propped against knees and backpacks to make assertive placards, though there are fewer demands than C sees in the east. GLASS-STEAGALL! and NO STUDENT DEBT! have been swapped out for anarchist signs. The people who hold them watch C pass, suspicious. She discovers the drummers by the Tree of Life. She pauses, listens. She tucks her chin low into her jacket collar and closes her eyes. A chill in her knees. The drums enter her body, vibrate in her ribs.

6

How rarely she finds herself downtown with free time! She crosses the street to gaze into an empty loft. Another is filled with art. She spends an evening exploring stores that are not her own, connecting the dots toward home. Perhaps the loan adviser—or the Professor's speech—has motivated research into market competition. She is sharpening her edge. Comparative advantage. The concept is blunt in the back of her mind, but she carries it like a blade.

In a hardware store, she wanders up and down aisles devoted to knobs, plunging palms into bins. She hums. More knobs are installed on the faces of phantom drawers that do not open. She tugs at each, just in case. Drags fingers over handles meant for turning showers on and off. *Hot is cold and cold is hot.* The heel of her hand thuds along the display. Just think. Installing all these holds. What a job! She might have enjoyed it. She would like to assemble something beautiful again. To see the world respond. *Push. Pull.* She feels, in the empty aisles of the store, more inspired than she has in years. She lifts handfuls of wires from a tray and wonders what else she might bring to life. A set of Christmas lights, cradled in her arms. Downstairs she finds the ovens. Rows and rows, like a shining graveyard. It occurs to her to open every door. She inspects the broilers and the gleaming grates. If she had a secret, she might very well store it here, in one of these unplugged tombs: French, industrial, stove tops electric or gas-powered. *Can I help you?* a salesman says. He adjusts his badge. C takes his measure. He doesn't want her to find his secret, she thinks, doesn't really want to help. I'm just looking, she says. I'm picky. He hesitates. C smiles and nods, then turns to go. The gnome trails her up the escalator, out the door, through the shifting forests of Broadway, and into a furniture store.

Later, sprawled on the floor of her own shop, surrounded by her purchases, C threads Christmas lights through a length of PVC pipe. Handfuls of knobs emerge from her pockets. They are part of the sharing economy—all baubles are. She works her thumbnail against the price stickers until they fall away, a confetti of neon orange, and arranges electrical equipment and hinges and tracks for installing drawers, then changes her mind and arranges again. The projector slings images onto the wall, and in its cone of light the gnome is pale, washed-out. She almost doesn't notice him, except she's used to having him around, even fears his absence now. She looks around the store and onto the street. "Hello, gnome?"

He turns slowly in his spotlight and does not respond. No shadow appears. C is beginning to wonder if he's left her, if she's upset him. She begins to cry. Then the gnome emerges from the cone of light. He grows denser, brighter, as he zips through the shop. He points at the wall, where an instruction manual appears, arrows modeling parts to whole. "What's that?"

7

It is morning when she wakes up, unshowered and already at work. Her contraptions are strewn across the floor, and she wonders what came over her last night. Stealing! Engineering! She scoops a pile of drawer knobs into a bowl and sets it on the desk, shoves the rest of the hardware behind the register. No one has to know.

The intention lingers, however. A combustible charge in the air. She watches it flicker in her periphery until she recognizes what it is: a will for production. She is revitalized—and filthy. The shop is cold and full of sun; bright packages are transformed into gold. Between two shelves of laminated stickers, she performs her stretches, calisthenics, expels the arthritic demons from her joints, the way she used to do before she sat down to weave. Afterward, sweating, nervous, she washes up in the tiny bath, pressing wads of soapy toilet paper to her underarms, between her legs, the sticky membranes behind her knees. How much effort a body takes! The sheer fact of it, stark in the coffin of the water closet, makes her pause. She looks in the mirror, where a patch of tarnish obscures her shoulder. All at once, her heart becomes a drain. Reservoirs of emotion flush through her veins and so register on internal meters after all. Her clothes and underarms damp, she thinks of Zo. Of the ridiculous theories the Professor stores in his head. It is just as ridiculous, perhaps, to mourn her friend, a woman with powder-blue nails who would allow a specimen like him to quite literally sweep her off her feet. But knowing it is foolish does not help her stop. She thinks of the Professor's grip on Zo's waist, of Zo's hand on her throat, the pressure of the palm against her trachea. Two beds. Two sets of hands. Her own hand slips between her legs. When she comes, her surprise is audible. She washes up again.

She opens the door to find Mah-rie standing in the entrance, reporting for her first day of work, reading a novel upside down, as if she's pulled it from her purse in haste. C looks around. She wonders how loud she was. She fakes an eccentric sneeze.

I'm early, Marie says, reaching for the door. I'll come back.

Oh no, you're fine. I'm just under the weather, is all.

Her assistant is a little shadow, dressed in black denim, black wool turtleneck, and a scarf to keep her hair from falling into her face as she lifts boxes from the floor. She hands an obstructive package to C, who slices the seal with a razor blade. Together, they restock puzzles (shelved) and packets of feathers (slipped tediously onto wire hooks). Marie mounts a stack of paint sets to reach the Rubik's Cubes. Those should go on sale, C says. Mah-rie marks them down, one by one. Orange stamps ignite from the sticker gun. The restocking goes more than twice as fast as when C is alone, suggesting that the effect of her audience is nonlinearly catalytic. She feels more focused with Marie around. She's even compelled to show off, to show off Marie. When it is time for the midmorning break, she takes her assistant around the corner to the bodega, introduces her to the owner. Anytime, he says, gesturing like a maestro to the grimy bathroom, which C uses every time her own is kaput. The coffee on the hot plate is fresh, the grounds still steaming in the pouch. The owner serves them two cups on the house. Anytime! Everything is going C's way. Mah-rie is like a kind of luck charm, a rabbit's foot dyed in the synthetic neon of youth, so incandescent that C seems to bask in the glow of it too.

When the weather is nice, C says, sipping coffee as they walk, I convert the store into a sidewalk café. Today is such a day. She sets the rack outside, erects the chalkboard by the door—LIFE REALLY IS SHORT—CREATE!—then directs Marie to move the stickers, a set of pinwheels, the plume of peacock feathers, and alphabetic beads in front of the windows outside the shop. Marie studies the beads in their tins. Running low on consonants, she says. The girls are all for initials these days, they decide; they've left the vowels behind. C makes a note on her inventory list. Then they sit down to wait, Marie outside with her coffee on her knee, and C by the register within. Marie is a vision in her black wool, black jeans, brown suede coat, and the pink silk scarf set against her auburn locks, lounging in the throne of a white plastic lawn chair. She takes the novel out, rights it, finds her place. Her long legs, culminating in the heels of her cowboy boots, stretch in front of her just far enough to interrupt passersby. People stop to talk to her. They compliment the floral pattern of the silk on her head. They purchase pencils, pinwheels, stickers. Two grown men stop for a set of playing cards. They tease her, What is she doing later?

Marie looks up at them sweetly through the veil of her lashes. Fuck off, she says.

Later, a student stops by, Marie's age. He studies a series of pastels and paint sets in the corner, where C keeps a small store of professional supplies. He lingers at the door, half-in, half-out, and turns his intense attention to the postcards Marie guards, fists thrust into the waxed cotton pockets of his coat. She ignores him expertly, turns a page in the novel she's brought. He clears his throat. He wants to announce himself: he paints. C looks up from her calculator to catch the exchange. She is figuring budgets that do not compute, though this seems entirely less concerning now that Mah-rie is on payroll.

The girl rests the book page-down against her chest and considers this painter. She shades her eyes, her hair spilling over the back of the lawn chair. I do too, she says. The boy asks her what she recommends. She walks him through the oil kits while C looks on with pride. He comes over to pay. She compliments him on his choice, rounds up before making change.

In the evening, she walks around the block to avail herself of the ATM that waives her withdrawal fee. Card denied. Back at the shop, she whips four twenties from the register, presses them into Mah-rie's hand.

You're very hired. How do you feel about conducting this under-the-table?

Mah-rie nods in agreement, then her face clouds beneath the pink of her scarf. What does that mean?

Just come back tomorrow, C says. Here's the key.

8

What a relief it is not to have to return to the store the following day! Mah-rie will be there, immaculately turned out, perfectly trained. C has left her phone number by the register on the back of an old receipt—*Call if you need anything*—and pulled down the grate. The night is hers. She can sleep in! It nearly floors her, standing there on the sidewalk outside her shop, to think of the time congealed within. She feels like sitting down to catch her breath, then she does, on the curb, a box of Cheerios between her knees. The sheer time she's put into the store appears to her suddenly, like a banner dropped from a building or a bridge, the whole composition revealed, where before she'd glimpsed but a corner of the real tapestry it was. It makes her dizzy. A day, tomorrow, next week—that was the scale on which she'd operated. Now she sees the whole: ten years all at once. Roll it back up. She's spent more hours of her life in the shop than in her own home. And tomorrow she will take the day off. It is this sense of freedom, the invisible hand of jubilance, maybe, that guides her downtown to Fran's. Before she knows it, she's walked past the train and past her stop into the cast-iron graveyard of high-rent, far-west, emptyish penthouses. Through the lit windows, she catches glimpses of the art on Fran's neighbors' walls. The whole of Tribeca is a kind of gallery at night: silent, underpopulated, the private attractions well lit and spaced out, so as not to crowd or overwhelm, everything untitled. She takes out her phone and calls from the stoop.

Fran, I'm outside. Are you home?

They sit at the table with the cereal and two glasses of wine. The apartment has one main room, a bedroom at the back, and the dining table runs through, the center of gravity, its surface raw cement. She thinks of the men who had to deliver it and feels glad she wasn't one of them. Or maybe they just made the thing in here. It's the kind of immutable furnishing you must construct a room around. The space is large and open and very empty, compressed beneath the raw rafters like the lower deck of a ship. It doesn't look like what C expected of a rich person's place. In fact it looks as if someone is moving out or in. Maybe that's the style. Dark patches mark recent evictions of former wall hangings. The outline of an armoire. I donated them, Francesca explains. All of them? Fran gives a sad little laugh. They let you write it off on your taxes.

She's running her pencil down the column of numbers C has dictated, the crumpled statements she's produced, while C sits beside her at the colossal dining table, still dazed by the success of the day. She feels light, clean, the rag of her worry wrung dry. There it is, the state of her own finances. Very undeductible. She grips her seat to scoot closer, in reach of the fruit bowl and Fran's accounting, but the chair won't move. When she looks down, she finds the legs are nailed to the floor.

Francesca, she says. What's with the chairs?

Fran drops the pencil, waves a hand. My family couldn't take it anymore, she says. She sits sideways in her own steadfast seat, chews a lip. Then reaches for her wineglass, her legs mingling with C's. Ignores the alarming arithmetic. C is grateful to her for skipping over the concern—perhaps this is what it means to be born with money, inherent optimism. Unlike the Madonna, Fran doesn't scold, demands no penance following the confession. *Count your age in rosaries . . .* She explains of the chairs that Mother caught on to her asset dump. That's it. No more. She even froze her account. We've had quite enough of that, Mother had said, snapping on a set of gloves to supervise the staking of the furniture. From now on, all the heirlooms will be fixed to the floor. This was last month, Fran says. She looks down at the chairs now, anxious, and adds, She even took my checkbook.

Well, they're very sturdy, C says.

It occurs to her, disloyally, that Francesca carries her wealth better than Zo. A florist has arranged a centerpiece of pearly pussy willow. The chairs and dining and end tables are all fastened to the floor. If C came into an inheritance like Fran's, the treasury of a tiny government, she supposes the first steps would be obvious: pay off her loans, her rent, her hospital bills, reactivate her health insurance. What then? Maybe, like Zo, she'd exercise the freedom of infinite revision. Maybe, like Fran, she'd try to give it away instead. Fran's excesses connote a permanence to which C wishes she were not so attracted. The fixed chairs, the remaining art on the walls, are in keeping with the stability of her financials. The apartment has grown into its own expense. As has Fran.

Her wealth is as integral as an organ. She'll never escape. And deep down, C has always known her own disdain was a kind of homage. She needed Fran, and Fran understood. She needed C too. Across the room hangs a modest weaving, not especially large, not especially pink, just pink enough to tastefully offset the silver of the willow boughs. It is an early piece of C's. A study for something else. Lots of refuse, as if the warp were a trawl that had caught feathers, buttons, macramé. The irregular weft blooms three-dimensionally, bursting in woolly pods like saltwater anemones. The background, washed out, graduates from muted blue to taupe, bright pink. It's called *Garden I*, if C remembers correctly.

I forgot you had this, she says.

Fran nods. She leans back in her chair, arms crossed, still holding her wine. You really were something, C. Then she looks back to the accounts they've reconstructed on a spare piece of stationery. This, on the other hand—it's a work of art in its own right, I'll give you that. Though unfortunately I can't sell it. But have you thought about that? The record of financial ruin—there's some potential there. Very process.

C is still looking at the tapestry, the irregular buds. I really was good, she agrees.

The sex is better than it was with Zo. The thought arrives while she and Fran are still in bed, and she gently pushes it away, concerned that Francesca, in turn, will compare her to her friend. It is possible they have settled for one another over a third party, which in a way only draws them closer. The more frequently one falls in love, the more likely one feels one is settling in the future. The only defense is to be first—and, barring that, the evidence of the present, the reality that

Francesca's touches are urgent and sincere. C focuses on the line of her upturned jaw, her shoulders, her breasts, the little mole on her back, normally hidden by a bra strap. She gives herself over to loving tasks. Fran reaches through the sheets and grabs her wrist. Ouch, ouch, not so fast, she says.

After, Fran finds silk housecoats for them both. They emerge as twins in matching robes, waists cinched. They sit on the floor in the front room, where the sofa legs, too, have been bolted to the hardwood. C checks a corner of the carpet and finds it has been nailed down as well. Fran draws up her knees. The silk slides across her like light. C likes to think that Fran is fully aware of how wonderful she looks, the effect of teal against her red hair. She's drawn it into a knot at the top of her head, secured it expertly with a single pin. A streak of white appears, taut against her temple. Her chest is still shimmery with sweat, the flash of it revealed when she leans over to switch on the lamp. She catches C watching her and smiles.

I like you, C. I really do.

You don't know what a mess I am.

Fran crosses her legs and laughs, rearranges the silk at her chest. Of course I do, she says.

But does she really? C tells her about the misorder of fifty Rubik's Cubes, the hospital, how she has not paid her October rent—nor September's, as a matter of fact. The landlord, of course, is eager to see her out, to scale the apartment to market rates. He's warned her multiple times. In fact, she has no warnings left. The misfortunes pile on so quickly that they begin to strike C as funny. The two can't help but laugh when she explains the etiology of her belly pains. Can't eat, can't shit, can't metabolize a thing. It's permanent, C says. Stand her in an inch of water in a vase; trim the stems to keep her fresh. She tells Francesca everything, or almost everything. When she runs out of bad news, reserving only the one story she dare not mention, she studies the patterns in the silk, the carpet, to avoid looking up at Fran.

Say I did close down. What would I do for rent?

Fran shrugs. Come live with me.

C laughs.

I'm serious, C. You have so many friends.

C's throat constricts. The silk hem of the robe darkens deeply. She glances up at the bookshelves. She ought to have collected books, she thinks, rather than scraps of fabric, rayon, wool. Books are better company. The windows across the room are mirrored with night, reflecting the two women on the floor.

That's the thing, she says.

Fran stands and, retying her robe, strides to the shelves. Let me show you something.

C suppresses the urge to tell Fran to stay. At the shelves, Fran rummages through some baskets, reaches for an old soapbox. She cradles it, churning through knickknacks with her free hand. Suddenly, C cries out, Stop!

An anthology drops, narrowly missing Fran's head. She looks up at the ceiling, gives the shelves a light kick to see that nothing else falls. Kicks them again. What the fuck, she says.

Satisfied that the furniture has repented, she brings the box to the carpet and continues searching until she finds what she was looking for: a plastic sandwich bag, and within it, a ring box. She holds it out to C and snaps open the velvet hinge.

It was my grandmother's, she says. I gave it to someone once.

C accepts the band in her palm. The inner circumference is fogged with a patina—the oils of someone else, presumably Fran's grandmother, or the woman to whom it was next presented. C has an idea of who that is. Now it lives in this plastic bag. A ruby, caught in the teeth of the crown, glitters dully in the lamplight. C holds it to the bulb and then hands it back to Fran.

It's lovely.

I'm just saying, I've lost people before too.

C nods. Fran, do me a favor. Lie down and close your eyes?

She complies.

Do you hear that too? C whispers.

They are quiet, searching the room. Fran is rigid with attention. Then she yawns, stretches her arms over her head. It's the neighbors, she says. I soundproofed the ceiling, but still, they're always vacuuming. It's a fucking compulsion.

9

The ring lingers in her mind like a prize. She doesn't return to the store for days. She calls sometimes to check in. Mah-rie? Everything is going well. They're selling Rubik's Cubes and pastel sets; expensive items are flying off the shelves. Only she has to go to class in the afternoon. No problem at all—she's not to miss school. C reminds her to lock up properly before she goes. Meanwhile, she stays at home and weaves. She packs, beginning with the kitchen: her dishes and silverware and the blender and the Dutch oven she hasn't used since Zo went through her bread-baking phase, just before the Crisis. Perhaps she plans to move in with Fran. What couple needs duplicate cleavers? Toss. One can trust that of anything C owns, Fran's version will be superior. Higher thread count in the sheets. How to choose what to keep when everything you own is shit? She tosses the knockoff Cuisinart. Perhaps she packs simply because it seems expedient. She's minimizing, paring down, ready to move if the opportunity arises, though no plans as of yet. The gnome bobs about the baseboards. "You shouldn't do that with the eyes," she tells him, wrapping her mother's mixing bowls in dishrags and lowering them into a crate.

"You shouldn't waste your time," he replies. They've reached a kind of stalemate, she thinks. Here they are, sharing the same compartment of her life. From now on, there will always be enough space—perhaps for Fran as well. They watch the news. One evening, she begins to unburden the beam of the loom. The piece unwinds, yard by yard. She is unspooling a whole mile of night, tinseled with other objects. There are lengths of Christmas lights, an ornament. A silver gum wrapper chewed into a time capsule of a few months before. Twine and string and one of Yi's flowers, crushed by the weight of the yards of fabric that continue to unwind, rattling with buttons and ribbon and bits of dried food. A desiccated chili, a russet potato, a cob of corn. The gnome tilts his head to change the channel.

"Whatever happened to those rainbows?" C asks.

He shrugs, keeps his new felt bowler hat firmly on his head. "It depends on the quality of the password salting—which is to say, on how afraid they are. And how often they update operating systems. In salted encrypting, each password is tagged with a unique hash that dissolves in water—in other words, when the user logs in—leaving just the plaintext stem. Still salted, however, they prevent the kind of precalculation required for rainbow functions. It's all very new. And we've learned to set low expectations for non-defense-related dot-gov extensions . . . " he continues in his own jargon, failing to invite her in.

C turns back to her loom, rethreads the warp to begin again. Fine, she thinks. She can keep her secrets too. Although—from whom?

10

Cross-legged on cold cement, a sheath of free literature in her hands, C draws the hood of her sweatshirt over her head and redirects the flashlight to the text. The question at hand, Reform or Revolution, is one she does not quite understand, though she gathers that the group is predisposed to the second. So is the woman who wrote the text they're reading. C is too detached from the discussion to fully absorb her reasoning, but she's attracted to her passion. She is in a high state of potential. She feels she could be convinced of anything, whatever creed, is sensitive even to the content of the Professor's oration. There is nothing left in her to resist conviction. She turns a smile on the woman who is still wearing the same green crepe dress. Her overcoat pools around her, displaying the herringbone pattern of the tweed. The discussion leader repeats her question. Can incrementalism end in revolution?

C looks across the square at the Big Red Thing. Oh, sure, she says. Or no. I agree.

The woman in crepe sighs. She reaches for C's wrist. C picks at the PB and J in her lap. She wishes for cereal. She thinks of the takeout containers in Yi's fridge: the salmon, creamed spinach, dumplings, and mac and cheese. The hot bar will be half-off in half an hour. Who will lead Yi across the street to read the buffet signs? She draws away. What is happening? When she notices the fingers on her wrist, she nearly screams, then realizes it is only the greenish woman, offering advice. Honey, she says, you should get some sleep.

11

She returns to the store for the rest of her hardware and to teach the painting class. After dusk, the pupils arrive. C feels so much affection for them, these talentless children and their inexplicable arrogance. To them, she has no other life. She is only a mannequin siloed in the prow of Sixth Ave. But the boy! That's why she's returned. For him, she is alert. The innocence of her pupils almost brings tears to her eyes. She smiles at the mothers who trust their children in her care. They too are innocent. The children present their cheeks to be kissed goodbye. C reaches for the shoebox in which the projector slides are stored. As she lowers it from the shelf, she thinks of Zo on the ladder, her bare heels sliding backward into the niches of her pumps.

C hasn't prepared; she's neglected her duty to her protégés. When she plugs in the projector, what appears are those images of ravaged apartments, split houses, compromised walls, the undoing of every renovation—how long ago, it seems, since they first saw these slides. They flip through photos of destroyed flats, gutted apartments, great ragged holes torn through parlors to offer views of an unwitting street. An urban scene replete in gray scale, white and black. At this point in the lesson, the children usually rejoice. Yes, we see it! they cry. We see the perspective! We see the flowers! We see the sky! They are trained to celebrate the balance of blue and orange. But today they are silent. They look at the ravaged scenes with the focused, unselfconscious awe that only children can conjure. The projector spits out a house in Jersey that the artist sawed in half. In the picture, the two separate wings have begun to sigh apart, revealing the rooms within. Electric stove and slip-covered sofa connote the small lives the bungalow used to contain.

What happened? a girl says.

C looks at her audience. She looks at the picture. She explains that the image was produced with an industrial saw, that no one was home, that the little house was soon to be demolished anyway. So it was okay. No one got hurt. The artist made art only of abandoned things. The children blink at her. C asks, Can you see any elements of composition that we've discussed? Do you see balance here?

The class is quiet. Evening has settled in the shop. The only source of light is the projector lamp. The ruined house is stark and bright against the wall. The little boy raises his hand. Did he have to ask permission? he says.

C looks at the picture. She honestly doesn't know. Of course, she replies.

She makes up the assignment on the spot, in part to distract herself from the pain. It sits there, hollow in her side, echoing. She breathes. C announces that today, they, too, will create compositions inspired by destruction. The children regain enthusiasm. They are to recreate the stillness of the ruins, though the drawings must maintain some element of form. The paints remain in the cabinet. Instead, C sets out graphite, erasers, paper styles with which to smudge the shadows. Then she returns, slightly hunched to relieve the discomfort in her belly. She focuses on something else: the girls begin to scribble wildly. They have ignored every instruction about form. Flowers appear, quick blossoms ravaged with a fist rubbed fast across the sketch. Perhaps they do not understand. They are drumming blooms into the paper and then scribbling to smudge them out, tearing new pages from the pads. Slow down, C says. She wants to tell them that destruction, too, is a kind of art. It takes care and focus and time. But this is all too much to ask. She tries to guide them. How to draw a flower of structural integrity that still appears destroyed? It is hopeless. The girls are not here to reshape the world. The boy silently attends to his easel, graphite creeping up his wrists. He glances every so often at the picture of the sawed house. On the drawing paper before him appears a reproduction of Manhattan, parted as if by lightning strike: a chasm has spatchcocked the island's spine. Dark clouds hang above the city, split.

12

She makes her way back downtown in the night. Traverses Tribeca's deserted streets. The people backlit in the apartments seem to her worriless and pure; no wonder she is the only one outside, restless. When she arrives, Fran is in her silk robe, ready for bed but fresh, as if she's been expecting company. C feels sick. Fran is lovely like this, at rest. You're so beautiful, C says, her voice straining as she guides her host past the inexpungible chairs; the cement dining table, so much like an altar; past her own weaving on the wall.

Where have you been? Fran asks in a flat tone.

At the Park, C says. Around.

In the dim bedroom, where curtains fall over cast-iron windows, the guilt condenses in the mold of her chest and takes on a heavy form. She sits on the bed. There is no denying, in the trial ongoing in her mind, how ready she is to abandon Fran, who is gentle and calm and kind, who really is stunning in her own way, her hair tumbling over the teal silk robe when she lets it down. There is also no denying how ready she is to stay. It can't be, C thinks, that she prefers cruelty to this. "I don't," she says aloud, involuntarily.

Fran pauses, puts a thumb to C's chin. What's that? She

brushes the hair from C's eyes, and the tenderness of the gesture elicits a confession.

C lays her head on Francesca's shoulder. I've fallen for all the wrong things, she says. They are quiet for a moment. Fran strokes her hair. They fall asleep like this, C still in her coat, her cheek on Fran's shoulder, Fran smoothing her hair.

It's okay, we have time, Fran says.

The pain returns at full volume some time after midnight. C wakes up unsure where she is and which of her sensory systems has been disturbed. They all hurt. The mirror of Fran's vanity is a ghost in the dark. C's trench coat is tangled at the bottom of the bed. She slips it on. Her first thought is to master the pain with breath. She lies still, breathes in, breathes out. Fran is asleep, her hair spilling across the pillow. She places two fingertips, light as petals, on Fran's eyes and feels the pupils darting back and forth beneath the lids. Then the pain constricts. She exhales, slips from the bed, slips on her jeans, and leaves the waist unbuttoned, thinking that perhaps she'll walk it off, it's only a cramp.

One hand braced against the wall, she guides herself out of the room to the bookshelves. She wants to see the ring again, kneels at the baskets and sifts through. The pain flashes like great foil sheets catching noon-bright sun. She finds a tape measure, a rubber band ball, a sewing kit, a woman's hairbrush. There it is: the velvet box. She crouches with it at the dining table and around the pain, which is gaining complexity and subroutines. The scattered newspapers, draped over cement, all say the same: the demands are fair, which only makes them trickier to deny. And who, anyway, could grant permission? C checks the dates. There is an article excerpted from every day, and the Big Red Thing is centered in each. It belongs to one of Fran's clients. She brings the newspaper clippings close to her face and breathes through the concerto being conducted in her organs. In the foreground of one picture, a man slides his hand into the back pocket of a woman's jeans. A purse swings from an elbow. It is impossible to identify who they are, but C is convinced—it has to be. Every couple she sees, really, is the Professor and Zo. Everything is evidence.

C pushes the articles away, clears some space, gives up, gives in, rests her head on the table. The concrete is cool against her cheek. She opens her eyes. The ring box is there, inches from her nose. She holds it tight in her palm, then opens it, extracts the jewel. She tries to focus on the dull luster of the stone, to empty herself into this object to escape the pain. Had Fran wanted her to have it? Is that what she meant? The agony reaches a new pitch, and she groans. Where is her visitor? He chooses now, of all moments, to abandon her.

She needs to delegate. She'd call out, but the pain consumes whatever it is she was about to ask. It seems impossible that her body could register anything more than it already has, yet somewhere, from the center of her agony, she begins to understand how truly alone she is.

Her clothes on, if barely, she steps outside, stands on the curb in her unzipped jeans and her bra and her unbuttoned coat, like someone escaping a fire or on the lam. The ring flashes mutedly on her hand as she raises an arm to hail a cab, fastens the collar of the trench coat with one hand. Minutes pass. She can hardly stand when finally a taxi draws alongside the sidewalk. Nearest hospital, she gasps.

Later, in the ER, she thinks, Not all hospitals are the same. There are no rooms here. They're short on staff. Eventually, someone puts her in the hallway on a cot. Do you have health insurance?

She used to, she says. She did; she does, but she cannot find her card. The lights are too bright. C lies for a long time in her coat, bra exposed, prodded now and then by nurses, paralyzed with pain. How stupid—what false advertising. She looks like a prostitute late for work, which— The gnome, bobbing faintly, does not disagree. He's comforting now, comical; he's here. C closes her eyes, desperate, wishing he'd go away. She hates his stupid boutonniere. He isn't real, she knows, not in a way she can depend on. Even now, he seems ready to flicker out. She recalls that all children hate their mothers in the end. The world is a disappointment. Police are arguing with a doctor at the front desk. The pain is intense, and it occurs to C she ought to change her tampon. She wonders why she didn't before she left. It is urgent. How could she forget? She slips her knees over the edge of the cot. Her body is a sleepwalker she is watching from afar. Soon she finds it cannot walk; it crawls. On her hands and knees, she inches down the hall. The gnome is anxious in the fluorescence. "Wait for help," he says. He squeezes his ears in distress. C would like to be comforted, and yet she is afraid. She is afraid that she does not know if she can conceal this thought from him. The ladies' room is at the end of a long linoleum tunnel, and reaching it will be sublime. She'll lock herself out. The reception looms overhead. Then a nurse with a wheelchair arrives and lifts C into it, wheels her back and lays her in the cot. C struggles at first—I'm almost there, she sobs, I have to change—then gives up, goes limp. Look how much progress she's made, undone all at once.

13

C is in the hospital for three days. They give her a piece of toast before she goes to see if she can keep it down. Very good, the nurses say. She thinks of the man with the sandwiches. *More, more.* When she's released, floating and light and empty, the hospital band leashed to her wrist, she drifts uptown to the store and tapes a sign to the window. Then she heads home to no heat and an eviction notice. She carries it into bed.

A draft sifts through the room. The gauzy curtains inflate like lungs. It's gotten cold, C thinks. The gnome nods, dejected. They are quiet. C pretends to be asleep. She has no idea what to pretend anymore, how much she is required, by design, to reveal of herself to the visitor. He is indigenous to her mind, after all—in which case it would seem she's attacked herself. She's not to be trusted, not even around the people she loves.

She's still wearing her coat. Beneath the sheets, she slips her hands into her pockets, as if readying for a journey. The lapels pull away, revealing the bra and the blanched bones of her chest. Where is her phone? "Left pocket," says the gnome. C opens the screen. She wants to talk to Zo from a safe distance. She dials once, twice. The phone rings and rings.

Yi opens the door on the second knock. She waves a hand in C's face when she tries to apologize. You're busy, Yi says, I'm busy. Yi points to the kitchen, which appears washed-up after a suburban storm. Every surface has disappeared beneath an array of blooms, cut flowers, petals, and leaves spilling to the floor. C clutches at her trench coat, wondering what's transpired since she's been gone—if Yi has lost her mind or the remainder of her sight. But she is only volunteering for the hospital fundraiser. Mothers Against Leukemia is selling bouquets, and the volunteers and med students have all chipped in, Yi's granddaughter included. C glances at the red galoshes lined up in the hall.

At the counter, centered in the pale November light, C snips the plastic stems and sorts the blooms by length. Yi gathers them into bouquets. Synthetic scraps and petals fall to the floor. She hadn't been able to tell from the door that the flowers are fake, the petals nylon and the stems wax-coated. Totally convincing! She still can't quite tell, holding the stems in her hands. Bulk orders have perfectly recreated the lusterless length of a rose. The false thorns make a convincing stab. Then she applies the scissors, and the ruse is revealed. The stems bend lazily but refuse to snap. At least one pair of scissors breaks, though the flower itself remains intact. How unyielding. Real flowers succumb. Living stems snap with a cry. Yi lifts a mock lily, pairs it with a handful of daisies and a spray of baby's breath, the plastic buds clacking as the sprig settles into place. She shakes it so she can hear the flowers harmonize, then secures the bouquet with a twist of ribbon, blue and pink.

They arrange bouquets for hours. The phone rings. They search the apartment, lifting newspapers, napkins, jars, and plastic scraps of foliage, looking for the receiver, but neither can commit, and the phone is not found. The bright tone of the answering machine arrives. Yi—a Yi from ten years before—welcomes messages. Be there soon, a voice says. Me too, C thinks. She rests her hands on Yi's counter and closes her eyes.

The gnome is hovering over her. He zooms closer until he is right in front of her face. "Stay alert," he says. His expression conveys certainty like the Professor's, but C knows what lies beneath: something not quite human, a profound indifference, nothing. She no longer feels afraid, but her affection for her visitor is much diminished. Of course she'll stay vigilant. One must stay awake to protect against miscategorization. *Do you know how many patients were misidentified last week?* the nurse at the hospital had yelled down the hall. A knock at the door, and a young woman enters, still in her scrubs. She glances at the open front of C's coat, the exposed bra beneath. Oh, she says, hesitant. You must be C.

Back home, she washes her hands in the sink and crawls back into bed. She'd forgotten about the granddaughter, had imagined herself and Yi as equals in their loneliness.

14

The gnome has taken leave to follow C everywhere. He comes to the grocery, the bank, the Park. The stolen ring glitters on C's hand. In the store, his erratic flight patterns are hemmed in by the crowded shelves. He avoids passing directly through solid objects, but sometimes there is no choice: he glides uncomfortably through the blade of a cardboard poster tube and is briefly severed. He examines the paints, the beads, fixes his suit in his reflection. C mostly ignores him. She has rarely felt so strongly how out of place he is among the objects of her world. He is surrounded by materials meant to be assembled, pleasingly arranged, and here he is, unable to lift a sequin. As he comes to a halt at the windows in the front, where the street extends beyond the glass like an exhibit in a zoo, C wonders if perhaps the gnome is not here for her at all. Perhaps he is only lost, in limbo, regurgitated from some other world to whose vibrations she is vulnerable. He nags. This is what she and Max might have been reduced to, had they stayed together. Although, were Max still around, it is unlikely the accounts would have gone so far south. Max had no head for numbers, but under his supervision, C would have been too embarrassed to allow things to slide this far. She imagines rock faces, cascades of slate. Her consciousness narrows through a closing gap; she and the gnome stare at the accounts spread across the desk. Neither can deny the discord represented there, nor can they muster the appropriate alarm.

"Why," the gnome asks, "did you order forty-two sets of oil pastels?"

"Four," C says. "I meant to order four." Equally inexplicable is the shipment of Rubik's Cubes. Fifty more lie stacked in a box.

At the bank, her state of distraction becomes more difficult to hide. She blinks a lot. Examines her hands. Glances at the ceiling, out the window, back at the desk. Swallows audibly. The loan adviser watches her with mild disgust. Are you all right? In the shop, when a customer arrives (and they are rarer and rarer now; the irregular hours have put them off), C seems like a woman who's recently picked up a harmless habit of talking to herself. It is to be expected. But in the blank cubicle of the bank, resolutely morose, her eccentricities are thrown into relief. The austerity of the decor seems intended to remind her that there is never anything to spare—*don't hope, don't wish.* In this environment, C's tics are hard to excuse. There isn't much for her to look at, save the candies in the bowl on the desk, or through the glass panel behind the loan adviser and into the next cubicle, where another adviser is hosting a client who also finds herself in straits, although not so dire as C's, who has been promoted from an exceptional to an irresolvable case. She can't help but watch the gnome skid across the ceiling, has trouble absorbing the news. She blinks seven times slowly. The loan adviser coughs.

Hospital bills, C says. Outside it's cold; it's cooled, the air conditioner has been extinguished. The gnome, stationed above the loan adviser's French twist, secure in its clip, is looking at the screen. He points to something. "This doesn't seem right." He looks at C. "There's a serious tax burden incurred from liquidating this," he says. "Are you sure you consented to that?"

C lifts the flap of her calfskin backpack and extracts a lollipop from a plastic bag. "It's already spent," she says.

The loan adviser swivels. What's that? C's eyes are too clear, too sane. The clarity alarms.

I am spent, she says.

The loan adviser turns the screen on its stand so C can see how far she has fallen into debt. We're going to have to repossess, she says.

C smiles. The gnome begins to laugh. He is rolling through the air. "She doesn't own anything!" he cries. They leave together, chuckling, C sucking on multiple lollipops at once.

What is a credit score but a kind of specter, an excerpt of the soul? C's floats along behind her like a shadow as she crosses her street, passes the housing block with its single rose, descends to the path along the river, heading south. The gnome is also present, fluttering fragilely, like a leaf. She is gathering spirits, a whole cadre of ghosts. She is open to them. Welcome, come on in. She walks along the river. Joggers pass. The trees have turned to flame. The water, deep and black, is chiseled with glass waves. Perhaps she will become a teacher, as her mother suggested all along. She'll work with the elderly in hospitals, with people like Yi, guiding blind hands through the paint; it is easy to see her erecting easels after school—but these futures remain frozen, because alternative income is not on C's mind. She sends a loving look toward her friend. The gnome is the perfect child. He doesn't eat, no longer even pretends to sleep. He is no burden at all; she needn't worry about feeding him tonight, though she craves the proof of touch. She reaches out a palm and sees the cloud of him tense and flinch and withdraw. At the edges of their shared consciousness, which are merging more completely now, like streams into rivers into seas, there remains a current of distrust. C's fear dissolves, diluted, into the expanded real estate of two souls, two minds; she outsources worry to the gnome, who is still struggling to understand what worry is. Their minds are linked now by the connective tissue of certain memories: keep accepting sandwiches because you have nowhere to go. The trees along the river cast an orange sheen onto C's face and skin, ignite bare neck and wrists. The water is dark and glinting and chipped with wind patterns. Bicycles pass in flashes of reflective tape. The gnome feels reproached, though he doesn't know why. It was never his responsibility to keep this woman alive.

Along the river, the skyline will soon be doing its beautiful, glowing, postcard thing. Ferries unload. Passengers trudge home to Jersey. Port Authority is a distant lantern on the other side. It's so much easier to see it all by night.

15

She walks. Over six miles, her phone accrues six messages. From the bank, from the landlord, from Fran, from parents wondering why class was canceled again and demanding refunds. Then it dies. Now she is part of the vaudevillian display. There is nothing left to do but perform. It is an act of generosity to break the monotony, to cleave a day into two acts that may be compared. All one needs in order to feel is juxtaposition, to fold a life along the perforated line of an event horizon. C accepts this calling. She is calm. The old trees sway overhead. She is warm inside her coat, the lining sticking to her dewy skin. The bra straps slide down her shoulders and are not corrected. She is so warm, hot. She undoes the buttons, the scarf, revels in the cold.

"Hello, gnome," she says aloud. He is bobbing at her side, though it's a shame she can't quite see him. She wonders if he's cold.

What is there to teach? This is an age for the monologue, for wisdom gotten cheap, the flimsy forms of people speaking nonsense. There's not so much in one's control, not much to do but crouch at the loom of one's own life and draw the shuttle through the preloaded pattern of the warp. *WYSIWYG!* And What You See Is All There Is.

The challenge is to think in threads, never see the whole. Don't look up. Every creation fails its original conception, especially when everyone already knows what you're going to become; they've been watching, anticipating. Foliage falls through the air. The sun transforms leaves to licks of flame and the wreckage lands at C's feet. She wades, climbs a hill through the brush, over a low wall. Meets cement. Buildings rise and compress the world. In Midtown, she steps into a department store. No one kicks her out. She moves through the slick glitter of the cosmetic counters in her bra and trench, chest bare, coat open, her belly soft and vulnerable. At a mirror, she draws a knob of lipstick across her lips. Sinks a sample brush into a tube of mascara and adorns her lashes. The perfumes are an enchantment. They have such immaterial names. *Allure. Temptation. Ecstasy.* A saleswoman shoos her away. She remembers how with Max, the sex was contained between satisfactory extremes, never too numb, never passionate—neither ecstasy nor salvation—but always tender in its caution and incapable of lasting harm. There was a time leading up to his departure, but before departure was inevitable, when she complained of a pressure in her cervix. It was a vague, dull, and distracting pain. She offered this information to him, and later, when he was leaving but before he left, the pressure subsided; things changed. In any case, he was thrusting differently, and the pain had stopped. Drifting through the department store, she is moved by his tenderness. What she cannot remember is why it disappeared or where it went. It seems to her it vanished of its own accord, abandoned her as does sometimes the gnome. She imagines Max's search history on female anatomy filtering through financial plumbing, flowing into the stock price of lifestyle products.

And here she is. But where is the gnome? She looks around her now, rouged cheekbones flashing in the fluorescent lights. The department store is a hall of mirrors carapaced with cosmetics. Every surface gleams. Magenta dresses coagulate into a fleshy entrance, beckoning. C closes her eyes. It is difficult to concentrate amid the shine and the brass, the accessories capped in gold. She forgets what she is looking for, reaches for another tube of lipstick and draws a deep gash along her wrist. Another mouth, misplaced! C admires the cosmetic wound. This is surely why flowers are so beautiful, why the little girls love them so: they do not have mouths. They do not consume, the original sin, they have no need for an organ so crude as the tongue. She hums in relief, admires her wrists. Soon she, too, will be a flower, will wreathe herself in petals, self-protected. She swats at the edges of this fantasy, as if to chase away a fly. The gnome darts out of the way. He is whispering, offering advice. But now he can't get in.

Two security guards show her to the exit. Thank you, there it is, how kind. She revolves through the glass doors and onto the street, face painted, scented like a botanical garden. The scarf is long lost, caught on a branch by the river: a little flag left behind. Naturally, she walks south. In the Garment District, she steps in to see a movie that she abandons halfway through, abandons half a bag of popcorn. At the ticket counter, she slips the attendant her stub. I only saw half! she says, pleading for a refund. I only saw half! Outside, the day is growing colder, darker, dimmer. Popcorn in her pocket.

She locates a kernel, and it dissolves on her tongue. The doctor told her not to eat it. *Nothing but milk and rice and white bread, toasted.* It doesn't make sense to her now. They likely misidentified the patient; they never knew who she was. The woman conflated with C, she thinks, is still vegetating in the hospital beds. The gnome glides behind her, a funeral cortege of one, or maybe one-third, or maybe a more meager fraction still, diminishing returns. On the steps of the post office, C scatters the remainder of the popcorn for the pigeons. People are spilling out of offices, train stations, the tinted doors of cagey notaries. The human and her visitor wish them well. C aches for her small apartment, her still-warm bed. She sends her love to Yi, then she steps into a deli for a handful of candy bars. She is ravenous. The candy gathers in her arms, her fists. Bright packages and cartons spill onto the counter at the register. She pays in cash-register cash and buys a lighter, a loosie cigarette. She checks her wallet to make sure she has enough—what is the price of gas? In the small mirror by the lotto tickets, she can see her red lips and her made-up eyes.

That's $13.44, the man says.

C gathers her purchases from the bulletproof ledge. Also, a bottle of Ketel One, she says. And a gallon of gas.

The gnome has learned a great deal about human life in the months he's trailed C. He understands the toaster, the dryer, the dangers of inserting a fork into the toaster to extract a slice of bread, and also recklessness: C fishes daily for her toast with forks. He understands the shower; sometimes *hot* means *hot* and other times *cold*. He is familiar with the origin of the universe as seen from a human perspective: nothing, nothing, then language, then the world. He has studied how little humans understand themselves, how incapable they are of thinking ahead, how fragile the architecture of the human mind is, riddled by rivers of desire whose currents always shift. Consume, consume—there is no static equilibrium of preference. If only they could abstain from activities that cause them harm, but apparently—he knows this too—there is some pleasure in the pain. He has seen children build their block towers only to topple them. Towers, he's concluded, are built to be smashed. He understands C's intentions as she traipses down Sixth Avenue, gnawing a candy bar, and by logical extension, he must approve of the plan. The city grows dense and narrow; they cross Liberty Street and absorb the energy of the Park, where everyone is gathering supplies. *This is happening . . . This is happening . . . This is happening now . . . !* He is fluent in the ideologies C has created for herself. But her thoughts are suddenly inaccessible to him. He hovers above the Park, the crowd, his host, and his ward. Mass-produced printouts make their way through the throng—he understands the Xerox too. It always was a wish of his to press his cheek, his chubby face, to the glass and xerox a copy of himself.

Address	Hex Dump	Disassembly	Comment
00830611	56	push esi	GNite Decrypted File
00830612	8B35 2803800	mov esi,dword	dimming; twilight before true dark; buildings
00830618	85F6	test esi, esi	daguerreotypes; sieves <<thrutype: light>>;
0083061A	74 4F	je short 0083066B	bridges, spires, sky-clad; red alarms to warn
0083061C	53	push ebx	flight patterns; effervesce; sunset; <<*click!*>>;
0083061D	57	push edi	long, red cloth laid out along the river; then
0083061E	807E 20 00	cmp byte ptr (esi+20), 0	streetlamps; extinguish; block by block; &pace.
00830622	74 90	je short 0083062D	= slow, steady spectacle rehearsed a thousand
00830624	56	push esi	times in elective imaginations: initial flash,
00830625	E8 42FFFFFF	call <GNitePELoader>	grid gone, puzzled calm; then mitigation; it
0083062A	59	pop ecx	takes too long to admit the end; E[x] = .gov
0083062B	EB 36	jmp short 0080662	keeps damage to itself the way u keep from
0083062D	FF76 08	push dword ptr [esi+8]	invalid the fact that she is dying; hospital
00830630	A1 E80283000	mov eax,dword ptr [8302E8]	fails; food system rots; distribution centers
00830635	8B3d	mov edi,dword ptr [8302D0]	cropping up; supply chains local; bottled water
0083063B	D0028300	movzx ebs,word ptr [esi+8]	brigades; militias; end state: *u can lose ur lives*
0083063F	0F75E 18	call eax	*waiting for the world to change!*; inevitable
00830641	FFD0	test eax,eax	sacrifice; count: preventable deaths every day;
00830643	85C0	je short 00830663	untraceable locations; soldiers; nonperishables:
00830645	74 1E	push ebx	whiskey protein powder, sacks of grain; turbines
00830646	53	push eax	<<*click!speed!overproduce!*>>; surge flows
00830647	50	call edi	downstream; turn an hourglass and flip;
00830649	FFD7	test eax, eax	to analog;

16

In offices, the exit signs are dulled. Computers go to sleep—desks abandoned, screens dead. The trading floor hasn't been this empty since the Crash. Confused people gather in the streets to watch the rest of the daylight fade, a final gasp of red. The panic is potential, an electric charge that suffuses the air. So far, public response manifests as a new interest in the world. They consider the systems beneath their feet. Workers mill on the sidewalk and light cigarettes. People who haven't smoked in years cross the street to delis for a pack. They are waiting. Someone somewhere is figuring it out. The authorities, nameless men in blue jumpsuits, are excavating tunnels, warehouses—wherever it is the electrical grid is kept. Its infrastructure is elusive, abstracted. Strange, however, that other cities have also caught the virus and plunged into an early night. Philadelphia falls. Albany, Tallahassee, San Antonio, LA, Cleveland. The news turns stale on dwindling phones that optimists have not yet turned off. The channels of communication: also dwindling. The updates are slowing down. The same authorities who have reassured the public that the outage will soon be solved have now begun to change their tune. Coordinated attack. The whole nation is losing steam. There is no backup plan, city halls across the country realize, for disseminating information once the lines are down. On the streets of New York, the situation seems absurdly innocent. No one's injured. No explosions. No deaths—not yet. Just an extended lunch break in the dim, the sense that something special has arrived: life suspended. What is the end in mind? The first flashes of fear begin to settle with the pitch of night—also awe, as people wander the city with candles and flashlights. Home goods stores are out of wicks. Commuters uptown begin the long trek south, those downtown, the reverse, each party imagining that power must be present on the other side of Thirty-Fourth. It is impossible to imagine that all of Manhattan is dark. People have to pee, shower, charge their phones. Some live on the twentieth floor; they linger at the elevators, hoping. The first two casualties in the hospital accrue—cardiac failure following the deaths of two mechanical hearts. Human blood is stagnant in the plastic tubes. The deadline for electrical restoration parodies the schedule for subway repairs: the ETA is pushed back from nine to ten to tomorrow at noon. Flashlights dart across Liberty Square, then less and less frequently as the reality sets in: you need to conserve. The invisible hand in action. Light is scarce.

Fear settles thick as midnight falls. The candles are lit. A few beams spar across cement. The stars are stark and strange, renovated. And there, in the Park, like a tear in the night—a single light turns on.

A voice shouts, full of emotion: a body generates this light, the torch of a single woman, burning. She is surrounded by spectators. They are so close they could warm their hands. Who was there to see the match struck? The crowd encircles the burning corpse, stumped. What does good taste warrant in response to a woman on fire? A few bystanders try on a scream. There are no heroics. No one intervenes. All one can do is watch and appreciate.

In the silence, the crowd begins to wonder with a single mind. Why did she do it? In the absence of an answer, cruder thoughts creep in. How long does it take a body to burn? Is she still alive? Was she attractive? Was she fat? The wick of the woman is still tall. A car alarm hoots naïvely into the night as the trunk erupts. The vehicles echo one another, exploding in a choral round. Screams harmonize. Fire, all the visitors observe, also makes a sound. It is lovely, unexpected: the flames sigh, hum, they make a quiet music of all that they digest. The crowd has never seen a flame so large. The glow illuminates their faces. Amid a soft and final night, here, a sudden sun.

```
DATA visitors;
   SELECT FROM "epilogue"
RUN;
```

The heat is off; the lights are off; the lines are long. In the months leading up to the GoodNite climax, there were those credulous few who'd hoarded goods—dry grains and flour and candles and kindling, analog hot plates, portable solar panels that fold up, pocket-size. Zo was not one of them. One would think she hadn't taken the threat seriously. But there is only false comfort, she finds, in relying on supplies that will soon expire. She would rather face the shortage all at once, she and the Professor both. They have rations: powdered milk, dry rice, some water still in the pipes, more from the FEMA distribution centers set up every half a mile. There are generator stations where people can charge their phones, batteries, whatever they choose, and they choose judiciously. The solar panels shine weakly in the winter sun. Ten minutes per person, and per person one device. It's less difficult than one would think, disseminating instructions when people do not have phones, although who knows what the situation looks like elsewhere. The understanding of what life is like has been reduced to the neighborhood, the block. Car batteries sprout wires. Zo is reminded of the stories her mother used to tell her about the rationing, the queues. That was their world: Tito and Bollywood and African fruit.

Mariachi vinyl. You lined up for bananas, the imagination hemmed in by import restrictions.

It is cold, early. The windows are open. There is no heat to save. Zo stands in the kitchen and slips a hand into pre-soaked rice. The grains crunch between her molars. She gives up, drinks the milk she's made, looks around at the vestiges of her life. The bureau, emptied of its linens. The walls, half-eggplant, half-ivory, amplify the sense of quiet ruin. Everything runs out in the end. She looks out at the silent rooftops, where the time reads dawn. How, in all of this, will she ever find her friend?

A signal in her soul has gone dead. She thinks of those insufferable alarms, how you can start an engine with a set of garden shears and voltage basics. But with her, no spark. Hard to say if this is true for others too. It's not something to talk about. She isn't even sure she can explain this empty feeling. This room, her plans, the carpentry equipment, the half-built desk with built-in drawers, crowned with a comb of pigeonholes, are all very foreign. She can't imagine the woman who had the energy to make these things. Her manic sublimation. When she scans herself for that restlessness now, nothing responds. In the pantry, she tilts a cardboard box on the shelf and checks the food supply. More rice. No fuel. Not till Thursday, probably. The rice is useless until then, unless they make a trade. She marks the calendar, pauses, unsure whether she's already marked off yesterday, in which case she's just nixed the now.

Back in the kitchen, she performs calisthenics until she can see her breath, then pours a little water from the plastic jug into a bowl to bathe. Hair damp, limbs loose, suppressing shivers, she looks back into her bedroom, where the Professor is still in bed. Potted plants are lined up along the sill, so many of them. When he moved in, he brought the whole collection. Zo helped. The thale-cress in the kitchen is wrapped in plastic to keep it warm. A leaf drops from a stem, and she examines it. She wonders how much longer until the whole crop dies of frost.

They've taken to debating the attacks. They intellectualize it; they have not lost their dignity just yet. They wonder how, for example, a ragtag group of programmers could have staged a hack on such a scale without the government taking note. They wonder who will benefit politically (the right), and who will lose out (the left, incumbent) in the next election. Neither complains about the hunger, the chill, the lines. To complain would be to acknowledge that this new world is permanent. Instead, they wait. One week goes by, two. A month into the outage, their conversations have begun to entertain the topic of duration—of the disaster, of their lives, of others'. How long will it last? They speculate. It will take only a few generators per state, they think, to keep most people alive. It's hard to say, however, when they have no information. Everything is hypothesis, as is always the case with the Professor. All this while, he's kept it up. The thale-cress is also an experiment. *When introduced to the green peach aphid, the* Arabidopsis thaliana *signals distress to neighboring plants*—or at least, so it does under lab conditions in the apartment. Zo stands at the door beneath the Madonna, before the rows of sprouts bundled in their plastic bedding. Perhaps they'll survive. *Arabidopsis thaliana* is so well-suited to study, the Professor has explained, because it grows at alarming speeds on nothing at all. It self-pollinates, disseminating genomes simple enough to sequence, complex enough to extrapolate to higher-order organisms. In particular, the species is known for conducting an active chorus of interbotanical conversation. When herbivores are detected in a distal leaf, the message travels along the stem: secrete phenol compounds to raise the alarm for the plant as a whole. How lovely, how cooperative, to issue collective orders through chemical regulation. There is no purer assembly of dynamic equilibrium, the Professor says, and how useful such methods would be to the authorities at a moment like this. The relaying of orders has taken a creative turn. Officials bike up and down the streets with bullhorns. They announce strong measures, a curfew, threats of fines. What fines? What does money mean when the digital capital stock has disappeared, and how many had any to start with besides? The ATMs are mute. At the start, people pried them open to harvest wads of cash like organs or eggs, but to what end, Zo would like to know, when no one is accepting bills. There is trade only in candles, dry grains. What was cash but electricity? Everyone's been issued a blank slate. There are no methods through which to enforce financial punishment, and so by fines, one presumes the authorities can only mean violence.

Each day, she hopes C will return. She'd like to make amends. How arbitrary that she should be living this altered reality with the Professor, instead of with her. Before, when everything took place at great speed, when whole lives, fortunes, entire nations, were leveled overnight, life had seemed so temporary, exploratory. She preferred the Professor then, when everything was an experiment. Now that time has settled, she can't help but wonder where C is. She has nightmares of C arriving while she is out queuing, and so she sends the Professor for water and rations instead, while she stays home to wait. Only C doesn't show. And so this morning, curfew or no, she's decided, she will go looking for her friend.

She pulls the armoire forward just enough to open the door. Outside, the houses on her block are silent and dark. She turns down Hudson, empty except for people sleeping in the niches of storefronts, lighting little fires under hot plates, unfolding solar wings to the weak dawn. At the intersection, beneath the awning of a shuttered gym, someone is—absurdly—exercising. He leaps, lands, reaches for the dumbbells at his feet. Four, six, ten. He lifts them high. She detours to Sixth, sees the torn awning long before she arrives. When she does, she sees that C's store has been ransacked. The grate is up. Zo tests the door and finds it unlocked—the thieves could have saved themselves the trouble of smashing the glass. The hinges open warmly, like good ghosts. She punches the cash register and ejects an empty drawer. If she were her friend, where would she hide? A lone Rubik's Cube lies on the floor. Zo picks it up, rotates the panels, completes a yellow face. The remaining sides are checkered, unruly. She checks the sign still taped to the doorframe emptied of its panes: TAKE.

She returns to her route, the Rubik's heavy in her bag. At crosswalks, clusters of people are burning furniture. She wonders why they're wasting resources on what is promising to be a sunny day. Her own pulse beats to the march of *save,*

save, save . . . It's nearly New Year's. The city will freeze. The worst is always yet to come. A shout tunnels down a side street, but Zo has trained herself not to look. She flinches when she hears the shot.

She continues up Broadway, ignores the small fights kindling on the sidewalks, propels herself forward, increasingly afraid of what she will find when she arrives. It is nine miles to C's. Broadway rises, inclines. The stores lean. She feels the strain in her legs. For weeks she hasn't walked farther than the length of her apartment, the few blocks to C's store. It occurs to Zo that after twenty years she hardly knows New York at all. She hooks left to the river, where people are harvesting firewood, combing the hillside bare. A line of tenants has formed a water brigade, passing buckets to a building on Riverside. Nearby, a woman is cursing a pair of men slowly closing in on her patch of land. Behind her, a small plastic hut: the little winter greenhouse she is guarding, plus a child, bundled in his Gore-Tex.

"Hey," Zo calls. She reaches the man nearest the loot and gives him a shove. He hardly registers the shock. She isn't trying to topple him, she can't, she wants only to jolt him back to civility. She fits the Rubik's Cube in a fist. A sneer appears on the chapped curl of his lips—all the men look wild now. His partner, looming over the greenhouse, lazily cocks a rifle. "Okay," Zo says. "Okay."

She takes the mother's hand, the mother grasps her son, and together, they back away, toe to heel, facing the rifleman. She's read somewhere that it's harder for them to shoot you when they can see your face. Across the street, they shelter behind a stoop. Zo clasps the mother's shoulders in her gloved hands. "Are you okay?" With a moan, the woman shoves Zo away.

Zo leaves them. She begins to recognize the shops. The empty bakery. The city becomes more residential, the apartments rise higher. The style is Tudor, Art Deco, Revival of Various Forms. She passes the public housing block, where a rose has wilted in the cold, and finds a small crowd. She braces herself. But these people are not rioting. They are noticeably calm.

They stand in the cold wearing whatever they have. Everyone is waiting. For the lights to come on. To board. To obey. It is hard to say exactly what anyone is waiting for, only that an air of expectancy persists. The crowd swivels its head on its neck, searching through the empty space for its visitors. They'd become such close friends, the visitors and everyone who could see them. They hold paper peonies now. Bright plastic bouquets that burn in the day's gray frost. The blooms seem from another world, supersaturated, digitally spliced in. They glow. Their health is otherworldly too. Zo hasn't seen a proper flower in so long, she's mesmerized, it's all she can do not to stare at the people holding them, who for their part stare across the way. Finally, Zo turns. What she sees is C's former building, rendered unrecognizable. The façade has been hidden behind a great mourning veil. The shroud spills from the roof, heavy and gossamer at once—it moves in the breeze, here stiffly like canvas, here flowing like silk. From across the street Zo can parse the different threads, the chenille, the satin, the crude craft yarn, the nylon, the wool. All in midnight. She notices the irregularities, the refuse that has been caught up in the net, trash bags, sloughed like ballgowns, and strings of unlit Christmas lights and desiccated vines and glass bottles and brass door knobs, trinkets. People come up to the edge of its world to feel, to lightly tug, test the strength of the weave in their hands, and find that it's elastic, responsive, it absorbs their touch. An old woman clutches at it while navigating the block with her cane. The whole tapestry is a seeing eye guide. The ornamental trash casts a dull glitter. The cold plastic bulbs on the holiday lights glint in the sun. She is desperate to plug it in. It's a graveyard, a tombstone that flutters in the wind. If only Zo could read the inscription, light it up like a neon sign. Find the solution in the junk.

Someone knows the answer. The solution must obtain. So the crowd would like to think. Though—if one may be allowed to editorialize—there is some relief, at least, in considering that their problems are circumscribed. That is to say, not yours.

All progress, so it seems, is coupled to regression elsewhere.

ANNI ALBERS
On Weaving

ACKNOWLEDGMENTS

I wish to thank my editor Jeremy M. Davies and my agent Chris Clemans, as well as Stefan Tobler, Alex Billington, Tom Flynn, Nichola Smalley, Emma Warhurst, and the entire team at And Other Stories. I am also grateful to Ushnish Ray, Anny Oberlink, Daniel Lefferts, Matthew Shen Goodman, Patrick Yumi Cottrell, Ben Purkert, Shivani Radhakrishnan, Kay Zhang, and the many others who lent their intelligence and expertise to the drafting process. I am grateful to Jenna Miller and Eduardo Santana for their generosity and support. Finally and always, thank you to Siddhartha Sinha.

Dear readers,

As well as relying on bookshop sales, And Other Stories relies on subscriptions from people like you for many of our books, whose stories other publishers often consider too risky to take on.

Our subscribers don't just make the books physically happen. They also help us approach booksellers, because we can demonstrate that our books already have readers and fans. And they give us the security to publish in line with our values, which are collaborative, imaginative and 'shamelessly literary'.

All of our subscribers:

- receive a first-edition copy of each of the books they subscribe to
- are thanked by name at the end of our subscriber-supported books
- receive little extras from us by way of thank you, for example: postcards created by our authors

BECOME A SUBSCRIBER, OR GIVE A SUBSCRIPTION TO A FRIEND

Visit andotherstories.org/subscriptions to help make our books happen. You can subscribe to books we're in the process of making. To purchase books we have already published, we urge you to support your local or favourite bookshop and order directly from them – the often unsung heroes of publishing.

OTHER WAYS TO GET INVOLVED

If you'd like to know about upcoming events and reading groups (our foreign-language reading groups help us choose books to publish, for example) you can:

- join our mailing list at: andotherstories.org
- follow us on Twitter: @andothertweets
- join us on Facebook: facebook.com/AndOtherStoriesBooks
- admire our books on Instagram: @andotherpics
- follow our blog: andotherstories.org/ampersand

THIS BOOK WAS MADE POSSIBLE
THANKS TO THE SUPPORT OF

Aaron McEnery
Aaron Schneider
Abigail Charlesworth
Abigail Walton
Adam Lenson
Adrian Kowalsky
Aifric Campbell
Aisha McLean
Ajay Sharma
Alan Felsenthal
Alan McMonagle
Alan Raine
Alastair Gillespie
Alastair Whitson
Albert Puente
Aleksi Rennes
Alex Fleming
Alex Liebman
Alex Lockwood
Alex Pearce
Alex Ramsey
Alex von Feldmann
Alexander Bunin
Alexander Williams
Alexandra Stewart
Alexandra Tammaro
Alexandra Tilden
Alexandra Webb
Alfred Tobler
Ali Ersahin
Ali Riley
Ali Smith
Ali Usman
Alice Morgan
Alice Radosh
Alice Smith
Alison Lock
Alison Winston
Aliya Rashid
Alyssa Rinaldi
Alyssa Tauber
Amado Floresca
Amaia Gabantxo
Amanda
Amanda Read
Amine Hamadache
Amitav Hajra
Amy and Jamie
Amy Benson
Amy Bojang
Amy Hatch
Amy Tabb
Ana Novak
Andrea Barlien
Andrea Brownstone
Andrea Oyarzabal Koppes
Andrea Reece
Andrew Kerr-Jarrett
Andrew Marston
Andrew McCallum
Andrew Ratomski
Andrew Place
Andrew Rego
Andrew Wright
Andy Corsham
Andy Marshall
Aneesa Higgins
Angelica Ribichini
Angus Walker
Anita Starosta
Anna Finneran
Anna French
Anna Hawthorne
Anna Milsom
Anna Zaranko
Anne Boileau Clarke
Anne Carus
Anne Craven
Anne Edyvean
Anne Frost
Anne-Marie Renshaw
Anne Ryden
Anne Withane
Annie McDermott
Anonymous
Anonymous
Anthony Cotton
Anthony Quinn
Antonia Lloyd-Jones
Antonia Saske
Antony Osgood
Antony Pearce
Aoife Boyd
April Hernandez
Arabella Bosworth
Archie Davies
Aron Negyesi
Aron Trauring
Arthur John Rowles
Asako Serizawa
Audrey Mash
Audrey Small
Barbara Bettsworth
Barbara Mellor

Barbara Robinson
Barbara Spicer
Barry John Fletcher
Barry Norton
Becky Cherriman
Becky Matthewson
Ben Buchwald
Ben Schofield
Ben Thornton
Ben Walter
Benjamin Judge
Benjamin Pester
Bernadette Smith
Beth Heim de Bera
Bianca Duec
Bianca Jackson
Bianca Winter
Bill Fletcher
Björn Warren
Bjørnar Djupevik Hagen
Blazej Jedras
Brenda Anderson
Briallen Hopper
Brian Anderson
Brian Byrne
Brian Callaghan
Brian Conn
Brian Smith
Bridget Maddison
Bridget Prentice
Buck Johnston
Burkhard Fehsenfeld
Caitlin Halpern
Callie Steven
Cameron Adams
Cameron Lindo
Camilla Imperiali
Carla Castanos
Carole Parkhouse
Carolina Pineiro
Caroline Lodge
Caroline Perry
Caroline Smith
Caroline West
Catharine Braithwaite
Catherine Campbell
Catherine Cleary
Catherine Lambert
Catherine Lautenbacher
Catherine Tandy
Catherine Tolo
Catherine Williamson
Cathryn Siegal-Bergman
Cathy Galvin
Cathy Sowell
Catie Kosinski
Catrine Bollerslev
Cecilia Rossi
Cecilia Uribe
Chantal Lyons
Chantal Wright
Charlene Huggins
Charles Dee Mitchell
Charles Fernyhough
Charles Kovach
Charles Rowe
Charlie Errock
Charlie Levin
Charlie Small
Charlie Webb
Charlotte Coulthard
Charlotte Holtam
Charlotte Ryland
Charlotte Whittle
China Miéville
Chris Gostick
Chris Gribble
Chris Holmes
Chris Johnstone
Chris Potts
Chris Senior
Chris Stergalas
Chris Stevenson
Chris Thornton
Christian Schuhmann
Christine Elliott
Christopher Allen
Christopher Smith
Christopher Stout
Ciarán Schütte
Claire Adams
Claire Brooksby
Claire Williams
Clarice Borges
Claudia Mazzoncini
Cliona Quigley
Colin Denyer
Colin Hewlett
Colin Matthews
Collin Brooke
Cornelia Svedman
Courtney Lilly
Craig Kennedy
Cris Cucerzan
Cynthia De La Torre
Cyrus Massoudi
Daisy Savage
Dale Wisely
Dan Parkinson
Daniel Coxon
Daniel Gillespie

Daniel Hahn
Daniel Hester-Smith
Daniel Sanford
Daniel Stewart
Daniel Syrovy
Daniel Venn
Daniela Steierberg
Darryll Rogers
Dave Lander
David Anderson
David Ball
David Cowan
David Darvasi
David Gould
David Greenlaw
David Gunnarsson
David Hebblethwaite
David Higgins
David Johnson-Davies
David Leverington
David F Long
David Miller
David Richardson
David Shriver
David Smith
Dawn Bass
Dean Taucher
Deb Unferth
Debbie Pinfold
Deborah Green
Deborah Herron
Deborah Wood
Declan Gardner
Declan O'Driscoll
Delaina Haslam
Denis Larose
Derek Sims
Derek Taylor-Vrsalovich
Dietrich Menzel
Dina Abdul-Wahab
Dinesh Prasad
Domenica Devine
Dominic Bailey
Dominic Nolan
Dominick Santa Cattarina
Dominique Hudson
Dorothy Bottrell
Dugald Mackie
Duncan Clubb
Duncan Macgregor
Duncan Marks
Dustin Hackfeld
Dustin Haviv
Dyanne Prinsen
Earl James
Ebba Tornérhielm
Ed Smith
Ed Tronick
Ekaterina Beliakova
Elaine Juzl
Elaine Rodrigues
Eleanor Maier
Elena Esparza
Elif Aganoglu
Elina Zicmane
Elisabeth Cook
Elizabeth Braswell
Elizabeth Coombes
Elizabeth Draper
Elizabeth Franz
Elizabeth Guss
Elizabeth Leach
Elizabeth Seals
Elizabeth Wood
Ellen Beardsworth
Ellie Goddard
Ellie Small
Emily Williams
Emma Bielecki
Emma Louise Grove
Emma Post
Emma Teale
Erica Mason
Erin Cameron Allen
Erin Louttit
Esmée de Heer
Esther Kinsky
Ethan Madarieta
Ethan White
Eva Mitchell
Evelyn Eldridge
Ewan Tant
Fawzia Kane
Fay Barrett
Faye Williams
Felicia Williams
Felix Valdivieso
Finbarr Farragher
Fiona Liddle
Fiona Mozley
Fiona Quinn
Fran Sanderson
Frances Christodoulou
Frances Harvey
Frances Thiessen
Francis Mathias
Frank Rodrigues
Frank van Orsouw
Freddie Radford
Friederike Knabe
Gala Copley
Gavin Collins
Gavin Smith

Gawain Espley
Gemma Bird
Genaro Palomo Jr
Geoff Thrower
Geoffrey Cohen
Geoffrey Urland
George McCaig
George Stanbury
Georgia Panteli
Georgia Shomidie
Georgina Hildick-Smith
Georgina Norton
Geraldine Brodie
Gerry Craddock
Gill Boag-Munroe
Gillian Grant
Gillian Stern
Gina Heathcote
Glen Bornais
Glenn Russell
Gordon Cameron
Gosia Pennar
Grace Cohen
Graham Blenkinsop
Graham R Foster
Hadil Balzan
Hamish Russell
Hannah Freeman
Hannah Harford-Wright
Hannah Jane Lownsbrough
Hannah Rapley
Hanora Bagnell
Hans Lazda
Harriet Stiles
Haydon Spenceley
Hayley Cox
Hazel Smoczynska
Heidi James
Helen Bailey
Helen Berry
Helena Buffery
Henrietta Dunsmuir
Henriette Magerstaedt
Henrike Laehnemann
Holly Down
Howard Robinson
Hyoung-Won Park
Ian McMillan
Ian Mond
Ian Randall
Ida Grochowska
Ifer Moore
Ines Alfano
Irene Mansfield
Irina Tzanova
Isabella Garment
Isabella Weibrecht
Isobel Dixon
Isobel Foxford
Ivy Lin
J Drew Hancock-Teed
JE Crispin
JW Mersky
Jacinta Perez Gavilan Torres
Jack Brown
Jacqueline Haskell
Jacqueline Lademann
Jacqueline Vint
Jacqui Jackson
Jake Baldwinson
Jake Newby
James Attlee
James Avery
James Beck
James Crossley
James Cubbon
James Greer
James Lehmann
James Leonard
James Lesniak
James Portlock
James Scudamore
James Silvestro
Jamie Cox
Jan Hicks
Jane Anderton
Jane Dolman
Jane Roberts
Jane Roberts
Jane Willborn
Jane Woollard
Janelle Ward
Janis Carpenter
Janna Eastwood
Jasmine Gideon
Jason Lever
Jason Montano
Jason Timermanis
Jason Whalley
Jayne Watson
Jean Liebenberg
Jeanne Guyon
Jeff Collins
Jen Calleja
Jen Hardwicke
Jenifer Logie
Jennie Goloboy
Jennifer Fosket
Jennifer Mills
Jennifer Watts

Jenny Huth
Jenny Newton
Jeremy Koenig
Jess Hazlewood
Jess Howard-Armitage
Jess Wilder
Jess Wood
Jesse Coleman
Jesse Hara
Jessica Gately
Jessica Kibler
Jessica Mello
Jessica Queree
Jethro Soutar
Jo Keyes
Jo Pinder
Joanna Luloff
Joao Pedro Bragatti Winckler
JoDee Brandon
Jodie Adams
Joe Huggins
Joel Garza
Joel Swerdlow
Joelle Young
Johannes Menzel
Johannes Georg Zipp
John Bennett
John Berube
John Bogg
John Conway
John Down
John Gent
John Hodgson
John Kelly
John Reid
John Royley
John Shadduck
John Shaw
John Steigerwald
John Wallace
John Walsh
John Winkelman
John Wyatt
Jolene Smith
Jon Riches
Jonathan Blaney
Jonathan Fiedler
Jonathan Harris
Jonathan Huston
Jonathan Phillips
Joni Chan
Jonny Kiehlmann
Jordana Carlin
Jorid Martinsen
Joseph Novak
Joseph Schreiber
Joseph Thomas
Josh Sumner
Joshua Davis
Joy Paul
Judith Gruet-Kaye
Judith Hannan
Judith Poxon
Judy Davies
Judy Rich
Julia Rochester
Julia Sutton-Mattocks
Julia Von Dem Knesebeck
Julian Hemming
Julian Molina
Julie Greenwalt
Juliet Birkbeck
Juliet Swann
Jupiter Jones
Juraj Janik
Justin Anderson
Justine Sherwood
KL Ee
Kaarina Hollo
Kaelyn Davis
Kaja R Anker-Rasch
Karen Gilbert
Karin Mckercher
Katarzyna Bartoszynska
Kate Attwooll
Kate Beswick
Kate Carlton-Reditt
Kate Morgan
Kate Procter
Kate Shires
Katharina Liehr
Katharine Robbins
Katherine Brabon
Katherine Sotejeff-Wilson
Kathryn Burruss
Kathryn Edwards
Kathryn Williams
Kathy Wright
Katia Wengraf
Katie Brown
Katie Freeman
Katie Grant
Katie Smart
Katy Robinson
Keith Walker
Ken Geniza
Kenneth Blythe
Kent McKernan
Kerry Parke
Kieran Rollin

Kieron James
Kim McGowan
Kirsten Hey
Kirsty Simpkins
Kris Ann Trimis
Kristen Tcherneshoff
Kristin Djuve
Krystale Tremblay-Moll
Krystine Phelps
Kylie Cook
Kyra Wilder
Lacy Wolfe
Lana Selby
Lara Vergnaud
Larry Wikoff
Laura Newman
Laura Pugh
Laura Rangeley
Laura Zlatos
Lauren Rea
Laurence Laluyaux
Lee Harbour
Leona Iosifidou
Leonora Randall
Liliana Lobato
Lily Blacksell
Lily Robert-Foley
Linda Milam
Lindsay Brammer
Lindsey Ford
Linnea Brown
Lisa Agostini
Lisa Dillman
Lisa Hess
Lisa Leahigh
Lisa Simpson
Liz Clifford
Liz Ketch
Liz Starbuck Greer
Liz Wilding
Lorna Bleach
Lottie Smith
Louise Evans
Louise Greenberg
Louise Jolliffe
Louise Smith
Luc Verstraete
Lucie Taylor
Lucinda Smith
Lucy Banks
Lucy Moffatt
Lucy Scott
Luke Healey
Lydia Trethewey
Lyndia Thomas
Lynn Fung
Lynn Martin
Lynn Ross
MP Boardman
Maeve Lambe
Maggie Kerkman
Maggie Livesey
Malgorzata Rokicka
Mandy Wight
Manu Chastelain
Marcel Inhoff
Margaret Jull Costa
Margo Gorman
Mari-Liis Calloway
Maria Ahnhem Farrar
Maria Lomunno
Maria Losada
Marie Cloutier
Marie Donnelly
Marie Harper
Marina Castledine
Marja S Laaksonen
Mark Bridgman
Mark Reynolds
Mark Sargent
Mark Scott
Mark Sheets
Mark Sztyber
Mark Waters
Martha W Hood
Martin Brown
Martin Price
Martin Eric Rodgers
Mary Addonizio
Mary Angela Brevidoro
Mary Clarke
Mary Heiss
Mary Wang
Maryse Meijer
Mathias Ruthner
Mathieu Trudeau
Matt Carruthers
Matt Davies
Matt Greene
Matt O'Connor
Matthew Adamson
Matthew Banash
Matthew Cooke
Matthew Eatough
Matthew Francis
Matthew Gill
Matthew Lowe
Matthew Woodman
Matthias Rosenberg
Maura Cheeks
Max Cairnduff
Max Longman
Meaghan Delahunt

Meg Lovelock
Megan Wittling
Mel Pryor
Melissa Beck
Melissa da Silveira Serpa
Melissa Stogsdill
Melissa Wan
Melynda Nuss
Michael Aguilar
Michael Bichko
Michael Boog
Michael James Eastwood
Michael Floyd
Michael Gavin
Michael Kuhn
Michael Schneiderman
Michaela Goff
Michelle Mercaldo
Michelle Perkins
Miguel Head
Miles Smith-Morris
Moira Weir
Molly Foster
Mona Arshi
Morayma Jimenez
Morgan Lyons
Moriah Haefner
Myles Nolan
N Tsolak
Nancy Foley
Nancy Jacobson
Nancy Kerkman
Nancy Oakes
Nargis McCarthy
Natalia Reyes
Natalie Ricks
Nathalie Teitler
Nathan McNamara
Nathan Rowley
Nathan Weida
Nicholas Brown
Nicholas Rutherford
Nick Chapman
Nick James
Nick Marshall
Nick Nelson & Rachel Eley
Nick Sidwell
Nick Twemlow
Nicola Cook
Nicola Hart
Nicola Mira
Nicola Sandiford
Nicola Scott
Nicole Matteini
Nigel Fishburn
Niki Sammut
Nina de la Mer
Nina Nickerson
Nina Todorova
Norman Batchelor
Norman Carter
Odilia Corneth
Olga Zilberbourg
Olivia Scott
Olivia Turon
Pamela Ritchie
Pamela Tao
Pankaj Mishra
Pat Bevins
Patrick Hawley
Paul Cray
Paul Ewing
Paul Flaig
Paul Jones
Paul Munday
Paul Myatt
Paul Nightingale
Paul Scott
Paul Segal
Paul Stallard
Pavlos Stavropoulos
Penelope Hewett Brown
Penelope Hewett-Brown
Peter Griffin
Peter Halliday
Peter Hayden
Peter McBain
Peter McCambridge
Peter Rowland
Peter Taplin
Peter Watson
Peter Wells
Petra Stapp
Phil Bartlett
Philip Herbert
Philip Nulty
Philip Warren
Philip Williams
Philipp Jarke
Phillipa Clements
Phoebe Millerwhite
Phyllis Reeve
Pia Figge
Piet Van Bockstal
Rachael de Moravia
Rachael Williams
Rachel Andrews
Rachel Carter
Rachel Darnley-Smith

Rachel Matheson
Rachel Van Riel
Rachel Watkins
Ralph Cowling
Ramona Pulsford
Ranbir Sidhu
Rebecca Carter
Rebecca Moss
Rebecca O'Reilly
Rebecca Peer
Rebecca Rosenthal
Rebecca Shaak
Rebecca Sӧregi
Rebekka Bremmer
Renee Thomas
Rhiannon Armstrong
Rich Sutherland
Richard Clark
Richard Ellis
Richard Gwyn
Richard Mann
Richard Mansell
Richard Priest
Richard Santos
Richard Shea
Richard Soundy
Richard White
Riley & Alyssa Manning
Rishi Dastidar
Rita Kaar
Rita O'Brien
Rob Kidd
Robert Gillett
Robert Hamilton
Robert Hannah
Robin McLean
Robin Taylor
Roger Newton
Roger Ramsden
Rory Williamson
Rosalind May
Rosalind Ramsay
Rose Crichton
Rosie Ernst Trustram
Rosie Pinhorn
Roxanne O'Del Ablett
Roz Simpson
Rupert Ziziros
Ruth Deyermond
Ryan Day
Ryan Oliver
SK Grout
ST Dabbagh
Sally Baker
Sally Foreman
Sally Warner
Sam Gordon
Samantha Pavlov
Samantha Walton
Samuel Crosby
Sara Bea
Sara Cheraghlou
Sara Kittleson
Sara Sherwood
Sara Warshawski
Sarah Arboleda
Sarah Brewer
Sarah Lucas
Sarah Pybus
Sarah Spitz
Scott Astrada
Scott Chiddister
Scott Henkle
Scott Russell
Scott Simpson
Sean Kottke
Sean McDonagh
Sean McGivern
Sean Myers
Shannon Knapp
Sharon Dogar
Sharon McCammon
Shauna Gilligan
Sheila Packa
Sian Hannah
Sienna Kang
Simon James
Simon Pitney
Simon Robertson
Siriol Hugh-Jones
Sophia Wickham
Stacy Rodgers
Stefanie Schrank
Stefano Mula
Stephan Eggum
Stephanie Miller
Stephanie Smee
Stephen Cowley
Stephen Pearsall
Steve Chapman
Steve Clough
Steve Dearden
Steve James
Steve Tuffnell
Steven Norton
Stewart Eastham
Stu Sherman
Stuart Grey
Stuart Wilkinson
Su Bonfanti
Sue Davies
Sunny Payson
Susan Jaken

Susan Winter
Suzanne Kirkham
Sylvie Zannier-Betts
Tania Hershman
Tara Roman
Tasmin Maitland
Teresa Werner
Tess Cohen
Tess Lewis
Tessa Lang
Thom Cuell
Thom Keep
Thomas Alt
Thomas Campbell
Thomas Mitchell
Thomas Smith
Thomas van den Bout
Tiffany Lehr
Tim Kelly
Tim Scott
Tina Rotherham-Winqvist
Toby Halsey
Toby Ryan
Tom Darby
Tom Doyle
Tom Franklin
Tom Gray
Tom Stafford
Tom Whatmore
Tory Jeffay
Tracy Heuring
Tracy Northup
Tracy Shapley
Trevor Wald
Val & Tom Flechtner
Valerie O'Riordan
Vanessa Fernandez Greene
Vanessa Fuller
Vanessa Heggie
Vanessa Nolan
Veronica Barnsley
Victor Meadowcroft
Victoria Eld
Victoria Goodbody
Victoria Huggins
Vijay Pattisapu
Vikki O'Neill
Wendy Langridge
Will Herbert
William Black
William Franklin
William Mackenzie
William Sitters
Yana Ellis
Yoora Yi Tenen
Zachary Maricondia
Zareena Amiruddin
Zoë Brasier

CURRENT & UPCOMING BOOKS

01 Juan Pablo Villalobos, *Down the Rabbit Hole*, trans. Rosalind Harvey

02 Clemens Meyer, *All the Lights*, trans. Katy Derbyshire

03 Deborah Levy, *Swimming Home*

04 Iosi Havilio, *Open Door*, trans. Beth Fowler

05 Oleg Zaionchkovsky, *Happiness is Possible*, trans. Andrew Bromfield

06 Carlos Gamerro, *The Islands*, trans. Ian Barnett

07 Christoph Simon, *Zbinden's Progress*, trans. Donal McLaughlin

08 Helen DeWitt, *Lightning Rods*

09 Deborah Levy, *Black Vodka: ten stories*

10 Oleg Pavlov, *Captain of the Steppe*, trans. Ian Appleby

11 Rodrigo de Souza Leão, *All Dogs are Blue*, trans. Zoë Perry and Stefan Tobler

12 Juan Pablo Villalobos, *Quesadillas*, trans. Rosalind Harvey

13 Iosi Havilio, *Paradises*, trans. Beth Fowler

14 Ivan Vladislavić, *Double Negative*

15 Benjamin Lytal, *A Map of Tulsa*

16 Ivan Vladislavić, *The Restless Supermarket*

17 Elvira Dones, *Sworn Virgin*, trans. Clarissa Botsford

18 Oleg Pavlov, *The Matiushin Case*, trans. Andrew Bromfield

19 Paulo Scott, *Nowhere People*, trans. Daniel Hahn

20 Deborah Levy, *An Amorous Discourse in the Suburbs of Hell*

21 Juan Tomás Ávila Laurel, *By Night the Mountain Burns*, trans. Jethro Soutar

22 SJ Naudé, *The Alphabet of Birds*, trans. the author

23 Niyati Keni, *Esperanza Street*

24 Yuri Herrera, *Signs Preceding the End of the World*, trans. Lisa Dillman

25 Carlos Gamerro, *The Adventure of the Busts of Eva Perón*, trans. Ian Barnett

26 Anne Cuneo, *Tregian's Ground*, trans. Roland Glasser and Louise Rogers Lalaurie

27 Angela Readman, *Don't Try This at Home*

28 Ivan Vladislavić, *101 Detectives*

29 Oleg Pavlov, *Requiem for a Soldier*, trans. Anna Gunin

30 Haroldo Conti, *Southeaster*, trans. Jon Lindsay Miles

31 Ivan Vladislavić, *The Folly*

32 Susana Moreira Marques, *Now and at the Hour of Our Death*, trans. Julia Sanches

33 Lina Wolff, *Bret Easton Ellis and the Other Dogs*, trans. Frank Perry

34 Anakana Schofield, *Martin John*

35 Joanna Walsh, *Vertigo*

36 Wolfgang Bauer, *Crossing the Sea*, trans. Sarah Pybus with photographs by Stanislav Krupař

37 Various, *Lunatics, Lovers and Poets: Twelve Stories after Cervantes and Shakespeare*

38 Yuri Herrera, *The Transmigration of Bodies*, trans. Lisa Dillman

39 César Aira, *The Seamstress and the Wind*, trans. Rosalie Knecht

40 Juan Pablo Villalobos, *I'll Sell You a Dog*, trans. Rosalind Harvey

41 Enrique Vila-Matas, *Vampire in Love*, trans. Margaret Jull Costa

42 Emmanuelle Pagano, *Trysting*, trans. Jennifer Higgins and Sophie Lewis

43 Arno Geiger, *The Old King in His Exile*, trans. Stefan Tobler

44 Michelle Tea, *Black Wave*

45 César Aira, *The Little Buddhist Monk*, trans. Nick Caistor

46 César Aira, *The Proof*, trans. Nick Caistor

47 Patty Yumi Cottrell, *Sorry to Disrupt the Peace*

48 Yuri Herrera, *Kingdom Cons*, trans. Lisa Dillman

49 Fleur Jaeggy, *I am the Brother of XX*, trans. Gini Alhadeff

50 Iosi Havilio, *Petite Fleur*, trans. Lorna Scott Fox

51 Juan Tomás Ávila Laurel, *The Gurugu Pledge*, trans. Jethro Soutar

52 Joanna Walsh, *Worlds from the Word's End*

53 Nicola Pugliese, *Malacqua*, trans. Shaun Whiteside

54 César Aira, *The Lime Tree*, trans. Chris Andrews

55 Ann Quin, *The Unmapped Country*

56 Fleur Jaeggy, *Sweet Days of Discipline*, trans. Tim Parks

57 Alicia Kopf, *Brother in Ice*, trans. Mara Faye Lethem

58 Christine Schutt, *Pure Hollywood*

59 Cristina Rivera Garza, *The Iliac Crest*, trans. Sarah Booker

60 Norah Lange, *People in the Room*, trans. Charlotte Whittle

61 Kathy Page, *Dear Evelyn*

62 Alia Trabucco Zerán, *The Remainder*, trans. Sophie Hughes

63 Amy Arnold, *Slip of a Fish*

64 Rita Indiana, *Tentacle*, trans. Achy Obejas

65 Angela Readman, *Something Like Breathing*

66 Gerald Murnane, *Border Districts*

67 Gerald Murnane, *Tamarisk Row*

68 César Aira, *Birthday*, trans. Chris Andrews

69 Ann Quin, *Berg*

70 Fleur Jaeggy, *Proleterka*, trans. Alastair McEwen

71 Olivia Rosenthal, *To Leave with the Reindeer*, trans. Sophie Lewis

72 Lina Wolff, *The Polyglot Lovers*, trans. Saskia Vogel

73 Mario Levrero, *Empty Words*, trans. Annie McDermott

74 Michelle Tea, *Against Memoir*

75 Cristina Rivera Garza, *The Taiga Syndrome*, trans. Suzanne Jill Levine and Aviva Kana

76 Hanne Ørstavik, *Love*, trans. Martin Aitken

77 Tim Etchells, *Endland*

78 Rita Indiana, *Made in Saturn*, trans. Sydney Hutchinson

79 Luke Brown, *Theft*

80 Gerald Murnane, *Collected Short Fiction*

81 Gerald Murnane, *Invisible Yet Enduring Lilacs*

82 James Attlee, *Isolarion*

83 Deb Olin Unferth, *Barn 8*

84 Juan Pablo Villalobos, *I Don't Expect Anyone to Believe Me*, trans. Daniel Hahn

85 Andrzej Tichý, *Wretchedness*, trans. Nichola Smalley

86 Yuri Herrera, *A Silent Fury: The El Bordo Mine Fire*, trans. Lisa Dillman

87 Lina Wolff, *Many People Die Like You*, trans. Saskia Vogel

88 Ann Quin, *Three*

89 Rachel Genn, *What You Could Have Won*

90 John Metcalf, *Medals and Prizes*

91 Claudia Hernández, *Slash and Burn*, trans. Julia Sanches

92 Ann Quin, *Passages*

93 Various, *This Is How We Come Back Stronger*

94 Eva Baltasar, *Permafrost*, trans. Julia Sanches

95 Norah Lange, *Notes from Childhood*, trans. Charlotte Whittle

96 James Attlee, *Under the Rainbow: Voices from the First Lockdown*

97 César Aira, *The Divorce*, trans. Chris Andrews

98 Mario Levrero, *The Luminous Novel*, trans. Annie McDermott

99 Tice Cin, *Keeping the House*

100 Yuri Herrera, *Three Novels*, trans. Lisa Dillman

101 Elisa Victoria, *Oldladyvoice*, trans. Charlotte Whittle

102 Sammy Wright, *Fit*

103 Robin McLean, *Pity the Beast*

104 Mona Arshi, *Somebody Loves You*

105 Paulo Scott, *Phenotypes*, trans. Daniel Hahn

106 Robert Aickman, *Go Back at Once*

107 Adrian Nathan West, *My Father's Diet*

108 Alia Trabucco Zerán, *When Women Kill: Four Crimes Retold*, trans. Sophie Hughes

109 Preti Taneja, *Aftermath*

110 Barry Hines, *The Gamekeeper*

111 Gerald Murnane, *Last Letter to a Reader*

112 Fleur Jaeggy, *The Water Statues*, trans. Gini Alhadeff

113 Najwa Barakat, *Mister N*, trans. Luke Leafgren

114 Jessi Jezewska Stevens, *The Visitors*

115 James Greer, *Bad Eminence*

116 Juan Pablo Villalobos, *Invasion of the Spirit People*, trans. Rosalind Harvey

117 Eva Baltasar, *Boulder*, trans. Julia Sanches

118 Ann Quin, *Tripticks*